CONCESSIONS

CONCESSIONS

DEBBIE DiGIOVANNI

RIVEROAK®
Good News in Fiction

An Imprint of Cook Communications Ministries
COLORADO SPRINGS, COLORADO • PARIS, ONTARIO
KINGSWAY COMMUNICATIONS, LTD., EASTBOURNE, ENGLAND

RiverOak® is an imprint of
Cook Communications Ministries, Colorado Springs, CO 80918
Cook Communications, Paris, Ontario
Kingsway Communications, Eastbourne, England

CONCESSIONS
© 2004 by Debbie DiGiovanni

Cover Design: UDG/DesignWorks
Cover Photo: © Getty Images

First Printing, 2004
Printed in the United States of America
1 2 3 4 5 6 7 8 9 10 Printing/Year 08 07 06 05 04

ISBN 1-589-19022-X

This book is dedicated to my little brother, Jim Carrico, and to my mentor, Miriam Pendergraft.

They are gone, but not forgotten; they are forever in my heart.

Acknowledgments

To Mike, Chandra, and Gianna for your constant love and support, and to my dear family everywhere.

To my biggest heroes: Pastor David Gerig and his precious wife, Cindy. To the rest of you blessed souls at Calvary Chapel who are as family to me. Particularly, to Carl and Jennifer McCormick and Phil and Peggy Higgins for your special part in my writing endeavor.

To Barb Eimer, my daily joy and inspiration. To my best and beautiful, Cindy Abiko. Also to Grace VanDitte, an anchor in my life; Karine Wagner, my brightest star; and Jamie Tennessee, one of my greatest gifts.

To my California queens: Becky Chang, Karen Netherlain, Lorna Griffin, Corrine Selberg, Kathy DeMarco, Florinda Osborn, and Pauline Hampton. And to my local queen, Patty Nelson.

To Tricia Goyer, Joanna Weaver, Rebecca Blasing, and Erica Faraone—true and gifted hearts. To Wanda Dyson for the vision. To Debbi Bedford for homemade soup and encouragement. To Dr. Larry Day for wisdom. To my Fairbanks advisors, one and all. To my editor, Jeff Dunn, who has been a friend. To my agent, Janet Grant, a classy lady.

To God, the lover of my soul, to whom all glory on heaven and earth is due.

1

*T*here is no sound in the house but the soft roar of fire in the potbellied stove that warms the room and the gentle ticking of a grandfather clock; a reminder that life moves on, no matter what our advice. There is no hurrying or slowing the seasons. They come as the Creator summons them.

I am nestled under a blanket in the sunroom my family calls the "Igloo." It is our winter haven, where nights are spent reading, knitting, working crossword puzzles, conversing, and sky gazing.

On this March night I watch the dancing sky, a green and yellow curtain extending high above the trees that surround our twenty-acre paradise. It is the Aurora Borealis. The Northern Lights of Alaska.

There is serenity in the stillness, but I am missing my family. My husband, Jack, and my young daughters have taken our Alaskan huskies, Max and Martha, for a walk. Our lovable duo, once champion sled dogs with finer names and pedigree lineages of which we are unaware, were rescued from the animal shelter. They rarely take to the trail these days, but in our estimation serve an equally useful purpose as beloved family pets.

Figures emerge from the forest, and I watch them edge toward the house. Three silhouettes stop and turn to view the gallery of lights. There is comfort in the thought that wherever we are in this world, we share the same sky.

For a time there is no movement. I feel as if the entire world is gazing at the heavens.

Lunging dogs break the enchantment. Jack holds them near and away from the scent of night creatures.

The teapot whistles shrilly. I pull it from the stove and pour boiling water over Godiva cocoa, stirring the mixture into the glazed teddy bear mugs with twisted faces that the girls home-crafted in our ceramics studio. After adorning the cocoa with whipped cream and chocolate sprinkles, I arrange the cookies we baked earlier on a matching pottery plate. The cookies were intended to be snowflakes, but they look more like misshapen trees. Life is about making special moments.

I hear laughter and running. The dogs barking and quieting at Jack's command. I run downstairs to greet my daughters.

The door flings open, and they fly in the mudroom, enveloping me in hugs of dry, sandy snow. They pull off their boots, piling them in my arms. I lay them on the rack.

Faith tears off her snow clothes and tosses them across the room. Hope hangs her things on the row of coat hooks made to size.

"Hang yours too, Faith."

She follows her big sister's example out of childhood duty.

I can't imagine two sisters as opposite as these, but they are equally endearing. Pride swells in a mother's heart when her job is done well. It is a pride I often feel.

The stairs creak as they walk stiffly, drawing heavy breaths. I pat their backsides affectionately, urging them on. They warm themselves by the flickering fire at the huge rock fireplace in the living room, shivering in their matching long underwear and double socks.

I place the cookie plate within reach. Faith snatches, Hope selects. They take mugs of cocoa and lick globs of whipped cream; blow their rosy cheeks redder to cool the hot chocolate. I watch their faces. Faith with her piercing dark eyes; Hope with a face of angelic goodness. I never tire of their beauty.

They finish their cookies and cocoa; I take the stoneware.

Faith wipes her mouth with the back of her hand and mops the leg of her long underwear a streak of brown, adding to the array of stains. Hope retrieves a napkin from the kitchen, dabs, and throws it in the trash.

"Bath, girls," and they tear down the hall.

"And don't forget your towels."

"We won't," calls Hope.

"We will," calls Faith. And a second later—"Not really."

They are eight and nine now and able to manage their own baths. I am not yet regretting the loss of their younger years.

I turn on the porch light and look through the window to see that the temperature reading is five degrees. The barn is lit, and though I cannot hear him, I know that Jack is whistling his tune.

Max and Martha will bed down easily, but the kenneled sled dogs Jack uses for winter touring require far more attention. We call them the "Illustrious Seven." Every night Jack prepares a cooked mixture of dry food mixed with salmon, and gives them doses of vitamin supplements. He inspects their pads for cuts, and in the colder weather covers them in booties to prevent frostbite.

Knowing that the routine is at least a twenty-minute chore,

I once again direct my attention to the night show, sipping on cocoa and warming under my blanket in the easy chair. I am feeling happy and fortunate tonight. Now and then I hear laughter burst down the hall and settle back into silence.

The Igloo is my porthole to the outdoor world, and my favorite place to be. The room is an encasement of glass with a high pyramid roof, and was built to withstand extreme temperatures in this land of extremes. In Fairbanks, where we live, the winter can dip to fifty below.

Some people call Fairbanks the end of the earth, and it may seem so. Fairbanks is south of the Arctic Circle, sixty-five degrees north latitude. Some describe it as a frozen wasteland. To me it is the beginning of the earth. Perpetual beauty and motion. A canvas of unending sky, stretching into infinity. And in my imagination, God with his magic paintbrush, dips into rainbow colors and paints the sky awash in arcs of unsurpassed glory; as if he understands that the long, frigid winter can wear on a soul, he prepared this figment of beauty with which he chose to adorn this barren region.

Not everyone shares this viewpoint. Some pay a price for the incessant darkness that pervades the long winter months. There are those who cannot endure the ice fog that hangs like smoke without a source when the subzero temperatures reign. To some, the crunch of snow is a miserable sound; to them, the stagnant inversion layers are suffocating.

They ache to be somewhere else—most anywhere else. Starved for purpose, they congregate at the bars and drink until they drown their sorrows or busy themselves with meaningless activities to divert their minds from madness.

Others survive without thinking. As if resolved that life is a habitual, nonsensical routine. Waking, eating, sleeping in the cold.

But most involve themselves in the endless winter activities that are the heart of Fairbanks. They are sports-minded individuals who enrich their lives with skiing, snowboarding, snowmobiling, sledding, ice fishing and dog mushing. Community-minded individuals who volunteer for the latest worthy cause. Creative individuals who enjoy the arts, ballet, and symphony.

And still there is time left for reflection. The desolate months of winter are a time to look deeper inside oneself. To become intimate friends or casual enemies with oneself. Either to water the soul or to dehydrate it.

One thing for sure. At the end of the season you know what you are made of. You've been stretched beyond your imagination and have neared your outer limits, and should have gained some constitution in the process.

Gold was discovered here a hundred years ago, and some believe that the summer is pure gold.

The first time your bare feet touch ground after months of being stuffed in closed shoes, you wiggle your toes to the air, position your face to the sun, and thank God. And then begins the nearly twenty-four hours of daylight and a short season of reprieve and living a more casual life of single-layered clothes—and ice to cool your drink (instead of for sculpture)—until, once again, you willingly submit to the inevitability of the changing seasons. Beginning again the continuing cycle of Alaskan life.

Every summer I have a winter's dream. Usually in August, when the memory of shoveling snow and ice skating to the mailbox has lessened. Not a night dream; a daydream. Pulled from the files of my fondest memories.

I remember the first full moon of the snowy season and the bold reflection of light across the land. How we dress in snowman's attire as we have done since the girls were toddlers. We move into the cold snap of the night and watch for movement. Sometimes we see moose or the shadow of a great horned owl in flight.

Jack carries the backpack with the snacks and the wood for the fire. We trek the quarter-mile to a place Hope named the Kingdom of the Trees, where the trees were once burned and have been sawed to stools.

Upon reaching our revered landscape, we twirl. As we twirl, Jack builds a fire. It is the same as I did with my sisters when we were children and my own father would build a fire, and my mother would dance with us.

We make 'smores and sit on stumps. There is laughter, and shared stories, hands held in a circle, and a prayer to the Giver of the glorious gifts. In the majesty of the openness we understand that we have something special—as special as anything in this world could be. As warm as the sun; as happy as a song; as lasting as a treasure.

The thought of leaving here never crosses my mind.

"Karan," Jack calls to me as he does whenever he steps in the door.

"In the Igloo," I answer.

I hear the drop of his heavy boots, thuds on the wall as he hangs his outer garb, thumps on the steps as he nears.

The green-yellow sky is now a stream of purple, rarely visible. I wonder where the colors go …

Jack appears, looking worn.

"Look, Jack. Purple." I point to the display.

"Beautiful," he says, less than enthusiastically.

"Are we blessed or what?"

I get up from the blue velvet chair, folding the blanket as he stands in a stupor. I reach to rub his shoulders. They are sturdy shoulders. The build of a hard-working man.

"You look tired, Jack. Sit down. I'll get you some cocoa."

"No cocoa," he says, as though it were poison.

"Alright then. Tea, Mr. LaRue?"

"No tea."

"What would you like then?"

"Something tropical."

He plops down and throws his feet recklessly over the arm of the chair, his face obviously distressed.

"What's wrong?"

"Endless hours of choking darkness, that's what wrong. Working like my dogs out there and never getting ahead."

"What exactly does 'getting ahead' mean? I haven't seen the Joneses around here lately. I think we do pretty well for ourselves."

I feel my face scrunching into a frown.

"We've lived here fourteen years now."

"You've lived here fourteen years; I've lived here my whole life. And your point is ..."

"I feel like I'm standing on the edge of nowhere, and if I take one more step I could drop into a bottomless pit."

He leans back in the chair and rocks in an annoying, discordant rhythm. I am trying to understand, but I do not. I cannot relate to his despair.

"Sometimes I feel like I'm living the same day over and over again."

His words hurt, like burning coals searing deep inside me.

"You say that as though our lives are some sort of punishment."

"It feels that way sometimes."

He stops his rocking, for which I am grateful. Then there is the sound of nothing for awhile.

I fashion my long brown hair in a high bun and hold it in position as I think, not wanting to overreact.

"Jack, I've never heard you talk like this."

"The truth is, I'm sick of it."

I am wounded at his directness; surprised at his animosity. I loosen my hair, and it cascades down my back.

I want to use cutting words. To accuse. Reprimand. When I was younger, I would have done just that. But I know the fruit of it. Facing opposite directions on opposite sides of the bed, silence over morning coffee, walking past each other in the hall and pretending not to notice.

I force myself to sit on the arm of his chair and look into his eyes.

Jack looks past me. Past the window. Past the sky.

"I feel this raging discontent."

I want to comfort him, but he does not want my comfort. I don't know what he wants.

I hold his chin and turn his head toward me.

"Can't you understand?" His eyes plead with me.

I play with the edges of his hair that is the color of corn silk and just as soft. I long to fix whatever is wrong.

"I thought you loved it here. Our life here," I say, reminding him what he so often speaks.

"I do love it," he says, reassuringly.

"You have an odd way of showing it."

His eyes soften along with his face.

"I'm sorry. I really am. I don't know what's wrong with me tonight. I just need a change."

"Like what?"

"I don't know. That's the thing; I don't know," he says, a pinch of frustration still audible in his voice.

Jack is not often frustrated. It's one of the things people comment on. How patient he is.

"Well, maybe it's seasonal disorder," I reason. "Solomon Jonas had it. He bought a tanning bed and—"

"Forgive me, please," he begs, realizing his folly. He pulls me into his lap and covers me in soft kisses. I secure my arms around his neck and look deeper into his eyes, trying to reach his thoughts.

He watches my tranquil face in wonder, knowing I have every right to be angry with him.

I grab an idea out of nowhere.

"Your cousin's wedding is in California in June."

"Bradford's wedding?"

"Why don't you go? It would be good for you."

Before he says it, I know what he will ask, and I answer it.

"We can handle the Illustrious Seven. You can give them a break from running."

His mind is vacillating, I can tell.

"A week would take a chunk out of my guide business, Karan. June is one of my busiest months."

"There's nothing scheduled yet; you can mark the week out."

He nearly smiles.

"Can we afford it?"

"Sure we can," though I'm not sure it's true.

He wants to go; I know he does.

"I think you should go," I say convincingly. I am trying to believe it myself.

"Three months … " he moans, as though it is an eternity away.

Before we finish our conversation the girls alight on us like butterflies. The play begins instinctively. Hugs. Tickles. Giggles. Jack is lost in the incomparable joy of fatherhood.

Within minutes he is on the floor with Faith on his back.

"Gee! Haw! Whoa!" Faith commands as she pretends Jack is a sled dog. Her long brown curls toss in every direction as he bounces her across the room.

Hope offers a dog biscuit. Her Nordic features match her father's, which he insists are strictly French. Old and royal French.

He didn't mean it. He just had a hard day. We all have hard days.

"Alright, you mushers; it's eight-thirty. Time for devotions and then bed," I say as I reach for the Bible.

"No. Please no," they complain predictably.

"You heard your mother," Jack says as he wriggles Faith off his back and draws me into his chest. There is an unspoken agreement of amnesty between us.

Our girls sandwich in the middle of our glorious hug. I am overtaken with a sense of completeness. I know everything is going to be all right.

There is nothing more precious than a family loving each other.

2

Months glide by as smooth as ice. The winter gives way to spring and warmer temperatures. The melting snow and ice cause water levels to rise. The town of Nenana, fifty miles south of Fairbanks, takes wagers on when the ice on the Tanana River will break up. The clock marks the official time the wooden tripod crashes through the icy surface, signifying the long-awaited arrival of spring. April 29 this year.

Darkness wanes, daylight expands. Migratory birds arrive.

There is no more talk of discontent or falling into bottomless pits. Jack is his usual attentive self, showering me with love and compliments.

On Mother's Day he and the girls set up a picnic in the Igloo with my favorite delicacies—French bread, brie, calamata olives, and fruit—which they arrange on Royal Albert china accented with our best silver settings on a red-checked tablecloth. They serve raspberry lemonade in goblets and minicheesecakes for desert. Jack wears jeans and a light blue starched shirt with a funny red bow tie. The girls wear flowery dresses with lace collars.

Faith makes up a game: Tell What You Like Best about

Living in Alaska. Jack says his favorite thing about Alaska is *us*. Hope names the game Alaska Glory. She loves to name things. Our green Suburban is named Pickles.

One night Jack paints my toenails in the moonlight and kisses them while barely dry. On a rainy afternoon he surprises me with a fondue pot of Swiss Gruyere. We take longer walks on the wooded trail encircling our spacious "house that Jack built" the year we married, sloshing through the spring muck. The girls call us on their walkie-talkies; they tell jokes that are too long but make us laugh.

I tell Jack I want to take up photography and learn to paint the sky.

He says he is looking forward to grooming more trails for the dogs and maybe adding a few to the team.

He seems happy.

We celebrate Father's Day with French donuts called beignets prepared from box mix and café au lait from a can Jack's mother sends us from New Orleans. Jack is from Louisiana and has a passion for fabulous food and strong coffee.

We make the girls steamers with English toffee flavoring. In the afternoon we attach the dogs to the four-wheeler and take them for a run.

The sled will serve no purpose until autumn. The snow on the ground has melted, and I am certain Jack's restlessness melted along with it.

The following day Jack wakes up early to catch his plane to California. I hear water running as I drift between sleep and consciousness. A few minutes later I distinguish a sound I believe is the zipping of his jacket. I open my eyes halfway to the shadows of the room, darkened from the drawn roman shades that block out the light.

Jack grabs his old green suitcase decorated with accumulated luggage tags, remnants from his travel days when he worked for a major construction company.

I packed for him as usual. Jack lacks all sense when it comes to matching. His recurrent question being, "Does red go with brown?"

Faith tiptoes in the room.

"What are you doing out of bed, angel girl?" Jacks whispers. "I told you girls good-bye last night. It's only for a little while."

"You have to take a piece of Alaska with you, Daddy. You can't go without Alaska," she says excitedly.

She hands him a small feather in the dimness.

He puts the keepsake in his pocket and pats it near to his heart. He tells her to hush or she will wake the world. He kisses her crown.

"Kiss Mommy for me, darling. I don't want to wake her. She is too beautiful to be awakened."

I try not to move, lest his illusion be broken. We said good-bye last night. A long, stirring goodbye with precious words between us. I asked him not to phone; it would only make me miss him more.

"Yes, Daddy; I'll kiss her big. And we can get our own breakfast. Hope makes pancakes now."

"Lots of syrup and globs of butter," he says. "But don't tell Mommy."

I close my eyes and think happy thoughts.

The Illustrious Seven behave remarkably well in Jack's absence. We let them loose in the adjoining fenced meadow to run free among the birch and wildflowers. They splash in the streambed with the girls.

The girls make up a holiday and honor the dogs with a party. They tie red ribbons around dog biscuits and fashion cone hats out of paper and strings. They paint them colorful designs, which the dogs do not seem to appreciate. Hope names the holiday Dog Days in Almost Summer.

I can't sleep in the house for missing Jack, so we sleep in the barn. The girls love it. They cuddle with Max and Martha and tell them secrets they say are only between children and dogs.

I get little sleep. Faith snores loudly, as does one of the dogs. The daylight extends into the night hours now and shines through my lids. I am dreamless and unrested.

Wild roses bloom in unexpected places, and raspberries lost two years to frost, emerge on unpruned vines. The girls collect smooth stones from the stream as though they are wonders. They ask me if butterflies sleep in their cocoons before they emerge and how the bugs outlast the winter.

I think of Jack. I wonder about his thoughts. If he misses Alaska and the sky.

*I*t is June 21, the longest day of the year and the day of Jack's homecoming. The girls are with their grand-mother. They will celebrate the summer equinox with a salmon bake, midnight baseball, and all-night celebration at the church. I would be celebrating too, if Jack were here.

Some equate the summer solstice celebration with some mystical religious connotation. Druids celebrated it as the wedding of heaven and earth. I prefer to look at it in bibli-cal terms, as the power of darkness being consumed by the supremacy of light. In practical terms it is the official day of summer. Mowers will be mowing; sunscreen will be poured in abundance; children will make lemonade stands out of cardboard; old ladies in wide-brimmed hats will weed their gardens.

Jack is late, beyond his promised arrival of seven o'clock. I am on the overgrown front lawn that is overdue for its first cutting. Stretched out comfortably on a soft worn blanket, I watch the sky.

It is peaceful here among the trees. There are no neighbors as far as the eye can see. The summer birds sing their evening song.

I want to stay awake so I can welcome Jack, but my eyelids give in to the heaviness that weighs them down for lack of sleep. Despite my best efforts, I drift into slumber.

At the feel of Jack's lips on my forehead, I awake. My eyes are unfocused and my thoughts dreamy, but I am aware of his consoling presence. Consumed in assuring peace, knowing he is safe and all is well.

We face each other with huge smiles. He smells of sweat, and his clothes are disheveled.

Max and Martha run from the barn to greet him, pressing their nuzzles against his chest. He pats their heads and orders them away.

"How was the trip?" I stretch and feel the air.

"Long. My flight out of LAX was delayed. It's nine o'clock already."

He gathers me in his arms for an extended moment of reunification.

"I'm glad you're back, sweetheart. So glad." I touch his face that is tanned and softer for the weather.

"I missed you immensely, Karan."

There is a look in his eyes I cannot determine.

He tries to smooth the wrinkles on his dark blue shirt, which I notice is new and Ralph Lauren polo. His black pants are also new. An impractical linen, hopelessly wrinkled. I don't mention it.

"The girls missed you, Jack."

"I thought of them every night. At seven o'clock I watched the sky just like I promised."

"You mean the smog?" I mock.

"They have skies in California too. Remarkable sunsets," he counters, almost offended.

"Tell me everything, Jack. Did Bradford get the nerves? Did the traffic drive you mad?"

"Yes and no."

I think it out until I am sure I am hearing right.

"So the traffic didn't bother you?"

"Actually I liked it. It made me feel like life was going on."

Something about the way he is looking at me when he says this feels wrong. His eyes are concentrating below his normal range of vision, somewhere in between my eyes and mouth. There is something behind his words. Something big and terrifying.

"I feel like life is going on here too."

Jack is acquainted with my intuitive nature. I can always tell when something is up, and he knows it. I read body language like some people read newspapers.

"You have an idea what I'm going to say, don't you?"

"Something I won't like?"

He dusts sticky hair off his face, the way he does when he is nervous. Fear envelops me, and I wring my hands in anticipation of his news.

"Bradford offered me a job. We're moving to California."

He says it quickly and succinctly, as though he must hurry to get the words out before he loses his courage.

I wonder if I am awake. I feel awake, but this is too unreal to be true.

I sputter, "I do hope you're joking."

His expression tells me he's not.

"I think it's best."

It sounds so impersonal, like something an accountant would say about filing a tax extension.

"You think it's best to tear us from everything we know and love?"

"Alaska does not have the only claim on beauty, you know. There are other beautiful places."

"Beautiful places? What are you really trying to say, Jack?"

"I make $40,000 here, maybe $50,000. Bradford says I can make $120,000— easy—in his construction business. And he offered me an advance so we can get settled."

"So it's about the money?"

Jack pulls blades of grass. Pulls them and throws them. Wildly. Randomly.

"That's part of it. Just think of all the things we can do. We will be able to send the girls to private school."

"The girls are homeschooled and happy."

He doesn't hear me.

"We can take more vacations and have newer cars. You can do some *real* shopping."

I stand up and brush the remains of grass pieces off my brown peasant blouse and matching cargo pants, staring at him incredulously.

"Just give me twenty dollars a day to spend at the mall,

and everything will be divine," I say, a definite edge to my voice.

"What?" he asks, naively.

"Everything I love is here, Jack. Everything."

He stands up and looks down, meeting my bewildered gaze.

"What about me for a change? I did it your way, now let's try mine."

I don't know what he's talking about. His way? My way?

"What is this … a competition? I thought this was a marriage."

"It is. A fantastic marriage."

We are standing toe to toe with bitter expressions on our faces, and his words seem an irony to me. Some wild idea has seized him. What the source of his madness is, I don't know. At thirty-five he is too young for a mid-life crisis and too old for youthful recklessness.

"Is this some game you've been playing with me? All these years I thought you were happy."

"I was. It's just that in the past few months I've realized … that there's more out there. That I can pursue my dreams."

"Isn't this your dream? Dog sledding tours in the winter; your guide business in the summer. It's what you always wanted, Jack."

His eyes travel to the dog lots where the Illustrious Seven are yipping cries of excitement, but he doesn't seem to care.

"Let me decide my own dreams, Karan; you decide yours."

"I know what my dream is. I'm living it—or at least I was until now. The bottomless pit you were afraid of falling into … you're pushing me into it head first."

"How you take it is up to you."

"In other words I have no choice?"

He lays his hands on my shoulders. I turn away. I will not look at my betrayer. This is the man who is supposed to protect me, to be devoted to my well-being, and he is ripping my life apart.

"Karan, listen to me." He catches my brown eyes and holds them with his intense blue. "If you battle me on this, we won't go. But I'm withering here. Day by day. Hour by hour. Drying up and dying."

I will not take a ride on his major guilt trip.

"Three months ago you said it was the darkness, and now with the everlasting daylight you are drying up?"

"All I know is, I don't want to be here anymore."

"You can't run away from whatever you're running from. It will follow you."

"I'm not running away. There's nothing to run away from. You just can't see how confining life is here because you've never been anywhere except Toronto and New Orleans."

"You're wrong, Jack. It's called godly contentment."

He fidgets.

"You know I sought the Lord on this, Karan. I prayed about it."

"Brownie points for you. I hope that cures your conscience."

"And I hope you can be the submissive wife you are called to be."

Jack never says such things, and I am shocked.

"How convenient that you think of that one verse and skip all the others, like loving your wife like Christ does the church."

"I'm doing what I think is right."

"Right for who?"

"For us, Karan. All of us."

I sigh, deep and long.

"I'm sleeping in the barn tonight. My stuff is already out there. We've been sleeping there because I couldn't stand being in the bed alone."

"Please, Karan. Don't do that."

"The girls are with my mother until four. Then Mom and I will go on our annual breakfast and shopping day, if you recall the tradition. There's chicken in the fridge. The girls made you lemonade and drew pictures of you with the dogs."

"That was sweet of them." He smiles.

I remember the dogs and panic.

"What about the dogs, Jack? What about the dogs?"

"George Cavanaugh has wanted to buy the team all year. The whole business in fact. Just before I left he was begging me—"

"That musher who throws dead moose on the porch for the dogs once a month and starves his wife and children for the Iditarod entry fee? If he needs a new team, it's because he wore his last team out. The guy doesn't even have water at his place; he has to haul it in from the river. Don't you think the dogs deserve better?"

He ignores my questions.

"Your mother will have to take Max and Martha; they won't thrive in California."

If the dogs cannot thrive in California, I am wondering why he thinks we will.

"I can't believe you're going to sell the dogs and business just like that," I say as I consider the absurdity of it. "And what about the house, Jack?"

"We can rent the house out. Someone from the university will grab it up."

I turn away and edge toward the refuge of the barn bordered by fruit trees with emerging buds.

Jack looks like he's going to follow, but doesn't.

"And my trees?"

"There are trees in California, Karan. Trees that keep their leaves year round and flowers that bloom mid-winter."

"You have an answer for everything, don't you?"

I watch him standing like a pillar, strong and unmovable.

"Answer this, Jack. What about my life?" I scream. "What about our lives?"

My voice reaches the trees and echoes back to me.

Tears well so deep I cannot see to the barn. Max and Martha sense my distress and overtake me in affection. I cringe at the thought of losing these loyal friends. I hug them tightly around the neck, feeling completely alone.

For the longest time, I lie immobile on a blanket over hay. The smell is sweet and reminds me of the girls.

So many emotions fly through my mind. I don't know which one to entertain, and so I let them fly until they finally land and disappear. Then I feel emptiness. A hollow, wrenching emptiness.

The opening of the barn door shows a portion of sky. The Northern Lights are no longer visible. It is a blue night sky with multi-layered clouds. I want to paint it.

How will I live without my sky? God, what should I do?

No audible voice. No clear message. The answer is in the stillness.

Be still.

I repeat the words in my mind.

Be still. Be still.

I am awakened in the night by the sensation of a presence. With my eyes still shut I strain for the pepper spray sitting nearby in a bucket in case it is a moose or bear. Unsure whether I should permit myself to be frightened, I open my eyes slowly. Jack is standing at the barn doorway in sunrise light. It must be after three o'clock. The sun has taken a quick bow and risen again.

"Karan," he whispers. "Can I join you?"

My heart slows its beat in relief.

"Alright," I say, but with hesitancy and suspicion.

The Illustrious Seven hear his voice from their kennel and bang against their quarters in frenzy. He commands them to be quiet, and, remarkably, they do. Max and Martha, at my side, do not move. They refuse to be disturbed.

Jack is wearing a terry robe. It is evident that he tried to sleep, but couldn't. He sits in the hay next to me and massages my shoulders. It feels wonderful, but I refuse to loosen them to his control. He pulls a drooping wild rose out of his pocket as a peace offering.

"Thank you," I say, with some animosity intended. I touch it to my nose and sniff. I twirl it between my fingers.

"I shouldn't have said the things I said." He looks at a patch of sky with this faraway look.

"You must believe them or you wouldn't have said them."

"I should have told you differently."

This is a defining moment. I will either throw a full-blown tantrum or succumb to the inevitable. I choose to succumb.

"It wouldn't have mattered how you told me, Jack."

"I know."

"But, regardless, I shouldn't have yelled at you." I draw my head down shyly and extend my blanket in invitation. He moves closer and strokes my hair.

"You look beautiful in the dawn."

I laugh, for my hair is a tangled mess and covered in straw.

"I was thinking the same of you."

I cannot fight Jack on this matter. He and I are one.

"You know you're tearing my heart out, Jack. But I'll leave it to you. I trust you with my life."

"Don't think I haven't struggled with this."

He covers me in his strong arms, and I allow myself to give in to my feelings for him.

"When Jack? When?"

I am afraid for the answer.

"Three or four weeks. As soon as we can."

Too soon! Much too soon!

I look up at the rafters in agony. Nothing less than agony.

Dread prevents me from asking where we will live, where he will work, what the churches will be like, and the dozens of other questions I have. If he shares the particulars, it will be real.

"I have one condition, Jack. You tell the girls. You tell them about the dogs. You tell them no midnight baseball. You tell them what it's like to be without seasons."

"I will," he says. "I will."

I see a tear stream down his face in the shadowy cast of the barn. His first admittance of regret, but there will be more; I am sure of it.

There are things I could say. I want to ask him if he kept Faith's feather, or if it is lying in a trashcan in California. But a man must be allowed his pride. He means none of this to hurt me. He wants a better life for us. Somehow he doesn't understand that this is our better life.

3

*B*right Sky Lane is a bumpy road, and long before a vehicle reaches our driveway we hear the sound. In my befuddled state, however, I hear nothing.

The truck door slams before I realize the vehicle is there.

"It's my mother, Jack. I want to tell her."

"I understand," he says.

We brush pieces of straw off each other and walk outside, hand in hand, pretending all is well.

My mother walks toward us looking younger than her sixty-eight years and remarkably exuberant for having had no sleep.

"Good morning, Mom. How was the celebration?"

We hug. She smells of bonfire smoke.

"All things good," she replies. "Glad to have you back in God's country, Jack."

"You bet," he says.

"The girls had a marvelous time, but melted into exhaustion the minute their bodies touched the upholstery. Much like you girls used to do."

She is referring to my sisters and me, and I beam at the

memory. Three leaning bodies floating into oblivion after a long celebration and the promise of a fun-filled summer.

"I'll carry them to their beds," Jack offers. "You two enjoy your breakfast. I'm going to bed myself."

"To bed? Haven't you two been to bed?" my mother asks.

I realize my resentment will not be easily subdued. I feel a wave overcoming me now and fight to suppress it, but lose to the magnetic pull of my emotions.

"The poor man has a lot on his mind, Mom."

I turn to Jack. "You look brutally fatigued, dear."

I hold a tight facial expression to disguise my disrespect.

He carries Faith's limp body in his arms and smiles in our direction, unaware of my mood.

"If you're tired, Karan, we can skip breakfast," my mother suggests with disappointment in her hazel eyes.

"I haven't missed one yet, and I'm not going to miss this one."

"Just thought I'd offer you the choice." Her eyes relight. "Pardon me for saying this, dear, but you look a wreck. And you've got straw in your hair."

"Thanks, Mom, for your honesty. Let me run in the house and run a rake through it. I'll be right out."

The mirror confirms my mother's observation. There are dark circles under my eyes that only sleep will cure. But I couldn't sleep if I wanted to. I am at the top of a roller coaster bearing full speed down a steep, winding track. I feel my eyes flicker in the intensity of emotion. Holding my arm out level, I watch my hand tremble.

After brushing my teeth, washing my face, fixing my hair, and dabbing on pink power blush, I emerge from the bathroom looking fairly put together. But I don't have the will to change my clothes. Failing to acknowledge Jack, I grab my purse.

"Have a good time, Karan," he says, lifting his head from his pillow, showing his dozy eyes and sinking back into comfort. His voice is calm, as though the morning was like any other.

It unnerves me that he can be so misled by his male predisposition as to think that everything is patched up with a few moments of tender words and affection.

"Mmmm," I hum. For if I speak, it will be what I am thinking.

If you want to know where I am just follow the trail to my bleeding heart.

On the way out, I stop at the girls' lavender-flowered room to watch them sleeping in twin beds.

Their breaths move up and down in opposite rhythms. The news of the move will be a shock to them. Alaska is all they know. All they ever expected to know. The thought is excruciating.

I pull myself away from their room and away from my thoughts. I close the heavy weather-safe door and lock the bolt from the outside. I walk slowly, kicking gravel.

My mother's old blue truck is running, and I strain to climb inside the high cab. It was once my father's truck. He's been dead twelve years now, and I still miss him—desperately.

I would not describe him as having been the ever-present father type. When I was young, he worked long hours as a welding inspector on the Alaska pipeline and came home dirty and tired, with few words to share. But on days when he had the time and energy, we would do the things fathers do with daughters when they have no sons. Fishing. Hiking. Camping. And family time together was always special.

"Ready for a man's breakfast?" my mother asks.

"Ready as I'll ever be."

And we bang down the road in the shockless antique, feeling every ridge in the road as a mountain peak, every hole as the Grand Canyon.

The drive to the restaurant is always quiet. Something about the early morning hours on the other side of summer demands reflection.

Our destination is the Eskimo Cafe. It didn't start out with the name. It started out as the Pipeline Cafe at the start of the pipeline construction in 1975. It was a place where pipeline workers flocked in mass. A company of rugged individualists from all parts of the country. Some short term, some permanent.

It wasn't for the food. It was passable at best. It was the stories and fellowship that the men appreciated. A break from the routine of construction camp life or just some R&R. Knowing there were others like them with different goals. Some in search of riches; others in search of adventure; and still others searching for what they were searching for. But all expecting to find it in the oil fields of Alaska.

When the construction of the pipeline was completed, and jobs ended suddenly, the name of the cafe stuck, and many of the workers stuck, even those with new occupations in the industry.

We happened upon the Pipeline Cafe by accident the year Daddy died and Jack and the girls were visiting his family in Louisiana. The summer festival had ended; it was just my mother and me, and 4:00 AM daylight.

I was driving Daddy's truck, the one Mom still owns. She yelled, "Stop. This is the place."

What place she was referring to, I didn't know. But I did as a good daughter would and parked in the dusty parking lot and followed her inside.

A dive would be too splendid a description for the restaurant. Dump would be a better word. But my mother wanted to stay, and so we did.

The first thing we saw was a tall, sour-faced waitress and customers, all male, some with filthy faces. They were clanking their silverware on their cracked cups for another round of coffee. I noticed that the plastic booths held together with pieces of duct tape hadn't been dusted in ages, some of the tables were covered in breadcrumbs, and ketchup was caked on the ketchup bottles. No question about it, men were in charge here.

I remember thinking, *If I order anything, it has to be prepackaged. Cornflakes or Total, or something like that.*

Mom asked the bee-hived waitress, "Do you know where Wally used to sit?"

"Why you're Lorna," she said, as if she didn't have to think to know.

"You're Ethel," was the reply.

There was extended eye contact, and what followed was nothing less than a celebratory reunion between strangers.

The men continued to clank their spoons, but Ethel ignored them. Red hair aflame and with a teasing smirk, she said, "You know, it was strictly for the atmosphere Wally ate here."

We grinned, for we knew it was true.

"He gave the best tips of any of my customers, and he talked about you every day he ate here, Lorna honey."

With her sour-faced expression vanished, the flashy waitress looked almost beautiful.

A customer yelled from across the diner, "Hey, Ethel, these eggs taste funny."

"Then why aren't you laughing, Charlie boy?" was her clever response.

The men roared until they were falling over. They even put their spoons down. A large, toothless, mean-looking man, I came to know as gentle Gilbert, grabbed the coffeepot and started pouring.

Mom loved Ethel's saucy wit, and they went flying down memory lane as it related to Wally Ray Plummer. Reliving his humor and his inextinguishable spirit of fun.

And every year on the twenty-second day of June, on or about the hour of 4:00 AM, it was the same. Reminiscing, jokes, and consistently bad food. I came to understand what my father saw in this happy little diner. It was the people.

We park in front of the Eskimo Cafe. The asphalt parking lot is packed with trucks and SUVs. Mother and I know it has been rebuilt, but the change is still staggering. The new structure bears no resemblance to the shoddy wood building that was torn down. It is white stucco, constructed in the shape of a slightly lopsided igloo. A huge illuminated sign bearing the name Eskimo Cafe with artificial smoke pouring out the top puts us on sensory overload.

"Tourist trap," we say together as we step out of the truck.

We walk inside and double-take the eclectic eatery. The interior is ice cream Neapolitan colors: brown, pink, and white vertical stripes. The customers are middle-class families, probably extending the summer celebration like us. There are no working-class citizens.

The sleepy-eyed hostess hands us menus and leads us to a table directly in front of Daddy's window with crate barrels made into chairs. We ask about Ethel, and, after an extended yawn, the pale, black-eyed girl says she doesn't work here anymore. *She retired when the new owners bought the place.*

It should be an exciting place for the bustle of activity, but the atmosphere suffers because it isn't Daddy's place anymore. In the old place with the old booth it was easy to imagine him dressed in his wool cap sipping on black coffee and reading his newspaper.

I have a feeling it will be the last time I will eat here, even if we weren't moving away.

Moving away. For twenty superb minutes I had nearly forgotten, and now it looms before me like a formidable glacier.

"Well, dear … the food looks good anyway." My mother makes a quick decision and closes the menu.

I scan the options. Everything on the menu starts with Eskimo: Eskimo potatoes, Eskimo French toast, Eskimo biscuits.

The blonde, teenage waitress is wearing a short, very tight black skirt and white squeeze top fringed with fur around the edges that makes a disastrous combination. She is smiling an imitation smile like her shoes are as tight as her uniform.

She spills cups of coffee in front of us we didn't ask for.

"What can I get for you two?"

I order Eskimo pancakes and ham I know I will not eat; my mother orders the Eskimo omelet with extra cheese. The waitress takes the menus that are in the shape of igloos and walks away with a swivel that looks rehearsed.

"I suppose they never thought about summer since we barely have one," I say.

"Hard to get into the spirit of the season in this iceberg palace," my mother agrees as she wipes up puddles of coffee.

I brave it.

"Mom, I have some incredibly bad news."

She squares her face in my direction.

"Yes, Karan."

The waitress interrupts, placing a bowl of peanuts in the middle of the table. We look at each other stupidly.

"You throw them."

"Throw them?"

"On the floor."

She demonstrates and swivels away.

I notice for the first time that the floor is strewn in sawdust and peanut shells. What peanuts have to do with Eskimos, I'm not sure. But it looks like great fun.

"Faith would love this place."

I watch people cracking and eating peanuts and throwing the shells. Slow and long; fast and sure. There are definite techniques to the art.

I crack a peanut, drop the contents in my mouth, and pitch the shell to hit an umbrella stand. I miss by miles. I am amused at my lack of direction; my mother is not.

Her eyes have not blinked. She is still staring at me, waiting patiently for me to share my shattering news. I realize that I have left her hanging with my suggestion that something is terribly wrong.

For lack of flowery phrases, I use Jack's words. "Bradford offered Jack a job. We're moving to California."

"Bradford? Who is Bradford?"

She wrinkles her nose.

"Jack's cousin."

"That's his first name?"

"Yes, Mom. That's his first name."

And then she startles in recognition.

"Moving to California?"

Her voice is loud, and I am embarrassed. But with Shania Twain singing in the background, people lost in conversation, and peanut shells being chucked, no one notices.

"When did you find this out?"

I look at my watch and count backward. "Seven hours ago, give or take a few minutes."

"I think I want to cry, Karan. I think I want to … but I am in a state of utter disbelief. This is contrary to all reasonable expectation. Implausible. Plaintive."

"And ridiculous," I add.

My mother has an extensive vocabulary. She was a librarian before my sisters and I came along.

"I was extremely upset when Jack told me, Mom. But his mind is set. And whether or not I think he's right, he's bent on it."

"Did you tell your sisters?"

"I haven't had a chance. Besides, I don't even know where Corrine is."

For a moment we say nothing.

I can see by the look on Mom's face that she is visiting another time in her mind. She breaks a peanut and flings it.

"I remember when your father moved us to Alaska. I always assumed we'd stay in Maine. We were both from there, went to the university there, and started our careers there. Then one day he came home and said he was giving up teaching. We were going to get rich off the Prudhoe Bay oil strike, and we know that never happened. Karan, to me, Alaska was as far as my imagination could stretch from the sea. My father was a fisherman, you know. We lived and breathed the sea."

"I know."

"More coffee?" the skinny waitress asks, even though our coffee has not been touched.

"No thank you," my mother says. I shake my head no.

Mom picks up her account where she left off.

"When your father told me the winter was mostly dark and the summer light, I burst into tears. I jumped in my car and drove to my favorite section of beach. He followed me there and told me it was something he had to do or die. *It was coursing through his veins*, he said. *Such a thirsty need that couldn't be quenched but for the taste of the real thing.* In those days, you followed your husband's dreams, and they either became yours or … "

"Or what?"

"I'm really not sure."

"Neither am I, Mom. Neither am I."

"It was 1968, which seems like yesterday to me. And let me tell you, sweetheart, it was a lonely, frozen planet for a thirty-three-year-old woman with a child and one on the way." Mom looks out the window, wrapped in old memories. "But I did eventually grow to love the place, and now you could tie a barge around my neck, and I wouldn't budge."

A part of me is lecturing the other parts of me. *You will not fall in love with California. You will not become a bronzed woman with long, red-painted nails.*

"So you won't come with us, Mom?"

I present a convincing look, brooding lip and all.

"To visit, but not to live. Never to live."

The waitress brings our food, but we hardly notice.

I look out Daddy's window and think how the landscape has changed. Casey's store is no longer there. A big Kmart stands in its place, and the streetlights are new. Some sleek-styled euro vapour lights replace the cast-iron black antique lights that were the charm of this area.

"I suppose nothing stays the same, does it?" I ask the air, for my mother is lost in her own thoughts.

"I'm going to miss my grandbabies," she laments.

"Things could be worse. After all, we still have our health." I follow my circular reasoning.

"I wouldn't mind reclining poolside right about mid-February," I hear my mother say.

We are immersed in the companionship of our swirling emotions, as our food gets cold.

"It's settled then?" she asks. "No changing Jack's mind?"

"Charbroiled and off the grill. You can stick a fork in it, Mom."

I grab mine and stab my ham.

4

*M*om's old truck is leaving a dust trail fifty feet long. The place is deserted; I am alone. I drag my body past the gazebo, past the wide flowerbeds coming up tiger lilies, dahlias, and daisies, brightening the landscape that has been void of color for so long. I climb up the stairs that connect to the wraparound deck with the hot tub and outdoor cedar furniture.

Max and Martha, overheated and panting, are sprawled out on an old kitchen rug by the front door. They acknowledge me with a whimper, but will not give up their shade. I pet their hot fur, feeling sorry that by the time they loose the bulk of it, autumn will be in danger of frost, and it will be time to grow back.

Throwing the screen door open, I kick sandals off my overused feet that have done too much walking for one day. Hot, thirsty, tired, and racked in excess everything, I walk resolutely to my oversized copper sink.

I turn on the tap and watch the well water fill my glass. The water wets my lips and then my throat, and seems like a liquid river, pure and divine, especially after drinking acrid city water all day that smells of chlorine.

On the counter is a note with Hope's scribbled writing, "Went to have haleebut tacos, Mommy. Back soon!"

I am feeling slightly guilty that I have left the job of bad-news-bearer to Jack. It seems that mothers have the distinguishable honor of being there during life's most harrowing events: vaccines, broken bones, and high fevers. And somehow I feel I should be there when my children's future is revealed—with Kleenex and candy to soften the blow.

But, whether I am there, or not, will not change the fact that we are moving. There are distant times when we are forced to watch and wait.

Like when Hope was a toddler and had this blood condition about sixteen letters long that starts with a *T* I could never pronounce. The doctors drained her of so much blood that her little veins were sorry streaks of a different color, and her lifeless body was so bruised she looked like she had been beaten. I could do nothing but go to the hospital cafeteria and weep over plastic cheese sandwiches. In the end, after much prayer, she was fine.

Or two summers back when Faith nursed a bird that thought our windows were sky and flew into it and broke its wing. We took it to the vet and did all the right things. And still, five days later, it died in her little hands, but only after singing one last note.

As parents, we feel so inadequate at times, so lacking in wisdom and power. We have to leave our cares to God or go crazy.

It's been less then twenty-four hours since Jack shared the devastating news, and with five hours sleep I don't feel like doing anything. I drop into the blue velvet chair in the Igloo and pick up one of the pieces of newspaper Jack left scattered about. Anything to divert my attention from the depressing messages my mind keeps returning to.

I don't want this. I don't like this. Why is this happening?

And there on the page I grab, in the Human Interest section of the *Daily News-Miner*, is a full-color photograph of the happiest man I've ever seen. He is holding a twenty-eight-pound Alaskan king salmon. And in a large bold caption I read, Reasons I Love Alaska!

On the next five pages is a string of opinions from Alaskan enthusiasts, revealing why Alaska is the biggest and the best place in the entire world. Singing the praises of the untamed land: everything from wildlife, to adventure, to no skunks or snakes, to having been born here.

I rip the paper in pieces and, against my tidy nature, leave them on the floor. I look around the room at all the things I love: homemade pottery, rustic signs, a bear rug, photographs of our own adventures, and wildlife paintings. Things that would look odd in a pastel-colored house in California.

I don't know what to do. Should I stop loving my life? Detach myself from my surroundings so I can bear the parting?

Pickles is coming up the road at lightning speed, taxing her shock absorbers. In summer Jack always drives too fast, as if to make up for the driving restrictions of winter.

I put on classical music my mother taught me to love: the London Symphony Orchestra's soothing composition of Beethoven's Moonlight Sonata. I sit close to the speakers and feel drawn to the somber notes as they vibrate through my body. But before the rendition is over, the LaRue clan is upon me.

The girls kiss me tenderly—one on each cheek—as if to

say that it's okay. As if they know that I am in need of comfort, when I, as their mother, should be comforting them. They step back and read my expression.

They have red eyes. Hope's are redder than Faith's. And they both look like they dressed under Dad's supervision. Their sundresses are rumpled; Faith's braids are crooked; Hope's ponytail is too low.

Jack's expression is thoughtful. He takes my hand and lifts me to him, but says nothing. Words can fail in times like these.

"I guess Daddy told you about California?" I meet their eyes in understanding, letting them know they have permission to grieve.

"Yes, Mommy," Hope says. They cling to me and shed tears; tiny tears that barely wet my blouse.

Jack throws his body on our blue corduroy couch and stretches generously.

Faith looks up to me with trusting eyes. "Mommy, do they have moose in California?"

I try to sound reassuring for their sake. "Not on front lawns, but maybe at the zoo."

"They have beautiful houses in California," Jack says, from the couch, as though beautiful houses outweigh the pleasure of moose.

The girls are not impressed. These are not children who are drawn toward material things. They're happy with a new book or a chocolate bar from the country store.

"And they have sunshine all the time," he adds.

"No snow fights? Even in winter?" Hope asks me, already knowing the answer.

"No snow fights, Hope."

"There are mountains with tons of snow and sledding."

Jack stands up and demonstrates the crest of a mountain with exaggerated arm movements. "Why they have everything little girls want."

"Everything, Jack? I seriously doubt it."

Hope is skeptical too. She is biting her nails, a habit she gave up ages ago.

"Big Bear is a hill away."

Slight exaggeration.

I turn off the music, and silence fills the room.

"Have you been to Big Bear, Jack? It's one of the most congested places in the world."

"Congested? It's not congested."

I notice he is wearing another new shirt. Ralph Lauren polo and white, with a red stain that may be Tabasco sauce.

"What kind of research did you do in the short time you were there? Did you hire a tour guide or something?"

He doesn't answer, but goes off on another train of appeasing thought—the candy-coated version.

"They have barbecues in winter, girls. And pool parties."

"But not halibut tacos," I say to balance the scale.

"Can you see the Big Dipper in California?" Hope checks the sky out of habit.

"Sometimes," I say, "but never in a green glow."

I walk to the sink for a glass of water even though I am not thirsty. I am waiting for Jack to counter with some splendid fact about California.

Beat my sky, Jack. Beat my sky. And he tries.

"There's a telescope at Mount Palomar Observatory. The Hale telescope. Almost the biggest in the world."

"How do you know this stuff?" I ask irritated, staring at the restless kitchen curtains flapping in the breeze and feeling the same way.

"Californiaiscool.com."

If I hear one more word about California ...

My water glass is overflowing and spilling on the floor. I grab a towel, toss it on the floor, and direct it with my feet.

This is becoming a contest, and Alaska is losing.

"A" comes before "C," I want to declare. But then I imagine Jack's clever comeback. *California was admitted to the union first—in 1850. Alaska was a territory until 1959. Therefore, Alaska became a state over a hundred years later.*

We know these facts because we've just been through a month of Hope reciting them every day in preparation for a homeschool history competition in which she placed third.

"One more thing," Jack says.

"What?" I have to ask.

"Disneyland!"

The girls jump like cheerleaders. We have satellite TV.

What can I say about Disneyland? All children love Mickey Mouse and Dumbo.

"Oh ... and the beach." He grins.

I give up. At least for the day.

*T*he girls are playing in the yard under revolving water in early morning sunshine. Their bathing suits are shining wet, and Max and Martha, shy of water, are barking from a safe distance.

When they come in, they will be covered in mosquito bites. I will use calamine lotion to relieve the itch and tell them not to scratch.

They look so happy and free. Resilient, pliant children. Have they forgotten?

Jack comes up behind me at the honey oak table and kisses my neck as I raise my mug to my lips. I spill my coffee and turn at him annoyed.

"Come on, Karan. When are you going to give this up?"

"Why don't you give me a copy of your grieving schedule so I can try to meet it?"

I grab a handful of napkins and sop the mess.

"I never knew you had such sarcastic wit."

"Well Jack, neither did I. I never had the chance to know. I've never been faced with anything so terrible."

"I'm taking you to a vacation paradise to live, and that's terrible?"

I shake my head, exasperated.

"Come here."

He pulls me by the hand and drags me downstairs into the girls' schoolroom with walls painted to look like a woodland scene and tables that look like sawed-off forest trees. He plants me in an undersized log chair and grabs a pointer. My knees are in my chest, and a lump is in my throat.

He pulls the roll-down map. It bounces a few times before it settles.

"Way up here is us. This little dot is Fairbanks." Jack reminds me of my sixth-grade geography teacher who assigned too much homework.

Where is he going with this?

"See this huge mass of land. That's the lower forty-eight."

He makes a triple circle with the stick.

"The rest of the world."

I roll my eyes.

He edges back up to Alaska.

"Now we have come to know this little dot very well, and we like this little dot."

"Yes we do."

He downscales to California.

I feel diminutive in this chair, like Alice in Wonderland after she drank the bottle not marked poison.

"This dot just in from the coast is Mission Viejo. There's a lot in this little dot. Wouldn't you like to get to know this little dot too? To know more than one place in your lifetime?"

"Are you done with your patronizing presentation? Because if you are, I have more important things to do ... like pack."

I stand and turn up my nose in insolence.

"You won't have any packing to do; I've hired movers to do everything."

"When did you hire movers?"

"Right after I rented the house," Jack says, tugging on his cell phone attached to his belt that seems a permanent accessory these days.

"I was gone twelve hours, and you rented the house?"

"To a professor I met at Harry's Halibut Kitchen. He'll take the house fully furnished, sight unseen. Down to the turkey baster. We've agreed on July 25 as a good move-in date. What do you think?"

I glare.

"He doesn't smoke."

"I suppose I would have found this out when they started packing boxes?"

"I wanted to save you the trouble. Honestly." He's got this little boy look in his eyes that smacks of wrongdoing.

He shifts his bare feet. He changes the subject.

"Listen, my pleasure princess, how would you like a vacation here in Alaska before we move?" He smiles and leans his head, friendly, and in such a way that I am caught in his charm.

Sounds like bribery, smells like bribery, tastes like bribery.

Oh well!

"Where?"

"Anywhere you want."

Two seconds of thought and I know the place.

"Prince William Sound to see the whales. I've always wanted to see the whales."

"They're yours," Jack says, as though handing me the stars.

5

*I*t is early afternoon in Prince William Sound, and the temperature is a pleasant sixty degrees. We are traveling at sixteen knots on the *Midnight Eclipse* atop relatively calm waters with the smell of saltwater filling our lungs. With my binoculars focused in a general easterly direction, I spy the mysterious creatures of the deep.

It's hard to believe that this is the epicenter of the second largest earthquake ever recorded, at magnitude 9.2. It's harder to believe that these are the waters of the 1989 *Exxon Valdez* oil spill where almost eleven million gallons of crude oil spread over ten thousand miles of ocean.

There is no sign of the chaos. Today earthquakes and oil spills are as far from my mind as moving was from my mind a month ago.

Secretly, I am hoping that after four days of family fun from the rustic home base of Whale Bone Lodge in Whittier (the access to Prince William Sound), Jack will be awakened from his illusion of greener pastures in warmer climates.

Tomorrow is our last day in this wildlife paradise, and the trip is everything I hoped it would be. It would take an entire book to depict our unreal adventures—the icebergs and abundant sea life; hiking to high alpine meadows; bear spotting; beachcombing.

We have yet to experience our exhaustion.

As we drove through the tunnel to Whittier, Jack wore a pinched face, which I assumed was the by-product of the obscene amount of grease the diners we patronized served us as breakfast, lunch, and dinner, respectively. Especially since he'd complained about it repeatedly.

My suspicions grew, however, when Jack's pinched face remained the next morning. But, after all, the pillows in this otherwise accommodating facility were paper-thin, and it had been a long trip the day before, so I let it go at that.

But while we were on the beach that same day eating the contents of a wicker basket lunch exquisitely packaged by the Whale Bone staff, and Jack still offered no explanation as to why his face was a permanent prune, I concluded he was purposely not enjoying himself to make a point. As if doing so would be admitting he loves Alaska.

It was Faith who said what I wanted to say.

"Daddy, you are just like Eeyore, and you're never like Eeyore!"

Faith has a knack for saying what's true in children's terms.

"Is there something going on in there that I can't see?"

She put her forehead to his chest as if to examine his heart. And instantly broke Jack's hardened spirit. Melted him like fire on ice.

"I guess I forgot how to play for a little while, sweetheart," he said, amused, and maybe a bit bewildered at her perception.

And for the rest of the trip we are as we should be.

The sky that night was an azure blue, and the waters a polished slab of blue marble. With the girls asleep, one on each of our laps, Jack looked at me with an intense expression of pleasure.

"Isn't God's beauty awesome?"

It was his first reference to God in weeks outside of our family devotions, which have been mechanically presented of late. And I asked God if he would please give Jack a little nudge to wake him from his rainbow dream, though I wasn't sure how God would do that. I just knew he could.

Jack stopped going to church weeks ago. He said the parishioners were losing sight of what was important. Something about spending too much on a bus for the youth when the roof was leaking and needing repairs first.

Most of our friends are from church, so "the church is messed up" routine is making the move easier for Jack than it should be.

I am the one who has to hear from the majority about "going outside," as the locals say. How we're "selling out" by choosing materialism over what's really important.

I look dumb and shrug and say, "Ask Jack." But Jack isn't there to ask, and so I just look dumb.

The problem now, however, as we sail in our sixty-foot vessel on our whale excursion, is purely physical. Jack is chalky beige, tending toward pale white. He gets seasick, and that is why Dramamine is his constant ally in the summer months when a great deal of his time is spent on fishing outings with eager clientele, most of them Californians and wealthy.

"Dramamine," he says, and puts his hand out as though I am an automatic pill dispenser.

"I don't have it. Didn't you bring it?"

"I didn't think of it," he says frustrated and wobbly kneed. "There aren't any waves out here in this narrow passage. So tell me, how can anyone get sick on a waveless sea?"

"Don't ask me; I'm not the one who gets sick."

We haven't argued since we left Fairbanks, even when Jack deserved to be argued with. I promised myself I would pack away my resentment for our mini-adventure.

And so I soften my words.

"I'm sorry I don't have any with me; I should have thought about it."

"No. I should have known better."

I touch his cheek in empathy.

"I've only been aboard a boat five hundred times and only once without my seasick pills. Ugh," he says, tightening his arms across his stomach. "Better get me a seasick bag just in case."

An older, platinum-haired lady wearing opaque hosiery and shiny black shoes spots the ashen look. Her huge diamond ring and gaudy bracelet tell me she is used to pleasure trips like cruises.

"You poor soul." She hands him a pill.

She walks away. I catch the brand label underfoot and think she spent too much money on her shoes. Jack swallows the pill without water and makes a funny face.

"Thank you," he tells her too late and clings to the railing as my shipmates and I watch the deep turquoise waters in reverence—all sixty-five of us tourist-types with disposal waterproof cameras around our necks and lightly tinted sunglasses for optimum nautical viewing.

Twenty minutes later, Jack is looking pink again. He stands up straight, his sea legs holding. He takes a full breath, stretches, and lifts his eyes upward for the first time to the rugged coastal mountains and the massive glaciers.

Hope begs, "Daddy, tell a whale joke."

I flinch. Jack's jokes are of the well-worn variety, leaning heavily toward corny.

"Why did the whale cross the road?"

"Why?" they ask in unison.

"To get to the other tide."

"A two-year-old wouldn't want to steal that joke, Daddy," Faith asserts.

And we all laugh.

In truth, Jack's nearsighted humor is one of the qualities that attracted me to him when we first met at the University of Alaska-Fairbanks.

At the time I had other things on my mind besides romance, like working forty hours a week at Maggie's Book Corner to pay for my education.

My daddy's hard-earned college fund, a glass jar packed with hundred-dollar bills, was mostly used on my sister, Corrine. She attended the University of Alaska, earned a forestry degree, and has since worked in a number of capacities in that field.

By the time my other sister, Tammy, went to the university, the college money paid her tuition through her freshman year when she met a stockbroker turned welder turned stockbroker. They married and moved to New York where she majored in children—four of them in the first five years of marriage.

And by the time it came to me, the money jar was as close to empty as empty can get, except for three crunched hundred-dollar bills pressed to the bottom of the glass. It might have covered the cost of my books.

I told Daddy he'd done well for us and not to worry. I refused his offer to borrow against his life insurance. We used the three hundred dollars to buy a new television set, not easily viewed from more than five feet away. At the time my parents didn't own a satellite dish, and good reception was intermittent stripes and fuzz. But we still laughed at *Candid Camera,* guessing half the time.

In my mind I am back at the university on an unusually warm day in May sitting on a bench reading seventeenth-century sonnets. Jack steps up looking drop-dead gorgeous, but then so did a lot of guys. Alaska has the highest male-to-female ratio of all the states, and the campus was swarming with good-looking men sold on the place, and young women trying to decide if the good-looking men were worth the hard life of Alaska.

"I'd like to take you for a walk," he said to me.

I wanted to laugh. You take dogs for walks, not women.

"Yes, I'm sure you would. To some secluded spot no one else knows about, right?"

The "Do you want to go for a walk?" routine had landed me in an alfalfa field one night when my date abandoned me after demonstrating his intentions and receiving a full-blown slap for his unwanted advances. I walked a mile to bang on a stranger's door. The owners were an elderly couple who might have thought I was a murderer. They finally agreed to call my parents, but only after I convinced them that I knew their great-niece from the university. I wasn't about to fall for the "go for a walk" line again.

"No, really," Jack declared, dropping his macho pose. "We can go anywhere you want to go."

"But, I don't even know you."

"Would you go out with me if I were Tom Hanks?"

"I would seriously consider it."

"But you don't know him either, so your logic is flawed."

I thought he was an idiot, possibly lacking in prospective dates.

"Look at me; I'm a nice guy. See." He showed his perfectly lined, pearly white teeth. "Floss every day and drink lots of milk."

"Your teeth are very nice," I said, believing it.

"I'm funny too. Almost as funny as Tom Hanks."

"Do you have better morals than Tom Hanks?"

"I don't keep up with Tom's morals, but I do volunteer at the animal shelter, finding homes for poor little unwanted puppy dogs."

"And I'm Mother Teresa's personal scribe."

"Okay. What would convince you that I'm a nice guy?"

I put my fertile imagination to work while he tried to look pure. And then I thought of what my youth leader once said was the perfect comeback. The one that would scare off in a hurry 99.9 percent of young men with unwholesome ideas.

"If you could quote all sixty-six books of the Bible."

He took off from Genesis and went straight through to Revelation without taking a breath, then sat down next to me, still showing his attractive grill. I found his blue eyes holding me the way they still do. I didn't say anything for a moment. I was decidedly quiet for the sake of self-preservation.

"I tell Bible jokes too."

Though I can't remember the one he told, I do remember that it was corny. So corny I nearly choked on my laughter.

"You're nuts; you know that?"

"I must admit I do know that."

"I suppose I could use a little humor," I said, gravitating toward my warmer side. "I'm an English lit major and am finding Milton duller than chewing on crayons."

"That's great," he said. His eyes lit up in boyish innocence, giving me a feeling of trust.

"Can it be someplace public?"

"Sure. As long as it doesn't cost … " He pulled out his wallet and counted his bills, then his change. "As long as it's not over $17.50. That's all the cash I have."

"I don't think I'll break your bank tonight. How about Pop-a-Taco?" The fast-food restaurant was a wannabe Jack in the Box, but with a clown that looked almost demented.

"I love their tacos and onion rings."

"That sounds like fun."

He tightened his hold on the book he was carrying, and I was trying to read the cover of it so I could better judge his character, but his arm was in the way. I found out later it was Jack London's *Call of the Wild*, the book that inspired his love of sled dogs.

"I'm a straight-laced Christian girl, and I may be boring."

"If you're any indication of boring, I think I'm going to like boring."

"Let's go then," I said. He took my hand, and we walked away kindred spirits. It hadn't occurred to either of us that we hadn't introduced ourselves, and wouldn't for nearly another hour.

Now I am clinging to Jack like the captivated schoolgirl I am remembering, wishing that things could stay the same. Staring at the frozen landscape that changes so slowly and wishing my life was as predictable. Wondering how long before I truly forgive Jack for changing things that don't need changing.

I lean my head against his chest and feel his heart beating steadily. I push a wisp of hair off his brow that tends to hang in that wrong spot and notice my hand is not the delicate hand it once was. I watch Jack's face. He's gained a few wrinkles, character to a man. His skin is tan, his eyes are soft blue, and his hair is the stuff surfers are made of. *He'll fit right in, in California; he looks made for it. But not me. Never me!*

Hope is talking porpoises. How they are smaller than dolphins. How their dorsal fins are triangular, and dolphins' are hooked. I am half listening. Demonstrating my interest with occasional nods and smiles in her direction. But I am watching the sea for my whales.

As she is speaking, several great humpback whales emerge from the deep, breaking the surface for air, and leaving a large ring of bubbles and fish flying for their lives.

The ship's temporary inhabitants move to one side to watch, and the ship leans precariously. The captain announces over the loudspeaker that we need to disperse, or the unequal weight distribution will tilt the boat. He strongly suggests that the waters are colder than we think, and the creatures not as friendly, and promises he won't be jumping in for us.

The crowd complies. But I retain my original viewing spot.

"Jack, this is what I came to see."

All the emotional drain of the past weeks flows from me. Nothing matters in this moment but the indescribable sight of these huge black sea monsters blowing through their top holes.

Jack, too, is mesmerized, and the girls, dressed in twin sailor outfits, are a picture with their jaws dropped and their eyes opened twice their normal size.

"Thank you for your cooperation, folks," the captain broadcasts. "Don't worry about the boat capsizing. It's never happened."

At least to him.

And now we see that there are five whales with gaping jaws, scooping krill and other small fish. With the glaciers in the background, it seems too incredible an experience. One reserved for kings and angels.

"Thank you, God!" I cry aloud.

Ever since my daddy told me the tales of the sea, of Moby Dick and his own Maine and Alaska experiences, I have wanted to see the majestic creatures.

I wish my mother were here, for she is the daughter of a fisherman, and I so want her to enjoy this moment, but she is bonding with the dogs.

"This is one of the best days I've ever had," Jack whispers in my ear in a voice of achy emotion.

I smile so wide it hurts.

I am hoping, desperately hoping, for Jack's words: *I think we should stay, Karan. Alaska is where we are meant to be.*

But the words never come, except in my overworked imagination.

6

he movers are packing my life away, and Jack says to relax.

"Here, have an Oreo." He plants one in my mouth, as though Oreos solve all the world's problems.

The girls are in the barn where they slept last night. I checked on them at 5:00 AM when I couldn't sleep. They were curled so close to the dogs I couldn't tell where fur ended and skin began.

I am feeling sick to my stomach. Coming to know parts of me, hidden and unknown. Places in my heart I didn't know existed before I was catapulted into this sad reality. I am an onion, layer upon layers. And every time I think the last layer is reached—there is another layer.

I nearly choke on Oreo crumbs as I chew unthinkingly. Jack asks if I'm okay.

Red-faced, I pour a glass of milk and swallow.

I choke a yes, and he seems satisfied. He goes back to instructing the movers.

"Wrap that computer monitor in bubble wrap. Make that double bubble wrap."

I haven't said a word about the way the movers are throwing our things around like plastic trinkets.

The thought of our belongings under the care of a pot-bellied man with a stringy goatee and small, close-set eyes I wouldn't trust to pick up my trash is rather disturbing.

What if the moving van is robbed? Or ends up in a ditch? Our books, pictures, and mementos. All the things that are suddenly more precious than gold could be lost to us forever.

Jack looks to be in complete control. I am allowing him to be master of this three-ring circus, and he is enjoying the role. He doesn't notice that I am disgruntled, just angry enough that he could see it if he wanted to.

He must be blind. Or so absorbed with his own agenda that his eyes are clouded over to what is happening. I am wondering who he is. My life partner. My best friend. The man I thought I knew better than any woman could know a man.

We do everything together. People call us inseparable and joke that we are welded so tight that it would take the jaws of life to pry us apart.

I call Jack my second skin. It is as if we are in this beautiful dance together and know each other's steps before they are executed. But now, for the first time, I see us separate and apart. What separates us is a philosophical point so essential to who I am that I cannot concede to it because I do not understand it.

Maybe my world is small, but is that wrong?

"You are as beautiful as the day I met you," Jack says, as I sit on a taped box wishing I could pack my emotions along with everything else.

I twist my lips upward to pretend a smile. I'm having a

hard time believing it. I'm having a hard time believing anything Jack says. I am the same; he has changed.

If he knew what I was thinking, he would be crushed. If he knew what I was thinking, we wouldn't be moving ... or would we still?

The plane is taking me to a place I do not want to go. I think of the millions who have been torn away more violently. Children from their parents. Men and women off to war. And feel incredibly sorry for them.

The girls have never been on a plane, and the thrill of adventure has overcome their grief for now. They are watching clouds and imagining them as animals; eating pretzels they say are the best they've ever tasted; drinking soda they are not allowed to drink at home.

Home ... where is home?

My eyes are closed to shut out the strange reality that we are in a flying contraption with an engine and flaps and rudders, moving through the sky at tremendous speed.

The engine thrusts the jet into the air; the air resists the motion in the form of aerodynamic drag ... I can hear my father explaining the dynamics as we watch airplanes taking off and landing while seated at the airport coffee shop. Still I have a hard time believing what goes so against my logic.

Out of the sore need to occupy my mind, I follow the tricks of my unguarded imagination. I picture myself in a Hollywood studio with shiny blue floors; Alex Trebek in a black suit with a mustard-colored tie looking dapper, gray hair perfectly placed. I am a contestant, and he is presenting the Final Jeopardy Question.

My hand is in writing position, trembling as he speaks.

The category is … plinking sound. "Where is Home?"

The question pops up on the screen behind him. He turns and states the question, "Known as the most treasured place on earth, this state ranks first in the nation in popularity of places to live."

And the music begins.

I write my answer assuredly, long before the music fades. I have bet everything on it.

Alaska is my response.

"Alaska," Alex says. "No, I'm sorry, Karan. The answer is California." Alex's look is sympathetic. "Alaska is a good try, but it ranks lower. Much lower."

I startle at the pilot's announcement that we are flying over someplace important. Jack is sleeping soundly, as always. Sleep comes easy to him. More than once I found him asleep on the library table in our college days.

Three more hours and we will be in Seattle to change planes.

We said goodbye to our home just as the sun was saying hello. It seemed empty without the dogs. A feeling of eerie isolation.

George Cavanaugh took the Illustrious Seven last night, and I took the girls out for one last halibut taco. We didn't want to be there when the dogs were taken away.

Faith said to pretend they are at training camp for the Yukon Quest. That they are being brushed with golden brushes and have red velvet beds and booties.

Hope pointed out that velvet was impractical for dogs. "You'd never get the dog hair out."

"So … " Faith replied.

Golden brushes? They'll be fortunate if they get brushed at all.

Later the girls and I dropped Max and Martha off at Mom's house. (Jack was conveniently busy.) The dogs, knowing the yard well, were happy running at first. The girls were trying to be brave, but I could see Hope's lip quivering and Faith fighting back tears.

"Goodbye," we called together and ran into the house. At the moment of parting, a whimper broke from Max, as if he knew. Then he and Martha just stood at the sliding glass door like they were crying. The look on their faces was practically human.

Jack says dogs don't know about partings; they serve one master as well as another. This is the same Jack who once told me that the bond between a man and his dog is stronger than steel.

Saying goodbye to Mom was a grievous moment, and there was no bravery exhibited on my part. It was a separation so painful I thought the hurt would linger forever. However, Mom eased the moment with wise words, as she always does, and offered an appropriate quote, as she always does.

"If you don't like something, change it; if you can't change it, change the way you think about it."

"Did one of the presidents say that?" I asked, certain I was right.

Mom chuckled.

"Mary Engelbreit, dear. I bought you her book of quotes for the plane ride. I know that planes make you nervous."

Mom didn't hold up so well when it came to telling the girls goodbye. But we decided to part with a prayer, and that calmed our spirits.

The bachelor professor is getting a good deal on his fully furnished retreat. He promised to polish the furniture with lemon oil, have the upholstery cleaned every six months, clean the oven regularly, and use Thompson's Water Seal on the decks. He seems a nice enough man. No obvious quirks, just this annoying habit of interrupting and thinking he knows more than we do, his less educated counterparts.

It's sad to say goodbye to the place when I haven't had a chance to love it properly. A house is more than a place you live; it's a piece of art. And the land is a companion with this ever-changing personality.

I can't get over the fact that a stranger will sleep in our bed, and that Jack is okay with it.

"He doesn't smoke," he told me again.

He is so far off target.

I wonder when Jack changed. Did he wake up one day dissatisfied? Was it the bitter cold or the fact that his coffee didn't stir well that day? Did he stub his toe? Or was it the Californian who called everyone "dude" and introduced him to sushi that swayed him to the pleasures of "golden living"?

Is there anything to be counted on but God and his grace?

I am spending too much time feeling sorry for myself. This has to stop!

The plane tosses in turbulence, like riding a mechanical bull. The girls are loving the ride. Watching them settles my fear.

Jack wakes up smiling. He's dying to share what he knows.

I finally ask about the job and the plans.

"It's about time," he says. "About time you asked."

He squeezes my hand and describes our new life in detail.

It sounds picture perfect, fairy tale stuff ... dreamy and appealing.

How can I let my heart concede to this unacceptable circumstance?

Concessions. The third word on Hope's summer vocabulary list, from the verb "concede" meaning to forfeit, compromise, surrender, give up, allow, grant. I think of all the synonyms loosely related to that word.

To lose yourself.

That is what I fear more than anything!

7

*J*ack promised pure California sunshine. Buckets of sunshine. Streams of golden rays pouring from the sky. It's pouring alright, but not buckets of sunshine. It's pouring so hard in Mission Viejo that the snails have come out. I stepped on three on the way in. They crunch an awful, mutilating sound. A sound that chills you, like fingernails on a chalkboard.

The weather has failed Jack, and I am happy. Yes, happy. I want him to know that his sunshine state is not *all* sunshine *all* the time.

Forget that it's the first time in twenty years that it's rained like this in July. That's what Cousin Bradford says. Round, liver-eyed Bradford with a huge gap between his teeth and hair implants on the back of his head that look like mini brown tassels.

I feel sorry for the girls. They are standing at French doors staring into a purely adult patio. A yard that appears untouchable with its granite walls, cobblestone walkways, artificial waterfalls, and exotic plants. For the first time in their lives they are aware that the world is not one big, wide-open space.

There are fences; large, concrete walls that are standard height and built to city code.

"Why do you have such high fences, Cousin Bradford? Is it because you get a lot of wind?" Faith asks.

"For privacy," he says, as though it should be obvious.

"We don't get hardly any wind in Fairbanks," says Hope.

It's easy to see the girls are homesick.

Bradford makes a suggestion. "We have a portable hammock in the TV room. You can pretend you're in the Caribbean on a white beach. Palm trees swaying. Reggae music playing in the background. A piña colada in your hand. Er … I mean a tropical pineapple and coconut drink."

"We've never had coconut," Hope says.

"Improvise."

The word is not on Hope's vocabulary list.

"Manage, honey."

She and Faith look up with confused expressions.

"Cope."

The expressions remain.

"Go watch the Disney Channel." He points down the hall.

This they understand.

I don't know Bradford well, but I can tell our stay is going to be strained.

In walks Delilah, Bradford's new wife. Yes, Delilah. What could possess parents to name a child such a tarnished name, I don't ask. But it fits her. She looks like she belongs on a stage in tinsel town as she comes prancing into her living room in a strapless red dress with an obvious blonde wig and too much makeup. Nothing subtle about her.

"Where are the children?" she asks first, in a tone noting concern that her things might be in danger of destruction.

"In the back, watching television," Bradford answers.

Add to her appearance her dislike of children. I am a mother; I know these things.

"Hello, Jack," Delilah smiles in his direction.

Jack returns a greeting.

"Hello." She looks at me surprised, like I am not what she expected.

"Hello," I say back.

"Thank God for automatics," she says, straightening her dress straps. "This rain could do a woman in."

"Automatics?" Jack and I ask together.

"Garage door openers."

"Of course. We have those in Alaska too."

Jack nudges me with his elbow for sounding so hoedown.

"So, have you found a house?" she asks. I'm not sure if she's hinting or just making conversation.

"They only arrived an hour ago, babe," Bradford chimes in, wrapping his arm around her and sticking out his chest, looking peacock proud.

"We'll start looking tomorrow," Jack says.

We stand for a long, awkward moment staring at nothing in particular.

The living room is vaulted ceilings and lots of glass and light. Beige, big, and fancy. But it feels claustrophobic to me.

I now wish it would stop raining so I could escape this rabbit hole.

Oh, to be back home in my own hammock staring at my beautiful sky with Max and Martha licking my toes with their slippery tongues.

Fool. Dreamer.

"Hungry?" Delilah asks. "I make a mean Thai stir-fry with coconut milk and peanut sauce."

Jack's face twists strangely. "No, we're fine; they fed us on the plane."

"They don't eat coconut," Bradford says looking worried, like maybe they shopped for the occasion.

"Yes, we do," I explain. "It's just not often because coconuts are expensive. Milk is $4.60 a gallon in Alaska."

"Why would anyone want to live in a place like that?" Delilah exclaims, patting her hair that doesn't move.

"There's more to life than coconuts," Jack says.

"Like ice fishing," she says cutely.

We force a laugh. After all, we are guests.

Jack, dressed in baggy beach shorts and a "Surfer Dude" T-shirt is trying to look Californian. He bought his new look last night at Marty's beach shop in the casual atmosphere of downtown Huntington Beach.

He's acting like a child, if you ask me. Using language like "gnarly to the max," which I have yet to understand the meaning of.

Jack was flattered—actually flattered—when Delilah's little sister, an underaged beach bunny, said, "No. You couldn't be from Alaska. You just couldn't be. Why you are positively Californian through and through."

I wonder what she thinks Alaskans are supposed to look like?

Then she went on to say that "surf rage" attacks are terrible these days. The surfers are territorial and feeling crowded. And the ancient surfers—those over thirty-five—are competing for waves that belong to Generation X.

Jack's expression was priceless.

I understood about the crowding, however. I was over-whelmed at the sticky crowds myself. Trying to understand why we waited an hour for a street-side table for people to crawl over us to get to their table. And the food tasted like any other, but to their account they did put maraschino cherries and colorful umbrellas in our soft drinks.

As we drive through Mission Viejo on a house-hunting mission in the sunshine that finally showed up, I am admittedly impressed. This place is beautiful; there's no denying it.

The houses in each subdivision look identical, down to the paint and door. The house numbers are the only way to tell that you're not at the neighbor's house, other than the color of the doormat.

It's what is called a planned community with a Master Plan for the purpose of conformity. Where people don't park on the grass and have to pick up their leashed dog's mess with plastic bags when they take him for a walk.

They should name this place the town of Perfect. It reminds me of a huge dollhouse neighborhood, but with real lawns, trees, and flowers—a Mayberry of a different kind.

But unlike Mayberry they don't wave as much, they lock their doors, and two miles down the road is a rush of traffic like Sheriff Andy Taylor couldn't have imagined.

We meet our realtor in front of a house that looks too expensive. She looks richer than anyone would want their realtor to look, and she talks through her nose. Maybe a nose job gone bad or a deviated septum. She's nice though. Very nice.

"What's the population in Mission Viejo?" Jack asks.

"Close to 100,000."

We walk up the steps of a peach-colored house with a red tile roof.

"A foreclosure," she says. "You could get such a deal."

"What's the price?" we ring together, instruments of curiosity.

"Only $629,000."

I gulp, and smile out of consideration; Jack acts like it's nothing.

"Excuse me, I left something in the car," she says. The BMW Z8 she is driving is well over $100,000 Jack tells me.

I raise my eyebrows. "She must make good on commissions."

"What do you think of the neighborhood, Karan?"

"I think we can't afford these prices. What would we use for a down payment?"

"We have funds."

"What funds?"

He looks at the street and then back to me.

"The college and retirement fund? You know we can't touch that money, Jack."

"Shh. The realtor will hear you."

"I don't care."

"I'll make up the difference, Karan. I'll put it back as soon as I can. But we need a decent down payment. We have to qualify."

Should I bother getting angry?

Pauline, our cheery realtor, guides us through the house, pointing out the granite counters, central vacuum system, crown molding, sunken tub, and covered patio.

All day we view similar houses with similar prices on similar streets. All day Jack is commenting how he loves this and loves that and asks about termites, plumbing, and roofing—things mostly guys and contractors ask about, and our realtor cannot answer.

"I'll check into that," Pauline keeps saying.

I miss the girls and wonder how they're doing. They're with Candy, Jack's aunt and Bradford's mother. This is a concern of mine. You see, Candy is a Louisiana born and bred California transplant who's convinced she's Hawaiian by way of visiting Hawaii, loving it, and renaming herself Nohea, which means lovely, and which nobody calls her.

She talks this Hawaiian slang that clashes with her blonde hair and dresses in some kind of Hawaiian dress she says is made of bark cloth. She is as laid back as a recliner and slow … a mix of Southern slow and island slow.

Aunt Candy's house looks strictly tribal, with tiki figure carvings, wall masks, spears, and bamboo curtains. Polynesian pillows in brown flowery fabrics are dispersed throughout the room on low couches, and a massive canoe is propped against the wall with paddles on each side. Coconut mugs on the table and bamboo silverware make you feel like Gilligan is coming to dinner.

Too much. Swedish, Chinese, or Samoan. It's just too much.

The girls were fascinated with the colorful décor, however. I am sure they will be wearing hula skirts and leis and wiggling their hips a lot when we pick them up.

I remember this Hawaiian guy who lived across the street from us when I was fourteen. His name was Kale, which reminded me of a vegetable, but he said it meant manly. He was a big guy who grunted a lot. And he was always talking about Huna, some type of shamanism practice. He claimed he could do healings.

I wonder if I should be terrified.

At the end of the day I come to two conclusions. One, that I need new sandals. My Wal-Mart flip-flops are killing me. The other conclusion I reach is that I am no longer making decisions about my life; Jack is making them for me. I feel like I'm being force-fed and have to say I like everything to please him.

He asks my opinion on something and sticks to his. This is a drastic change. What he used to say was, "Let's pray about it." We had this forty-eight-hour rule about big decisions like computers and cars. No more. He sold Pickles to the professor and told me about it on the plane.

"Let's take it," he says as we stand in the back yard of a house I think I like but don't remember if it had four or five bedrooms.

"Uh ... "

"It's great, Karan. What more do you want?"

I shrug my shoulders, which somehow relays approval to Jack.

"We'll take it," he says to Pauline with a voice of declaration.

"I'll write up an offer," she says, accumulating paperwork from her briefcase.

"Congratulations."

She shakes our hands with unrestrained enthusiasm.

Did we just buy a house?

8

*D*elilah can't cook, but thinks she can. She's says we're eating banana pancakes, but the mushy substance on our plates resembles nothing remotely close to food.

Jack escaped by way of Aunt Candy's old Volkswagen Bug. He took the girls down to the lake to feed the ducks and told me they would pick up Egg McMuffins later. After Delilah's Thai affair the other night, he said he couldn't spare the three Tums left in the bottle; he needs to save them for tonight's meal. Delilah says we're having Middle Eastern: roasted lamb, couscous, and peppers.

As she puts the marinated meat in the fridge, Bradford shows his gap teeth and says. "You're so international, babe."

Delilah giggles and stuffs her hands in the pockets of her apron with the bold caption, "Best Cook in the World"—obviously a gift from Bradford.

Bradford stuffs pancakes in his mouth and drips syrup all over.

"Your house is going to be great," he says to me, an unfortunate glob of food visible. "And only three miles away."

"Yeah, great." I try to smile.

"A quick escrow, I hear." Delilah looks hopeful.

"Thirty days or less."

"Thirty days, huh," she says as though she is counting the hours until we leave.

We cramp their style; it's obvious. They are newlyweds; we have children. I understand the situation. I am less than thrilled with my newfound relatives myself. These people are so different from the people I know, and three miles away seems next door in Alaskan dimensions.

"Gotta go. Time is money." Bradford takes one last monstrous bite and swallows so hard his Adam's apple bobbles. Then he turns to me and says, "Jack will be doing this soon."

I hope not; it's Sunday.

He kisses Delilah and smacks her backside.

She slaps his hand, loving it.

I'm feeling like I shouldn't be here.

I look at the beige wall and the flower-etched stone clock that says Hawaii. It was not her choice—Delilah pointed out as she sat next to me at the dinner table the other night—her Woodstock-loving mother-in-law gave it to them as a gift, and Bradford will not allow her to give it to Goodwill.

Bradford, overhearing, said in his mother's defense, "Nineteen sixty-nine was a good year, Del. Neil Armstrong landed on the moon."

"His mother is a perennial bloomer," she whispered in my ear, like it was supposed to make sense to me.

I pretended to cough for lack of something suitable to say.

With everyone gone but Delilah, I feel suddenly uncomfortable. Sitting in a stranger's kitchen with no plans for the day. No transportation. And so I ask if she was born here. Boy is that a mistake.

Delilah pulls off her apron and pulls up a chair and gets this hurt look in her eye, like when someone says something mean and hurts your feelings.

Then she proceeds to share with me in a voice that is tenser than the apple-sweet voice she practices, how her father was a trucker in Phoenix, Arizona, and she grew up dirt poor. How they ate nothing but macaroni and cheese for weeks at a time and lived in a house of particleboard, walls so thin they'd shake when her father would walk in his steel-toed boots.

Do truckers wear steel-toed boots?

And when she starts telling me that her mittens had holes, and her poor little fingers froze because they couldn't afford new ones, I start thinking she's getting her stories mixed up. Because the last time I checked, the low in Phoenix mid-winter exceeds Fairbank's high.

"That's why I love to cook," she says. "So I can enjoy all the good food I couldn't have when I was a child."

"That's fascinating," I say, but I can't help staring at her eyebrows. They're too thin, and the left one is distractingly crooked.

She gets up and starts piling dishes for the maid. "I love international cuisine. I met Bradford at an international establishment, you know?"

"Really?" I suppress an urge to laugh.

Jack told me confidentially that they met in a nightclub called the Tequila Rumba on Pico Boulevard in Los Angeles. The international food was probably nachos.

I'd like to feel sorry for her, but I can't. For one thing she's a habitual liar, and, even if I have misjudged her honesty, I know for sure she hasn't gained an ounce of character from her underprivileged background. It seems to have had the reverse effect and turned her into a spoiled, snobby socialite, without the social life.

I just want to be home leading my own simple life, not here in La-La Land analyzing people and their motives.

My thoughts turn toward Alaska and the long days of summer. Midnight barbecues, swinging on the porch with Mom, tending my garden, and the company of the dogs.

We should be in church today. I long to hear Pastor Davies tell me, once again, that God is good and in control, even when it doesn't feel that way.

I have a feeling life is about to get complicated.

When Delilah catches me staring at the wall after breakfast, she offers to drop me off somewhere.

"At a bakery would be nice. For some thinking time," I say, certain she didn't see me pouring the bitter liquid she called coffee down the drain when she left the room.

So she drops me off at Bagels by Judi with her cell phone and tells me to call her when I'm ready to be picked up.

I order coffee and a bagel. Grab a decorating magazine from the steel rack and move outside to sunshine, plopping my feet on an iron chair. Trying to think up a plan of attack between sips of flavored coffee, I rotate my shoes like a window wiper.

I am hoping for a brilliant range of decorating ideas for my new house from the inspiring magazine pages, but my heart is not in it. I am drawing a blank.

"Can I borrow that chair next to you?" a voice behind me asks. I turn around and notice her well-coordinated outfit. And for a moment I seriously consider offering to pay this stranger to sit down and offer me decorating advice.

"Where do you live?" I ask desperately.

"Why, do I know you?"

"Well—"

Before I can finish she answers, "Rudy's Mobile Home Park in Death Valley. We're visiting relatives. I think you have me confused with someone else."

I smile and let her take the chair and stick my nose back in the colorful pages.

I don't want to pick out new furniture and analyze swatches for window coverings because the owner took the ones she was supposed to leave. I don't want to pick out new pictures and measure for shelves and decide what long distance plan to choose and whether to get a water softener and repaint the white walls a warmer color.

The new house is wonderful, and I know I should be grateful. But I feel like I was ripped out of my happy environment and dropped in a strange land and expected to flourish.

If only uprooted people were like flowers, we'd transplant easier.

Soak bare roots for about an hour; remove from container; introduce the flower to its new soil; massage roots; water. Watch it grow big and beautiful in its new surroundings!

But people aren't like flowers.

If it's a matter of will, I'm in trouble.

Not that I'm thick headed, at least I've never thought of myself that way. But I know what I love; I didn't have to go searching for it. I was pleased with my life; it had substance and purpose.

The emptiness hasn't left me; it just shifts. I haven't felt full of life since that day on the sea with the whales. I can't accept the fact that this is my situation. But the thing about acceptance is it doesn't change a thing whether you do or don't. What we want doesn't always match what is. Otherwise, chocolate would be low-calorie food, and vacations to Italy would cost a dollar.

"Would you mind giving up that chair you have your feet on?" a woman in a bright orange tube top asks.

I give it up, no questions asked.

*S*hopping with Aunt Candy is like taking a vacation in a tropical paradise with none of the fun. I didn't know there were so many Polynesian stores in Southern California.

"You'll love this next store," she says. "They have the absolute neatest stuff."

We walk into her living room, magnified ten times.

"Karan, this would be perfect next to that couch you said you liked."

Aunt Candy is holding an ornate lamp made of bamboo. A menagerie of glued seashells for a shade.

"I don't think that would go with our colors," I say, imagining it in her living room.

"Can we have it in our room?" Faith asks.

"It's too expensive, Faith; I'm sure of it," I say in a tone she's used to hearing when she asks for things she cannot have. I'm hoping it is too expensive.

Aunt Candy reads the price tag.

"It's on me; I insist."

And Faith is pleased.

Since I can't ditch Aunt Candy, because she is our transportation, I manage to redirect our focus by suggesting Pier 1 Imports. A match for both of us. Aunt Candy keeps picking up Polynesian; I pick up contemporary. She admires the bamboo basket, I admire the wire basket. She adores the big flower prints; I prefer the dark plaids.

In the end I have nothing to show for the day, except tired feet. I think tomorrow I'll leave the girls with Aunt Candy (after praying over them) and head to the mall.

Jack's not worried about the money, so why should I be concerned? Apparently he thinks we are rolling in it. "Buy all the furniture and appliances you want. I'll cover it." Our carefully determined budget and adherence to debt-free living based on Christian principles has all been lost to the call of reckless abandon.

I don't like sleeping in a borrowed bed, but from now on I will be. Whether it's Bradford's house, or our new house; it won't be mine. Not really. My house is somewhere else. A stranger is locking my doors.

Jack's breath is on my neck, and I should feel close to him, but I don't. I feel as far from him as China is from here. I want to tell him things that are on my heart that he used to want to know, but doesn't ask about any more. I think he fears my answers. It's easier for him to be far away so he can tune out what he wants to.

If I could see into his heart like Faith alluded to that day on the beach, what would I see? Black pieces crumbling to dust? Does he see his heart changing colors? Our world growing into an overgrown jungle? These are the questions I want to ask him. These are the questions I wouldn't dare.

We talk and smile the same, but say different things. Nothing of consequence. And it occurs to me in watching couples that many of them relate this way. That what Jack and I had—what our family had—was one in a million. An intimacy that went beyond the normal intimacy level. It was uncommonly special.

Jack used to take me to the meadow where our home in Alaska now sits. At the time it was just bare land owned by some guy in Wisconsin who never visited, and not for sale. We used to pray to God right there, knees on the earth, that he would bequeath it to us somehow because it seemed to us the most beautiful place on earth.

When Daddy was dying of the greedy cancer that took him in seven short weeks, he told us to buy the property of our dreams, love God and each other, and be happy. He had an excellent life insurance policy, and the proceeds, even after being split between my mom and sisters, would be enough. Finally, one day just after his death, we visited the property and saw a "For Sale" sign and bought it, just as Daddy wanted. With the money left over, Jack built our house.

No small miracle.

But before we owned the land, Jack and I used to visit and pretend it was ours. He would talk about his adventures growing up in Louisiana. Say the most poetic things that I, being a poet myself, appreciated. He'd talk about how it feels to wet your feet in mucky water among the cattails and dragonflies; how a starry night makes you want to eat the stars like candy; how when the wind blows it has this lonely, isolated sound that sings.

Poetry would flow from his free-thinking spirit, and I would drink it in and feel full. I wanted to be a part of him so badly it hurt.

Jack called us dreamers of gold. We lived in a world that belonged to us alone, to which there was no key and no time. Just being together was enough, and the thoughts of good things to come. We were convinced that only heaven could exceed our ecstasy. Surpass our romantic land of castle visions.

And now Jack has shut the castle door so tight there's no air to breathe, and I, his damsel in distress, am calling, "Jack, please come back to me!"

"Karan? You're awake. I can feel it."

He faces me. I can see by the moonlight his eyes are partially closed.

"Yes, I am."

"Thinking?"

"Yes … thinking."

"Well, stop it, will you? You're keeping me awake. I have a lot to do tomorrow."

He rolls over and sighs heavy, and I know the poetry is gone from him.

9

It is Sunday morning, and the pastor is preaching in white shorts and a Tommy Hilfiger shirt. He's sweating beads. From twenty feet away I can see drips trickling.

The place is hot, like a sauna. And he's spending way too much time on the subject of money. Specifically for the new church building.

He describes this vision of mahogany pews, stained-glass windows, and air conditioning. The eyes of the congregation stare straight ahead as though they are used to hearing it and are dreaming the announcement time away.

I'm just trying not to faint. I think the money could be better spent on air conditioning *now* so he can keep the congregation he has. But maybe that's the idea; they'll contribute more just at the thought of cool air.

As we stand up to sing, I feel awkward and overdressed. I thought they might dress fancier in affluent neighborhoods, but they seem to take the lead of the pastor, mostly in shorts. Jack, standing next to me, is also in shorts. He said I was overdressed. I am waiting for a haughtily delivered "I told you so" from him after the service.

I am wearing a black silk dress, which is the only fancy dress I own. I feel wrapped in yards of the featherweight fabric. I tug at my pearl necklace and earrings, alternating between the two. The only real jewelry I own. I feel like the queen of Sheba adorned in precious gems.

I shouldn't have asked the tired-looking cashier for a recommendation. Her face looked dead, like most of the pew warmers now. But she had a fish symbol pin on her collar.

Back home, the church is lively. It's this fantastic place where people love and support each other. You can't escape a service without being consumed in warm hugs and authentic expressions of caring.

Our pastor, Lance Davies, is a brown-skinned Alaskan Native. He is an Athabascan Indian, but his call is to minister to the white people. He says, jokingly, that it is because his own people could not stand his shrill voice. And it's true; his voice is shrill—like a woman's. If you didn't know him, it might be considered annoying, but he preaches like he has a map to the human heart.

Pastor Davies is a little man with buggy eyes, and we call him the "Crane." For cranes have a loud, shrill voice that can be heard for miles away. And on days when he has a particularly anointed message and goes on too long, he smiles and says, "God graced me with a long windpipe, congregation. And pestered you, I'm afraid."

I can't help wondering if this pastor didn't print his sermon off the Internet. I know I've heard it before. And he's banging the pulpit. I don't know if it's in emphasis or to cover up bad preaching. All I know is that it's not edifying and is magnifying my headache from the mix of strong perfume.

The heat is suffocating, and I use my bulletin to fan myself as the mediocre sermon concludes. I look down nonchalantly to read my watch. The balding preacher gives the benediction, and the organist plays solemn notes.

In three minutes the crowd dissipates in the same way an auditorium clears after a bad elementary school concert. People are in a desperate hurry to get out of here. That tells me, in and of itself, that these people are not connected. Their time might be better spent reading the Bible.

Exiting the sardine-can lobby, their conversation turns to worldly living.

"I'm sailing Newport this afternoon. Wanna come?" I hear a man with a raspy voice ask. "Just bought a forty-four-foot yacht."

A big woman in fashion-abhorrent vertical stripes comments on her brownie recipe. "The trick is the amaretto; it's the ingredient people can't distinguish. And you can add a teaspoon of almond extract … but it's optional."

No one even mentions the sermon. As though the message didn't penetrate past the tips of their ears.

We won't be returning to this church. That's for sure.

*W*ell that was interesting," Jack says as we walk in the door of the empty house that looks too unlived in for six people staying there. Delilah and Bradford are not churchgoers. Bradford is working, and Delilah is shopping, so the note in the entryway says. The smell of chili permeates and breaks the illusion that we are on a model home tour.

"Let's go to a restaurant, quick. Before we have to eat that stuff."

I want to agree with Jack, that we had best escape our

gaseous fate, but my correcting instincts tell me I must stand true to proper etiquette.

"Take off your shoes, girls. We're eating here."

Jack grimaces, pulls the Velcro straps off his sandals and places them on the deodorized shoe rack that Delilah recently purchased, explaining that it would keep our shoes fresh and tidy, and her entryway less cluttered.

"Delilah's food gives me a tummy ache, Mommy," Faith claims.

I speak adult sense, a habit I can't seem to break. "We are their guests, sweetheart, and I appreciate how you have been very polite about the food. Even if you don't care for something, you continue to be polite."

"I'm polite too, Mommy," Hope says. "But hungry."

"We'll buy you some granola bars, and you can keep them in your room. But don't get crumbs in the carpet."

"Okay!" Hope and Faith chime together and hug like starving children.

"What was that we had for breakfast anyway?" The whites of Jack's eyes expand unnaturally.

"Stuffed French toast."

"Are you sure?"

"According to Delilah."

"It was like melted sugar over bread."

"She tries," I say to be nice.

"Cousin Bradford said I had 'preeme duna tendencies,'" Faith tattles, pulling at her long braid.

"Prima donna?" I ask.

"Yes, Mommy."

"I heard him too," charges Hope. "Is it bad?"

My protective motherly instincts rise up in defense mode.

"I'm sure he was joking, Karan." Jack leans down to child eye level. "He likes to joke, honey," he says to Faith.

I'm not so sure.

"His face didn't look like joking," she says and tilts her head and squeezes one eye shut.

Jack moves into the kitchen, and we follow him. He examines the pot of chili and utters a mumble of disgust.

"Jack, you will talk to Bradford." I speak disapproval with my eyes.

"So he called Faith a genius ... what's the big deal? From the Latin, girls, meaning 'those first gifted.'"

I pour myself a glass of water from the Sparklett's dispenser.

"You know full well the connotation, Jack"

"You sat directly behind me in Latin. Remember, Karan?"

"I remember that decrepit professor with the yellow bow tie who found English deplorable. 'Latin is the root of the romance languages,' he used to say at least ten times a day."

"And you used to copy my paper."

"I did not," I state adamantly.

"She did, girls. Your mother is a cheat from way back."

Normally I would laugh at Jack's playful teasing, but as of late Jack has been avalanching me with elbow pokes, and I suspect he has underlying resentments of which he is not even aware.

I take a long swallow of water and change the subject. "Where shall we dine?"

"But you said—" Jack begins.

"McDonalds!" the girls yell in agreement.

McDonalds. The girls want to eat under the golden arches

every opportunity, and it occurs to me that maybe that's because it's familiar.

The girls are doing well. Too well. I think because it feels like a vacation to them still.

I worry more about Hope. Faith speaks her mind, but Hope holds it all in. Yesterday at the mall she saw a stuffed animal that looked like Max and Martha. She didn't say a word, just kept stroking the thing as though it were real.

"Alright, sweethearts. Chicken McNuggets here we come," I say exuberantly.

Fatty, greasy, artery-clogging fast food. Yuk. The thought is about as appealing as Delilah's chili.

"Come on, cheat girl and my two geniuses."

Jack throws his sandals back on, and I throw another well-practiced look.

The chenille patch bedspread on which I am lying is soft, and the room is a relaxed décor, warmth unlike Delilah. The muscles in my neck are tense because Jack doesn't rub necks or feet anymore, and I miss his touch. I miss Mom, too. Not having her near is a bitter ache to me.

I am elated when I answer the phone and recognize Mom's voice by her cheery "Good morning."

"This room smells like you, Mom. Like lilacs. And it's purple, your favorite color. I think I'll decorate a room like this in my new house. Maybe our bedroom, though I'm not sure Jack would appreciate it."

"Lilacs … your father used to bring me lilacs; pale lavender lilacs off our shrubs in the spring. He knew I longed for the greenery of Maine. Then he would quote, 'In the spring a young man's fancy lightly turns to thoughts of love.'"

"Tennyson, right, Mom?"

"That's right, dear."

I move from my back to my side, trying to find a comfortable position for what I know will be a marathon conversation.

"Daddy was a hopeless romantic."

"He was," Mom agrees. "He'd get up before me and place lilacs in beautiful vases around our bedroom, sometimes several of them. The aroma was a garden. And in the winter he'd bring me pictures of lilacs, cards with lilacs, lilac bath salts."

I am drinking in the description.

"Your father said they were a symbol of our love because they bloomed so sweet and abundantly."

"I didn't know the story, Mom. But I remember the scent well."

"These days I have a time keeping the moose away. They love the things."

"I hope the professor is keeping my yard from the ravages of hungry moose."

"And your flower is the red rose, isn't it, dear? I remember when Jack came home with two dozen one year."

"He doesn't bring me flowers anymore."

"Why, last September on your birthday … "

"But things have changed since then. He's not the same man."

"That's nonsense, Karan. Why, Jack is a treasure if I ever saw one."

"I'm serious, Mom."

In search of a more comfortable position, I fluff the goose down pillows and arrange them against the brass headboard, lie back, and wing one elbow out.

"Well, if he's changed one way, he can change back."

"I hope so, because I'm growing weary of sleeping with a stranger."

"Women are external, Karan. Why, we can't keep what's going on inside from showing. But men have internal changes."

"I think they keep their feelings hidden on purpose, Mom. It's a pride issue."

"I don't. I think they're not as attuned as women, and they don't like feeling out of control; it makes them feel trapped. So they start thinking they need all the things they didn't fulfill in their youth to solve it, because men like solutions and want to prove themselves."

"But Jack is so young."

"That's just it, Karan; he wants to do these things while he's young. Have success, or experience … whatever it is he's searching for. Reassess his life course, as we all do to different degrees.

"So, why can't he join a men's Bible study?"

"Because then he would have to share his weaknesses and admit them to himself."

"Hmmm."

"Women tend to gather to heal; men tend to isolate themselves and withdraw from those they love."

"I think what you're saying is true, Mom. But it scares me."

"I checked out a book at the library on the subject once when Margo was having problems with her husband. He eventually got over it, and they're better for it."

"Could that happen to Jack?"

"Jack is fine, dear. When he buys a Harley and starts wearing leather, that's when you worry." Mom laughs, and the dogs bark in the background.

"Yeah, I guess."

*J*ack is wearing leather, and I'd like to die. "Bradley's jacket," he says. "Atrocious, isn't it?"

"Yes," I say thankfully. "Grotesque," I add, to ensure there is no doubt on the subject. "Nothing worse than an older man trying to be young."

"Bradley is only thirty-five; same as me. That's not exactly old."

"Old enough to start pretending he's young."

He hangs it back up in the coat closet.

"I was looking for my cell phone; have you seen it? Anything I leave out for more then two seconds, Delilah moves."

"It's on your belt clip, Jack."

He looks down surprised; yanks it to be sure.

"I'm meeting Bradford at the office. We're going to go over some things. I start officially tomorrow, you know. You won't be seeing as much of me."

He flares his nostrils, unaware of the habit.

"I don't know what I'm going to do with all this time on my hands." I say it jokingly; Jack takes it seriously.

"Maybe you can go to the beauty parlor. Aunt Candy will watch the girls."

He pulls bills from his wallet and stuffs them in my hand.

"Why? Do I look like I need a beauty parlor?"

"No, I just thought that's what women like to do here."

I take the money anyway.

"I'll use it to get switch plates like the ones we have back home."

"Home? You're going to have to stop referring to our old house as home."

"It is home; we still own the place."

Silence on the other end.

I cozy up to Jack, but his body tenses, as if to sense my ulterior motives.

"Do you think we could afford to keep both houses and spend our summers there?"

"The professor has a lease, Karan. And, besides, we need the rental income. If we stayed there, we would be losing rent."

I pull back and stare out into the street, hug myself in a poor attempt at self-comfort.

"Well, it will always be *my* home. It's the house Daddy meant for us, and I don't think it's fair that you expect me to forget it."

"We have to make sound financial decisions. The stock market is low, and we need to be wise with our money. Sentimental value can't be banked; rent can."

Money and *Forbes* talk. And who's this talking about being wise with our money? As he checks his reflection in the mirror, he seems like a stranger.

"You have our whole life mapped out for us, Jack. Let me know when you pick out our grave plots. I want to make sure they're in the shade."

"You're becoming bitter, Karan, and it doesn't suit you."

"Well I absolutely have no reason, do I?"

"None that I can see."

"Look, I don't want to argue, Jack."

"You're the one—"

We hear the sound of heels clattering along the pavement and recognize the footsteps as Delilah's stilettos.

"Just one month in the summer then, Jack? When the professor is on vacation or something?"

"You said you don't want to argue, so ice it, will you?"

Where is Jack coming up with this college slang?

10

I read a poem once about how life can be like a revolving door going around in a vicious circle until you're dizzy in its hold. You start out slow, and the propulsion carries you, until you're spinning out of control and can't stop.

When I was a young girl, my rich Aunt Athena took me to stay at a fancy Toronto hotel with revolving doors. I remember being in this elegant lobby with huge chandeliers and what looked to me like the magic carpets of Aladdin's tales.

Aunt Athena was occupied with hordes of expensive luggage, and an entourage was following her, which always seemed to be the case, though I'm not sure why.

I started going around in the revolving door and thinking it a blast, until I couldn't stop the thing. I was sure I was going to fall right over myself and be crushed by steel and glass. My aunt would scold me for being unladylike and, after taking me to the hospital, would punish me for the rest of the trip.

I remember the nice bellhop helping me by grabbing hold of the door, and me smashing up against the glass and later having a nasty bruise, which I attributed to banging into the bathroom door.

I was glad that my aunt, in her big fur coat and cat-eye glasses, didn't witness my misbehavior. She was busy bossing people around; something she did very well.

That revolving door has been my life lately.

Three weeks ago our belongings arrived. The pot-bellied driver, looking shabby and possibly a little drunk, showed up at 2:35 AM pounding on Bradford's door. What a scene that caused. Delilah flew into the living room without her wig in Victoria's Secret lingerie and some kind of cold cream on her face; Bradford was right behind her, still sleepy, with a stick in his hand ready to knock a robber in the head.

"Go back to bed, guys," Jack suggested. "It's just the movers; we can handle it."

"At this time of the morning? Are you all nuts?" Bradford asked, seething.

"Hey," the driver said. "I work cheap, and this is what you get. I don't set the time, I just drive."

"Well, be as quiet as you can," Bradford entreated, holding his hands in prayer position and looking up. "This is a high-rent district, you know."

"You'll have to move the cars out of the garage first," the mover's helper publicized, to Bradford's obvious dismay.

So Bradford's garage was packed floor to ceiling with our boxes, and Delilah was furious that she had to park her Mercedes in the driveway. She said her car would be positively ruined by bird mess.

In Alaska they'd laugh you out of the state for avoiding bird mess.

The heat was turned up on Delilah's already simmering resentments, so after this incident she stopped cooking meals out of spite. We thought it hilarious because we were barely tolerating her food anyway. We ate out for all our meals after that, and I fell in love with this Italian restaurant we've eaten at three times.

The day after the boxes arrived, Bradford asked again about the closing on the house and offered to arrange for the movers. Then he asked when we were getting a car. Hint, hint.

We had been borrowing Aunt Candy's Volkswagen Bug, and Delilah, through thin California walls, said that they were becoming the humiliation of the neighborhood with that psychedelic junk heap in front of her house. It was bad enough she had to have the thing parked there when Bradford's mother came to visit.

Bradford put Jack in touch with a buddy of his who he said could get us a good deal on a car. Two hours after meeting Bradford's friend, Jack came back driving a brand-new gold-colored GMC Yukon he said was cheap, though he didn't tell me how cheap, cheap was.

Apparently, stricter emission standards are being imposed on SUVs in California because of global warming Alaskans don't seem to fret so much about, thus the great deal. Californians hate the guzzlers—even though the sales don't seem to reflect this hatred—and some car dealerships are even eliminating them altogether.

Jack said we would need two cars and asked if I wanted to buy Aunt Candy's car because she might want an SUV too. Aunt Candy's funky yellow Bug has Hawaiian decals on the windows and a sticker on the back that reads, "Proud to be Hawaiian."

"I don't think so."

And Jack didn't seem to understand why.

"A van might be more practical," I said, trying to stabilize my worried voice.

"Sure," he said, after thinking a minute. "A van would work."

Bradford's movers (supposedly scheduled for eight o'clock) showed up at the suspicious hour of five o'clock this morning, which might have been a payback for Bradford's 2:35 AM awakening. Especially since he was fully awake when they arrived, snacking on leftover blueberry pie, and appeared to be enjoying the pandemonium.

The movers, dressed in street clothes, demanded $2,800 before leaving the driveway. I may not know what I'm talking about, but it seems an outrageous price for moving us a total of three miles. Of course, the invoice was presented *after* the boxes were already in the truck.

So here I am in my new house with boxes in every room.

My first acquaintance with the house was with our doorbell, a custom chime that sounded like a flock of confused geese. After several annoying rings from deliverymen who all seemed to show up at the same time and still felt compelled to each try our doorbell, I was intent on disconnecting the pesky contraption.

The one help Jack was to me this morning before he left for work was reinstalling the computer, so I was able to download how-to instructions from the pesky doorbell Internet site, which served me well until Step F, when in frustration I yanked the wires right out of the stucco.

I hardly remember half of the furniture delivered today, or where I ordered it, because I made the decisions in such a rush. According to my unreliable calculations, I purchased one piece of furniture every three hours of my waking hours during the period of a week.

When most of furnishings were arranged, I noticed my decorating was an assortment of pieces that looked fabulous apart but when put together looked like a seven-toned blue room ordered from a catalog by my nearsighted Great-Aunt Mildred.

The first deliveryman to show up, and the last to leave, installed a whopper of an entertainment system that Jack apparently ordered and forgot to mention. It must be expensive because the man, who kept pulling up his traveling pants, was drooling over it like it was some privilege to own it. How could Jack fail to mention a forty-two-inch home theater system with surround sound? Our TV in Alaska was a standard nineteen inches.

How much will all this cost? Stop this revolving door!

Three hours later, and I am taking part in a sit-down. But not to stage a protest—though that is a thought. I am frazzled to an unhealthy crisp, my hair is in a scarf, and the girls are dragging neighborhood children in who say they are hungry and thirsty and have to use our bathroom.

I am two minutes from insanity when I remember to pray.

Lord, I know you have a purpose in all this. And you don't have to tell me what it is this very moment. But sometime soon, please!

Suddenly in walks my new neighbor, about thirty, beautiful and smiling, a casserole dish balanced in one hand, and a big paper bag falling out of her right arm—lemons spilling everywhere. I am hoping her cooking is better than Delilah's, because we are very hungry, and I don't feel like cooking. In fact, I don't know if I could even find the stove through the clutter.

"I'm Cindy from across the street. You don't like lemons by any chance, do you? Because we have a lemon tree that's producing threefold this year."

"Suck 'em for fun," I say.

She laughs like my sister, Tammy.

"And the casserole ... eat it or not. I promise I won't be offended."

"Thank you. We're starving."

"Thank Betty Crocker."

Her wide blue eyes sparkle.

"Pardon me if I don't get up. Pardon me if I don't ever get up," I say, experiencing a lead body that refuses to cooperate with my brain's instructions.

"I'll put it on the counter." She walks into the kitchen.

"You'll have to clear a spot," I call to her.

"Hey, this looks like my kitchen after I hosted my husband's Christmas party last year. Makes me feel right at home," she calls back.

She walks up to my rumpled form and gives me a compassionate look.

"Join me on the floor?"

"Sure, neighbor. How about some lemonade?" she asks as she scoops lemons from my carpet.

Maybe this is one of the purposes, I think, watching Cindy amble around the room. I've never had a best friend. Lots of friends, sure. To lunch with, or shop with, or be with because of our association with kids or church, but not to tell secrets to or share my inner thought life with. Not the kind of friend you call on the phone just to talk or buy jewelry for.

Jack has always been my best friend, and with the girls and Mom we were a complete family. I never felt the need to include anyone else. And now, with Mom so far away and Jack absent in mind and body, I need someone to bounce ideas off. Someone to share with. Someone to have some fun with and experience *me*. Whoever the revised, rearranged, reconfigured me is.

Cindy and I stand near her hi-tech barbecue in a garden setting indicative of her colorful nature. In the background her daughters, Samantha and Meagan, who happily are the same ages as my daughters, are splashing in her pool.

I am pretending to have a good time, but am preoccupied by circumstance.

The food is gathering flies, and the guys aren't home yet. The hamburger buns are drying, the potato salad is warm, and the ice is melting.

"We did say six o'clock, didn't we?"

"Yes," says Cindy, "but these are guys, Karan. They have no concept of time. Steve doesn't, anyway. Sometimes he calls and says he'll be home at six o'clock, and four hours later he walks in the door."

"I thought most people worked nine to five."

"The thing is, he can't get anything done during the day. With phone calls, e-mails and employees needing a minute of his time every minute. He really has no choice but to work long hours if he wants to pay our exorbitant mortgage and keep me at home."

I am obviously naïve about business practices and time-clock living.

"When do you get to see each other?"

She flips a burger. Fire flashes and dies. Her mascara melts under her eyes, and she wipes it a smudgy mess, but I don't feel I know her well enough yet to tell her.

"I see Steve on weekends, his lunch hour, kids' recitals, vacations ... and barbecues like this one I plan and he's always late to."

"Really?"

Mosquitoes fly and land. I slap. I slap.

"But he's there to tuck the girls in at night; I appreciate that about him. Though sometimes they have to stay up awfully late to see him."

She squints her eyes from the rising heat.

"What about Jack?"

"In winter he had dog sledding tours and was only gone a few hours at a time. In the summer when he did wilderness tours and fishing charters he usually arranged them so we would still have family time. Lots of midnight barbecues."

"Well, he's a company man now."

"That's what scares me."

"Steve's had a heart attack already, and he's only thirty-eight. He's on high blood pressure and stress medication and has a special diet he never sticks to. I worry about him. I read the other day that 70 percent of all illnesses are stress related."

"Cindy, I'm sorry for saying this, but I don't want a life like that."

"It's got its perks. Guilt presents, you know."

"Guilt presents?"

"See, he's so distracted that he forgets something important like an anniversary or birthday, and so I just get a better present. I used to get upset when Steve would forget, but then I learned to work the system."

"I don't know, Cindy. I don't believe in manipulation."

"Give it six months, and you'll feel differently."

There is no way.

The kids step out of the pool looking like wet catalog models.

"We're starving. Can we eat please, Mom?" Samantha asks, a pleading expression on her golden-tanned face.

"Go ahead, kids," Cindy says.

And they start building mile-high burgers, too big for their stomachs, and dripping water from the pool all over us.

I look away, troubled.

"Trust me, Karan, neither of them will get home until nine o'clock or later."

"I don't know about Steve, but Jack isn't like that, Cindy. He knows how I feel, and he feels the same way. 'Family first' is our motto."

"If you say so ... "

Her eyes betray her doubt.

The girls are watching *Parent Trap*, the older version, and funnier in my opinion. Cindy and I are trying to pass the time with idle chatter. The crickets are making summer noises, and the neighborhood is still except for an occasional barking dog or passing car. And, oh yes, it's past nine o'clock and dark.

Cindy was right. No Steve, no Jack.

I am now planning my response. Trying to decide whether I should be mad and speak it, or be mad and sulk it.

The least I deserve is a phone call.

"Don't feel bad, Karan. The first five times are the hardest."

I cannot speak, for anger is swelling my vocal cords three times their normal size.

"And remember, there's always the prospect of bigger diamonds and Maui."

11

We are playing in the snow. Jack is smashing white powder on my wool-covered head. I feel the sensation of cold and ice running down my neck. I grab handfuls of dust and cover him in snow. He brushes it off, and I try to pack a snowball, but the snow is too dry.

Jack grabs me and wrestles me down to the freeze. I watch our vaporous breaths appear and vanish, and then we collapse.

The girls are watching, enamored with the play. They jump on us as we play dead. Faith takes the opportunity and smashes snow in Jack's face. He tickles her in revenge. Her laugh echoes wider than it does in the summer. And we are wet and shivering, but we don't care.

It is my August dream.

Jack is sprawled out soundly on our king-size bed in darkness so thick I cannot see the shadow of his face. The night is hot and sticky. The ceiling fan is inadequate, and he is snoring ferociously, the way he snores when he is exhausted. Sleep is not an option for me.

I have this urge to touch Jack's chest, and do. I feel his breath moving up and down and his heart beating in regular rhythm. I'm glad to feel it after hearing Cindy speak of heart attacks.

It used to be that I would wake Jack up when I had a dream or a special thought in the night. He asked me to. We'd talk about it in the darkness. In the still world the words seemed more clarified and intimate. Sometimes we'd hold each other without speaking at all, just watch the Northern Lights out the window. Jack positioned the house that way for that very purpose.

He's probably forgotten the beauty of the past. If he hasn't, I wonder how he keeps it from memory, for to me it is a song continually playing.

I am awake so long I see the room change from darkness to shadows to light. And now I see more clearly the work set before me. A mass of boxes still to be unpacked.

Funny, how Jack arranged packing our life with the movers, but the unpacking is left to me.

*J*am controlling my anger, but I'd like to spit. For weeks while staying at Bradford's house (after Delilah's refusal to cook), we went out for every meal. And now with the house a disaster and so much work that it cannot possibly get done, Jack, in this sweet voice, is asking for a bacon and cheese omelet with twice-buttered toast.

Doesn't he realize I haven't even unpacked the dishes yet?

"How about a good old-fashioned Egg McMuffin instead?"

"I'll grab a bagel on my way to the office," he says peevishly, and leaves me without a goodbye kiss, which could become habit. This day is starting badly, and I fear it will end even worse.

*T*wo days later, and I'm just now getting to the boxes. I try to unpack methodically, until I realize the boxes are marked wrong. The boxes marked "kitchen" contain bathroom towels, the boxes in the bathroom have kitchen utensils, and a box marked "living room" is a mix of all the rooms.

God, help me!

Cindy takes the girls and later calls and offers to help.

"Thanks, but no thanks, Cindy. I have to face this disaster alone."

By noon I've accomplished more than expected, and by 7:00 PM when the girls walk in the door and I direct them to the bathtub, things are looking much better, but I am looking a wreck. Jack isn't home again, but he does call.

"Sorry, Karan. I have a little more to do than I thought. I'll be home by nine o'clock; I promise."

Just as Cindy said would happen.

I sleep in an empty bed because I am so tired I couldn't stay awake if I tried. And what's the point? We would just argue, and I'm much too tired to argue.

*T*he next morning after I have missed another goodbye kiss from Jack, Cindy walks up and comments on my fragile expression as I pull mail from the black metal box.

"You know what you need, Karan?"

"A new husband?"

Disappointment shows on my face.

"No ... a hobby."

"I had hobbies in Alaska. I made crafts and knitted, I was an avid gardener, I did volunteer work ... and we had a pottery studio."

"Well, what do you have here?"

"A pottery studio?"

"No silly. Madeline Grayson who used to live in this house was a photographer. You have a whole setup here."

"I guess I do. I haven't explored the garage yet. But I did glide by the curtained room the first day we saw the house before I found an unsolicited pen in my hand."

"So, what are you waiting for?"

"I've been wanting to take up photography." I tap my chin in thought. "But I wouldn't know where to start."

"Start with wildlife."

"You don't have any wildlife around here."

"Are you kidding? We have tons of it."

"Where?"

"I'll show you. Tomorrow I'll take you and the girls there personally."

"Okay," I say, dying to know.

*V*enice Beach is the wildest beach in California, and possibly anywhere. And Cindy was right; there's tons of wildlife here. Just not the kind I was thinking of.

"This place certainly is a zoo." I can tell this a mile away. "Cindy, did you bring the bananas?"

"No, but I brought some coins. We're going to need them," Cindy says, jiggling her purse.

"Whoa … do we get to spend that?" asks Meagan, under ladybug shades.

"Not for spending, girls."

"We're going to throw it around," announces Samantha, almost as tall as her mother.

"Cool," says Faith.

As the boardwalk comes into view, I can see we are heading

into a new land. A bizarre scene of chaos against a serene backdrop of white sand and milky blue sea that seems to ease the severity.

The girls hold my hands tight, not sure what to make of it all.

Everywhere we look, oddity abounds: the chain saw juggler, the fire breather, some guy painted silver pretending to be a statue. Costumed performers parade oblivious to the early afternoon heat, but fully aware of the stares. The attention is what they seek, what empowers them to show such an embarrassing display of extreme exhibitionism.

"Let me get to my camera, girls," I say, and I peel their fingers from my hands and pull my Canon Sure Shot out of a small, ragged black case, feeling like a typical tourist.

Cindy smiles at me in reassurance.

My first click is slow and hesitant, a reacquainting with my mediocre machine. I catch a robust belly dancer as she glides by in a gold bra and belt over a full red skirt, pretending to be delicate.

I move my camera with the crowd and settle on another subject. This time the click feels natural. I shift between subjects, snapping in pulse with the movement.

My goal is to capture the activity of the crowd, the temper of the Los Angeles locals. But all the time I am wondering about their lives. Where they live, their belief system, and what they have hanging on their walls.

"I have no clue what I'm doing, Cindy," I say as I snap.

"Don't worry about it. Develop these at Kmart. You can learn the craft later. Just enjoy."

Hope and Faith haven't said much. It dawns on me they've rarely seen a woman smoke, much less micro-bikini-clad women and muscle men in shiny thongs.

They stare at me for a long moment while Cindy and her daughters chat like magpies and sip on gigantic sodas.

To break my daughters' guarded moods I catch their hands and spin them, twirling like we do under our home sky. A smile emerges on Hope's sweet face, and Faith breaks free in a dance like the Irish clog dancers you see on TV, as a stream of passersby applaud her efforts.

Faith bows, and we continue on our way, laughter blowing past us as we try adventure on for size.

A man wearing a tunic and playing a guitar on roller skates comes up behind me, performing for the camera. When he's done, he stands in front of us like I'm supposed to know something.

Cindy hands out money. "Drop the coins, girls," she says, sounding like a pro.

They do. And Meagan asks for more.

He skates away, making an impressive figure eight for an encore.

Not five steps away we greet more carnival characters: face-painted musicians, throwback hippies, and grotesquely oversized musclemen. We step over a sleeping homeless man and watch people engaged in health club sports.

"So this was supposed to be like Venice, Italy? I'll bet it's not what its founder had in mind."

"You never want to come here at night," Cindy says, as we weave through the crowd with our girls in tow. "This place is filled with gangs and drug dealers ... and sins take place out on the beach too seedy to mention."

"Don't worry; I wasn't planning on a night visit," I say.

"In fact, it's illegal to walk on the beach after dark because of all that."

"Really?" I stifle my imagination. "Amazing, how far the wicked heart will travel to make an experience when just sitting on the endless sand with the palm trees swaying should be enough."

"I know. I know, Karan."

"And I think we've had enough."

"I have to use the bathroom," Meagan says looking anguished.

"That's another reason to leave," says Cindy. "The bathrooms here are filthy."

"Yuk," I say, appalled at the prospect.

"I'm hungry," Samantha, the whinier of the two sisters, cries.

"Let's go to Fisherman's Wharf in San Pedro instead, Sam. We can have a late lunch there."

Noticing a woman shedding her top on the beach a few yards away, and seeing no cops around to stop her brazen self-exposure, I grab the girls and head the opposite direction.

"San Pedro's a good idea, Cindy. More of a family environment." I strain on the last of my words and throw my head so she will catch my view.

"Ooops. I didn't remember this," she says apologetically.

"No, it's okay. It was an experience, for sure. One that I do not plan repeating."

"I have to go to the bathroom," repeats Meagan.

*S*o where were you today?" Jack asks with a snip as we walk in the door, dropping beach bags and sand everywhere and smelling of fish. "I was home at six o'clock, and you were out playing, obviously, because I don't smell food cooking."

"Go take a bath, girls. Please."

Jack doesn't even say hello to them, and their sunburned faces show that they are crushed.

"I took a little break today. I'm taking up photography, so we visited Venice Beach and—"

Jack interrupts my explanation.

"You took *my* daughters to Venice Beach without consulting me?"

I study Jack's face like the faces I studied earlier on the beach. I feel an argument coming on and, like a runaway sled dog, I know it will not be stopped.

"Consulting you, Jack? You haven't consulted me on one decision since we've been here, and I need your permission to go to the beach?"

"That place is a magnet for loonies."

"I won't dispute that, but you didn't let me finish—"

"What kind of sense do you have, Karan?"

"The sense to know that you're not going to listen."

"I can see you're in a bad mood."

"Bad mood?" I raise my chest in rebellion. "Bad mood, Jack, was waking up the other day with ten thousand boxes to unpack and no help from you."

"I'm sorry. I didn't think to help, but I am earning a living, you know. We have a mortgage note to meet."

"And who decided that?"

"We did."

"We did?"

"Of course, we did!"

"Of course, we didn't!"

We fold arms and stare from a reasonable distance.

"I thought that once we were here, you'd change your mind about things and—"

"Become elated about it?"

"Sort of."

"Hearts are not wind-up toys, Jack. But I'm not miserable, if that makes you feel better."

"It does."

"Tell me, Jack, what do you think you're going to gain out of working yourself to death?"

"Freedom."

"You had freedom in Alaska. We have a house that is paid for. You owned a dream of a business, and you earned enough money to keep us, the girls, and the dogs, and still have *some* money to save. Sure you worked hard, but you loved it, as I seem to recall."

"What can I say? People change, Karan. It's called growth."

"It's called walking backwards."

"Not to me, sweetheart. I'm walking ahead."

"So, let me get this straight, Jack. We live in a beautiful house with amenities galore that I can't keep up with and nicer weather than back home. But to maintain this lifestyle, you'll be working like a dog, which you claimed you didn't want to do in Alaska, and you're okay with it?"

"Yeah, I guess so."

"And so family is no longer your top priority."

"I'm not saying that. There will be weekends and vacations."

"And music recitals?"

"If the girls are into it."

"That answers my questions."

"Good. That's what I'm here for."

"I'm taking a shower. I've got to shampoo this fish and smoke out of my hair."

Jack tries to communicate something with a guttural grunt.

Where did I put my manual on raising husbands?

12

Jack went off to work, the girls went out to play, and I am back in bed deciding whether it's worth getting up again. Lack of motivation is half of it. The fight with Jack last night didn't help. And the toilet seat he left standing up on purpose cinched it for me.

I feel depressed, emotionally weak. Doubtful about my future. And, strangest of all, it's hard for me to pray at this time when I need God most.

The last time I felt this despondent was during Hope's illness, a week that lasted a year.

As I lie staring at the ceiling I think about life cycles. How they come and go like seasons. I think about a lot of things, but mostly I think how much I thought I knew and how little I do know.

Last spring we studied recent history with Hope, and the 1970s in particular. She was shocked that Jack and I were actually alive during a time when record players and transistor radios were the standard audio entertainment.

The unit on the newspaper heiress, Patty Hearst, was a remarkable study of human nature. Here was a beautiful, rich woman kidnapped in broad daylight in 1974 at the hands of the radical Symbionese Liberation Army, and several months later, she was robbing a bank with her abductors and calling herself Tania.

Major change of identity. Even though that must have been the last thing she thought would ever happen to her.

I'm not comparing my predicament to being kidnapped, nor do I intend to hold up a bank anytime soon. But I do wonder, again, who I am becoming and whether circumstance can change us against our wills.

I'm afraid I'll forget my former life like a child forgets a deceased parent she once loved.

Everybody experiences pain, but when you're the one experiencing it, the reality is hard to dismiss.

I close my eyes and after a silent moment of practiced peace, I look hard at the wall. I find the will to pray, and in that prayer I find strength to face the day.

Sometimes it has to be enough to face that one long day.

I pour a cup of coffee, which is the first thing I usually do after prayer and devotions. Aunt Candy says I should give it up. But not now. I can't stand to lose another one of my favorite things.

I stir the coffee several times to milky color, and then I sip and enjoy before I think about all the work still to be done.

The front door opens and shuts. Hope comes up to me with a daisy in her hand as she did often in Alaska.

"I thought you might need this today, Mommy."

"I do Hope. I do."

I wipe a tear before it runs too far.

"I love you, Mommy," she says and walks toward the door. Then she turns to me to be sure I'm okay.

"I love you too, Hope," I say.

She closes the door.

I grab on to her tailcoat of hope, and marvel again at how she is the meaning of her name. My spirit rises like an air balloon. The change in me is instant. I confess my offense to God for doubting his ever-present care.

*S*omething remarkable happens in September, and it's not falling leaves or football.

Children go from sleeping in to waking up early. From drinking lemonade to gulping a breakfast drink. From riding their bikes to riding a schoolbus.

And though I said I would never do it, though I promised myself I would commit to the honor of teaching my own children and being their primary influence, I am fixing them a sack lunch, kissing them at the bus curb, and sending them off to be taught by a school system that won't allow prayer but embraces Halloween and Santa Claus.

Jack said private school is more expensive than he thought, and he heard that the public schools in this area score high on standardized tests, and I don't doubt it. But I believe he's missing the point.

Then he handed me a brochure from a private school to prove the cost (which had to have been the most expensive school in the area) and made a quick getaway before I could ask any questions.

The truth is, I don't have the will to fight it. My daughters are well grounded in the Word, academically secure, socially adaptable, and that's what matters most. I'm sure they'll do fine.

I'm choosing my fights carefully at this point, like they say to do with teenagers.

So now I have all this time on my hands that I've never had before, because I finally got the house arranged and the furniture polished. I even found time to hang Aunt Candy's housewarming gift—a driftwood sign with a Hawaiian saying I don't know the meaning of—on the wall in the laundry room where it is least likely to be seen.

I don't watch Oprah, and cleaning doesn't take me all day. The big undertakings, like those family photos in boxes in the attic that need organizing, have sat in those same boxes for years now; I think they can wait.

My neighbor, Pam, down the street suggested I start some home projects. She's a hyper Martha Stewart fan who grows herbs on her windowsills, makes homemade wreaths for her front door, and is never seen without bundles of fabric or a tape measure in her hand.

And though I'm not a fan of Martha Stewart, at home in Alaska I did enjoy a feeling of intimate homemaking, creating a private world of elegance and indulgence for my family. I loved presenting those special touches that flavor living like scented candles, chocolates on pillows, and folded napkins at dinner.

But this house is just a house to me. A place we live, eat, and sleep. A place where we don't pay as much attention to each other as we should. It has a feeling of "temporary," as though I could walk away from it tomorrow without thinking too hard or caring too much.

Cindy gave me a booklet with community classes like photography and art. I pull it from the stack of papers collecting in the miscellaneous drawer in the kitchen, mostly school notices. I flip the pages, find myself a suitable photography class, and walk across the street to Cindy's house.

She's watching Oprah.

"Come on in," she says.

I sit down on her brown leather couch and tell her about the class.

"That's what you need, Karan. I'd go with you, but I take a Pilates class at that same time in the same center."

"Maybe we can drive together and have frozen yogurt afterward," I suggest.

"And share secrets?" she asks, half watching me, half interested in the show.

"Yeah, we can share secrets."

A look of curiosity. "Do you have any?"

"No," I say with certainty, "but I can make some up."

And she laughs like my sister Tammy.

Jack forgets my birthday, the beast. But when he comes home at eight o'clock, the cake the girls baked under Cindy's supervision, the balloons, the streamers, and a huge sign that says "Happy Birthday Mommy" are a clue.

"Oh my. I forgot something important, didn't I?"

And I'm scheming like Cindy.

"I'll take a camera. A Minolta Maxxum 5 SLR camera," I hear someone say in my voice.

"Well, okay," says Jack, as though he's getting off easy.

"Have a piece of cake," I say.

I should have asked for the Canon EOS-1V. My teacher says it's expensive, but takes high-quality pictures.

I spend a lot of time in the dark these days mixing solutions, swirling paper in trays, and hanging proofs.

I'm not yet the artist, the master photographer I aim to be.

But I am amazed, and so is my instructor, at my natural ability to capture pictures with an artful eye.

A picture of Jack is coming into focus now. It is of him in our blue velvet easy chair, which is the only piece of furniture I insisted on moving from Alaska because it is the most comfortable chair I have ever sat in and because it has sentimental value.

The frame was taken after a hard day's work, and he's looking annoyed that I'm taking his picture. There's a lot to be said in this print. He's talking through his expression, or lack thereof.

He's saying silently, *My time is mine now, and I'm going after what I want, and you can't stop me,* and a dozen other adolescent boy thoughts that makes me happy I'm raising girls.

I don't care. Because my expectations of Jack have gone from him holding the moon up in the sky, to maybe him remembering to buy me an anniversary present and possibly taking the trash out—if he thinks of it.

I remember the words he spoke that longest day of summer when he pulled blades of grass, and I sat next to him dumbfounded. That day that is permanently etched in my mind.

I did it your way, now let's try mine.

Okay, Bud. Two can play at this game. That little wife who spent hours over a hot stove making your favorite chicken cacciatore. Crying over onions. Dicing. Stirring. Imagining how you'd love it. You don't need her anymore. After all, Italy Brothers now makes it in a can, and its just as good as slaving over it. So there!

My own mother wouldn't know me these days.

Of course, I'd never actually say these things to his face. I'm not that brave or rebellious—yet.

Besides being an amateur photographer, I am now a chauffeur. Picking up and dropping off kids at dance classes, music lessons, swimming lessons, and birthday parties. Sitting in my van waiting outside a given location on a given day reading photography magazines. Waiting. Waiting my life away. And when I'm totally bored, talking with other mothers, one of whom asked me if Alaska is in America.

These mothers go on and on like their lives depend on their children's success. They tell me how their daughters are destined for Juilliard, even though they can't stay in step with the "Good Ship Lollypop" number, how they're entering them on *Star Search,* even though they can't sing a note. Yadda, yadda, yadda!

I suppose all these lessons can't hurt them. They may become cultured women who marry doctors, preferably specializing in geriatrics so they can care for us when we're old.

13

Cindy and I are loading the girls in the van. They are tanned little girls now, with Ocean Pacific shirts and beach thongs. They chew bubble gum, eat Sour Balls, think *American Idol* is cool, and hate homework. All the things you'd expect.

It's been the same every Sunday since I started attending church with Cindy. While we're at church, the guys go golfing. We cook lunch; the guys eat it. We clean up; the guys talk golf.

Jack explained to me that since he has to work so hard during the week, he needs this time to unwind. He'd like to go to church and all, but he prays in the car and listens to Chuck Swindoll—sometimes. He and God are just fine. God understands his mental health situation. Even the Creator took a day off.

He explained to me again last week, with a putter in his hand, that if I don't give him this opportunity to blow off steam, he'd eventually be on Prozac like Steve. This is interesting since Steve golfs with him and, based on his theory, shouldn't be stressed.

I don't ask questions. I don't question Jack about anything, really. I'm not even sure what he does. His title is project manager, and it has something to do with constructing some new-fangled steel buildings that are all the rage. And I know it's commercial, not residential.

The only other thing I know is that work makes Jack very cranky and nasty, even to the girls. His favorite new saying is, "How can a family of four generate so many dishes?"

After church and an inspiring message from the book of James on controlling the tongue, we pull in the driveway, and Cindy makes a suggestion I like.

"Let's leave the girls with the guys and have lunch, just the two of us."

I think about it.

"We deserve it, you know."

"Alright," I say, bravely. "Who's going to tell them?"

"I will," offers Cindy.

"That's good, Cindy, because Jack won't say no to you."

"Come on, girls. Your dads will fix you lunch."

The girls run into the house. Jack and Steve are lounging on the patio drinking iced tea. Jack is animated, defending his golf game.

All four girls call, "Hi, Daddy," and run down the hall, legs everywhere.

We stand at the open French doors, flies making their way in the house due to male lack of thought. Cindy's stature is confident; I am a wet noodle.

"The macaroni and cheese is in the cupboards, boys. See ya."

They look at each other confused and then to us.

Cindy turns to me, "You do have macaroni and cheese, don't you?"

"Yup." I say.

"Ha, ha, ha," Steve exclaims.

"You think we're joking?" Cindy gives a satisfied smirk. "Think again."

And Jack just stares like no woman has ever talked to a man that way before.

She bowls out the door. I exit like a culpable prison escapee.

On the lawn the openness stirs us to adventure.

"Olive Garden, Red Lobster, or El Torito?" Cindy asks, flinging her hair in the air.

"I think Olive Garden."

"Come over to my house to change into something more fun," Cindy suggests. "You can borrow something of mine."

But I decline, after seeing her wardrobe. Ten times more daring than my own.

Lunch is wonderful. I eat shrimp and crab ravioli; Cindy has Fettuccine Alfredo.

"These breadsticks should be illegal," I say, after eating three.

We don't have any best-friend secrets or deep thoughts to share, but we talk a lot and laugh and make jokes about the guys, which make me feel guilty, especially after today's sermon.

And then we order a rich and yummy dessert that makes me feel even guiltier.

"You're one big bundle of guilt, Karan. Loosen up."

"I just want to do the right things in life. Serve God, love humanity, and pick up stray animals. But Black Tie Mousse Cake after the truckload of calories I just ingested. That's in the gray area."

"You can serve God, love humanity, pick up stray animals, and still have fun. Show me in the Bible, Karan, where it says you can't have fun."

"I'll check my Strong's concordance and let you know."

As we leave the restaurant, Cindy says, "It's only two o'clock. We should stay out longer so the guys can stew some more."

I'm not as sure as she is about this matter because I think Steve has been stewing for a number of years, and Jack is newer at it.

"Oh, please, Karan."

And I wonder if Cindy is a bad influence on me. Maybe she's a carnal Christian. The church ladies in Alaska are not so liberated. And even though the book of Ephesians can be taken out of context (mostly by men), it does say that wives are to submit to their husbands. I'm sort of confused.

At the mall I step out of a jewelry store. It's the kind of place where they pierce your ears for free, but then you have to buy the earrings. Most of the customers are teenagers.

I find Cindy waiting on the bench looking like a teenager herself in embroidered denim jeans with leather laces at the waist, a pink tee, and wicker sandals.

"I have something for you, Cindy."

"A present?"

"It's nothing big."

She opens the box with the miniature red ribbon on top. "Oh my goodness, it's so cute, Karan. And it says best friends."

She makes this face like she might cry.

"One side of the heart is for you and one side for me."

She cries.

"See, I never had a girl best friend; not really," I admit. "I was the thinker type growing up, and people could never understand that about me. I used to sit under trees writing poetry and doodling."

"That's because deep down you're an artist, and it was just over their heads."

"See, that's why I love you, Cindy. You flatter me. Even if it's not true."

We put on our necklaces, feeling best-friend special.

Cindy looks at me too serious, and I wonder what she's thinking.

"Karan, I didn't want to share this before, but the moment we met I knew we were going to be best friends."

"Me too."

We squeeze hands, ignoring the shoppers drifting by.

"See, I had a best friend, and her name was Karen, but she spelled it with an 'e.' When I met you, you reminded me so much of her. The way you talk, your humor … your long silky hair and all."

"That's nice," I say, wondering if I have some competition and feeling jealous for a mini-second. "So where is she now?"

"She died tragically, just like in the song."

"What song?"

"This fifties song, 'Teen Angel.'"

I recall it faintly.

"See, Karen had this ring that belonged to her mother who died when she was five, so it had real sentimental value. The ring was too big; that's why she didn't wear it. But because it was her mother's birthday, she did that day."

I listen intently, trying to hear over the foot traffic and

crowd noise. I acknowledge my attention with a double nod of understanding.

"Karen and her boyfriend were walking along the railroad tracks at dusk where we lived in Indiana."

"Yeah?"

"Anyway, the ring slipped off Karen's finger and fell under the track, and … "

She struggles to continue.

"Take your time, Cindy."

She breathes deep and releases her breath slowly.

" … they were rounding a bend in the tracks, and so they didn't see the train, and the train didn't see them until it was right on them. Travis jumped off the track just in time, but Karen was distracted in grabbing the ring. He called for her, but it was too late, and … "

Cindy stops mid-sentence.

"Oh my gosh, that's terrible."

"I was staying with my aunt that summer here in California."

"I'm sorry, Cindy. I'm so sorry."

I rest my hand on her knee.

"Trains can't stop on a dime; it takes over a mile, you know."

"What happened to Travis?"

Cindy's eyes are the glossy blue of an icy lake.

"Travis went through intense guilt therapy. Later he married a girl he'd known since he was ten, but he never got over Karen. Every year he visits the place on the anniversary of her death with his wife. She's a nice person to do that, don't you think?"

My eyes are welled up, and Cindy is wiping hers with a napkin.

"I'm honored that you would think of me in the same special way you thought of her, Cindy. I know I can't take her place, but people deserve to be remembered."

She throws her cup and napkin away with a look I've never seen on her face.

"I didn't want to share it with you before, Karan, because I didn't want you to think I liked you because of her."

"I wouldn't have thought that."

"Anyway, since I've gotten to know you, you're different from Karen in many ways."

"Like what?"

"She was this free bird. A modern day Anne of Green Gables."

"It's sad she didn't grow into a woman."

"That is sad, Karan. She wanted to be a missionary."

She plays with the hem of her jeans.

"I remember her obituary by heart. It said she had an abundance of warmth, contagious optimism, and dreamed of making a difference."

"Quite a person."

"Oh … and that she had a weakness for jelly donuts." She pauses. "Seriously, it did say that."

"Sounds like I could strive to be more like her."

"You will be. But you care too much about what other people think to truly know what's inside you, and she pretended nothing."

"That's so deep; it freaks me out."

"There. That reminds me of Karen; what you just said. She would have said something like that."

.

14

Somehow it feels like it should be snowing. It being the middle of October, I expected some significant change of weather. For the first time in a while I long for the Northern Lights and the dogs and halibut tacos. Of course, I never stop missing my mother. We talk on the phone once a week. She tells me to be careful with my feelings, and I'm still trying to figure out exactly what that means.

Pastor Davies sends me tapes of his messages and, in truth, they are better than my current pastor's, Pastor Abraham, which Jack says is a ridiculous name for a pastor. Like he can help it.

Pastor Davies's messages are truthful and full of meat. Pastor Abraham leaves me with less to chew on. My take on it is that Pastor Abraham has to gear his messages to a rich, spoiled congregation who prefer cheesecake to beef stew. Feel good messages to tough reality sermons.

When Jack and I are in the car together, which is rarely, I try to put Pastor Davies's messages on and play them. Usually Jack beats me to it and punches on some radical radio station he's pre-programmed in or throws in a questionable CD:

hip-hop, rap, the kind of music he used to rail at the church youth for listening to.

How can someone who once loved God so much, who lived God, talked about God, endlessly and passionately, not even notice that God is not in his life?

When we lived in Alaska, Jack couldn't go to sleep without reading at least a chapter of the Bible. Here in California, I started doing my devotions in the morning because Jack said the light bothered his eyes. And the girls, sadly, are on their own.

People wonder how the family deteriorates. As fast as a wink, I'm afraid.

So this new Jack, who looks basically the same as the old Jack except for trendier clothes that match and more expensive sunglasses, doesn't talk much. I hardly know when he's in the house because he's in the study most of the time on the Internet or reading financial magazines, which he never read up to now. All the outdoor magazines he used to love are as new as the day they arrived in the mail.

I can't recall the last meal Jack had with us. Work is his catchall excuse for everything that could be interpreted as bad parenting. I think it would serve him well to wear a sign around his neck that says, "Sorry—no time. Gotta earn a living!"

I send the girls into the study with food and drink, hoping Jack will understand that he needs to pay them *some* attention, but they don't stay in there long. They come back with long faces.

It has to affect them. To go from being so utterly loved to being totally ignored must weigh on their tender hearts.

Jack notices when they leave their things lying around or

are too noisy. He is missing out on opportunities that will be lost forever, and I am powerless to change it.

The beach is different from the landscape I'm used to. Painting it is strange. Cindy and I are taking a class together, and I'm trying to find what's deep inside me. So far what I've found is that I was born to paint … after I got past the fruit and vegetables and skipped the day of figure art class when I saw a muscular man wrapped in a towel looking paid.

How I didn't know I could paint before, I'm not sure. Mom says she always knew I had extraordinary talent. She still has my kindergarten finger paintings and a note from my seventh-grade teacher that says she should enroll me in art classes.

"Forgive me for not doing it, Karan. At the time there were other priorities," she said regrettably, as though I might have been a Picasso or Rembrandt.

"It's okay, Mom. Really. It didn't ruin my life."

I squeeze a dab of blue from a metal tube and mix it on my palette. Brushing soft-edged strokes on the canvas, I watch my paintbrush bring the seascape alive.

"That is massively good, Karan."

I examine Cindy's canvas. Dry, poorly developed strokes.

"Your scene is good too."

"Yeah, right. Mine is just a block of blue. But you, Karan, you paint like you see something more than what's in front of your eyes."

"Cindy, did you know that the early painters had to paint from memory? They couldn't leave their studios?"

"Why?"

"Tubes weren't invented until 1841. They stored paint in pig's bladders. Maybe you missed that class."

"Disgusting."

"Imagine the vision they had. They did sketches, but all the color was by memory. The contrast, the light. Absolutely amazing."

"All I know is that Grandma Moses started in her seventies."

I dab my brush in white paint.

"Next time we'll come at sunset, when there's more color."

Cindy dips her brush in too much paint.

"I think I'll go abstract," she says. "Then I can slap paint and call it art. And when I'm dead you can interpret my paintings. You have such a way with words."

I don't think you should do this," Jack says with great authority in his voice one day as I'm turning what was to be the girls' schoolroom into an art studio.

"Why not?" I ask. "You have your study; why shouldn't I have a room? What would you propose?"

"The girls need their own rooms."

"You know that's not true. They wouldn't be able to sleep without each other."

"Well, anyway, what do you see in dripping paint on a canvas? I just don't get it."

He examines the brushes and paints. Doesn't even ask to see my art.

"Because you don't get it means I shouldn't do it? I don't get what you're doing."

He shakes his head.

"You know that green stuff that pays the bills."

"You mean that useless paper you're throwing around like Mardi Gras candy?"

"Photography and painting. Do you really need them both?"

"Yeah, that is pretty outrageous, Jack. I should go work in a bar instead."

"Meow," he says, and slams the door.

Lots of doors slamming around here these days, and the girls are asking why.

Jack says he's checking to see if the WD-40 is curing the squeaks.

The natives are hungry.

Aunt Candy is carrying a Hawaiian ham, and I am carrying the sweet potato bake.

Thanksgiving Hawaiian style.

The table is set on a green-blue floral tablecloth with bamboo place mats and seashells scattered about. A tropical centerpiece with flowers cut fresh from Aunt Candy's garden sparks a celebratory mood. The girls are wearing handmade leis, and we are all donned in Hawaiian attire at the request of the hostess.

"A bunch of banana leaves, and we'd have it going on here," says Jack.

"Oh, I did forget the banana leaves, didn't I?" Aunt Candy replies innocently.

Bradford, bamboo fork in hand, laments, "When you said three o'clock for dinner, Ma, I thought you meant three o'clock. I'm starving."

"Hold on, son; good food takes time."

"Speaking of good food," says Delilah, "you'll be begging for my Hawaiian egg bread recipe."

It's obvious to me she's competing with her mother-in-law.

The first thing Delilah said as she strutted in the door looking like a Hawaiian barmaid was, "I made a coconut pudding that's to die for."

Bradford was right behind her carrying dishes like a careless juggler.

We settle around the colorful feast.

"Ho Ka 'Ono!" Aunt Candy says.

"What?" we ask together.

"That means, 'Let's eat; it's so good.'"

I nuzzle Jack in time to stop Bradford's aim on the ham.

"How about a prayer?" he interrupts. Bradford puts down his fork, but only after we all stare him down.

"Good idea," says Aunt Candy. "I know a Hawaiian prayer."

I knew she would say just that, and so I did my research.

"I got this prayer off the Internet," I say, as I try to hold the paper steady in my nervousness. "It was a Christian prayer Robert Louis Stevenson wrote for a Hawaiian thanksgiving feast sometime in the 1880s."

I am hoping it won't be an issue.

Aunt Candy presents a thoughtful look. "I think King Kamehameha would approve."

I am so relieved.

"Jack, will you do the honor?" I hand him the printed sheet.

His mellow voice consumes the room in a pure melodic flow.

"Lord, behold our family here gathered. We thank Thee for this place in which we dwell; for the love that unites us; for the peace accorded to us this day; for the hope with which we expect the morning; for the health, the work, the food, and the bright skies that make our lives delightful; and for our friends in all parts of the world. Amen."

It is beautiful, we all agree, as Bradford stabs the ham, splattering juice in his clumsy way.

Jack is so different without an agenda. I think he senses it too—the peace of not trying so hard.

"Want to go for a walk?" he asks after the meal, the first line he ever used on me back at the university that day of fond remembrance.

"Me?" I ask, which sounds silly, but I'm not used to the attention.

"Yes, you, my hibiscus flower. You look absolutely beautiful."

It's the first time he's said anything complimentary to me in months, outside of "nice outfit" with a question mark, meaning "how much did you pay for that?" This would be a double standard since I hardly buy anything, and his closet is brimming with expensive labels I never ask the price of.

But tonight his affection is real.

Aunt Candy has the girls occupied with a Hawaiian board game called Surfs Up.

"This can only be played once in a while, girls. I want to keep it looking good. It's part of my vintage Hawaiian collection."

"Oooooh," they exclaim as they handle the colorful pieces.

It's a beautiful park at sunset. Sweater weather, and absent of clouds and people.

I am shy, like this is our first date and I don't know what to say. We haven't been speaking nice to each other, and so there's this trust factor that's missing, at least with me.

"Nice night."

"Yeah, real nice."

Jack holds my hand, and we walk. It doesn't come as naturally as it should.

The grass is still green and the trees fully leaved, which I find amazing.

"Good dinner too, except for the pudding." Jack puckers.

"Wasn't that awful?" I agree.

"I took one bite and said I was full, and I was, actually."

"I couldn't do it. Delilah looked absolutely puppy dog, and so I choked it down for her sake. But I'm sure she got the salt and sugar mixed up."

"Why did you do that? She hasn't been very nice to you."

"She's had a hard life, you know. She probably never had proper Thanksgivings, what with living in a particle-board house with holes in her mittens in Phoenix."

We laugh.

We haven't laughed in a long time, and it feels good.

"Look, Jack. A bird nest fell out of the tree. Should we leave it?"

"We have to. If we touch it, we could spoil it."

"I guess so."

I study Jack's profile as we stroll. It is carved, almost chiseled. Everything about it is beautiful. If marriage could get by on beauty alone, ours would be heaven.

But beauty can't run the world or solve hunger. It just sits there looking good.

"Don't you miss it, Jack? Don't you ever miss it?"

The question must be asked.

"Miss what?"

And I wonder if he means it.

"Alaska. Our first life; the one we knew before. The passion we knew before."

His hand goes limp.

"We have passion. I've got my work and golf, and you've got photography and sculpture. We talked about it."

"Painting, Jack."

"Yeah, I know … painting."

"Those are separate passions."

He stops and stares like I just uttered the most inappropriate sentence ever.

"You are too much, Karan. Just too much."

I feel a rise turning me red, a flash of heat burning in me.

"Excuse me for sucking air, as you would say."

"Look, I'm taking you for a walk, what more do you want?"

The magic is broken; the sky has fallen; I have turned back into a pumpkin.

"Let's go back to the house," he says, and drops my hand and walks ahead of me.

If this were Narnia and I were a flying horse …

15

*L*ove can't be bought, and this is something everybody knows—everybody except Jack.

It's 2:00 AM Christmas morning, and we are wrapping presents.

We told the girls last night that if they left their rooms for any reason we would cover them in maple syrup, tie them in twine, and leave them to the wild animals in our back yard (of which there are none).

We don't believe in Santa Claus. That's one thing Jack and I agree on. Cindy says we're ogres. Absolute ogres.

I haven't seen the loot. Jack went on a shopping spree yesterday. He called me on his cell at one o'clock and told me to "go over to Cindy's house, or something," so we wouldn't be home when he came home with the presents. I wasn't happy to be excluded. We usually do the shopping together, and much earlier than Christmas Eve. But he hasn't been so playful in months. He's more excited than the girls.

It's 3:30 AM, and we're still wrapping. Fingers locked in claws, neck tensed, feet asleep from suppressed blood circulation.

Faith calls from a cracked door down the hall.

"Can we come out?"

"No," I say, with a voice played mean. "Get back in your room, or I'm grabbing the syrup."

Faith slams the door. She and Hope giggle uncontrollably.

Christmas is my favorite holiday, but the truth is, I'm missing Alaska like I've never missed it. An Alaskan Christmas can't be beat. I love cutting our own tree from the white dusted forest; fresh-cut trees always make the house smell piney. Waking up cold and bundling together by a roaring fireplace with a warm mug in my hand. In the afternoon there's sledding, snow fights, and snowmen when the snow is wet enough. And after night has settled in, we have cookies and eggnog and make angels in the snow to be revealed in the morning light.

But you're not in Alaska anymore, I tell myself like Dorothy in Oz. *There's no place like home, and this is home. Jack says so.*

Every time I think we're done wrapping, Jack comes back from the garage with his arms full of more presents, and I'm getting worried. He spends like we are millionaires, and there is no discussing it with him.

By 4:30 AM the preparations are in order. The tree is gleaming, an unnecessary fire is burning, the presents are perfectly positioned, and holiday music is playing winter songs about snow, sleigh bells, and sledding.

"Okay, girls," and they run like stampeding buffalo and give tremendous hugs. They stare at this massive mountain, disbelieving it's all for them.

"Go ahead. Rip," Jack says, forgetting our annual prayer and Christmas story. The real one.

It's like they're not sure about all this.

The first presents they fly through, saying things like "This is neat!" and "Way cool!"

Jack carries bikes in from the garage. They test them on for size and jump up and down in their matching cherry pie pajamas.

Then they resume ripping. One game after another. One Barbie after another. Spy pens. Silly Putty. Computer software. Super Nintendo and other video games I'm not sure of. There are CD headsets and music I wonder about. Things that need assembling. Boy toys like Spiderman vision glasses and Super Soakers that I suspect are more for Jack than the girls.

The excitement is starting to wear. I can tell they're getting tired of ripping. They are taking nonchalant glances and throwing boxes around, leaving piles and piles of ribbons and paper to be trashed.

And here is Jack in his glory explaining how all the contraptions work. Installing batteries, tightening screws.

He stops and looks at me.

"Close your eyes, Karan. The next gift is for you."

I close my eyes and open them in what truly is a surprise. The basket is exquisitely packaged, like the baskets Jack designs every year. But it's the contents that steal my speech. It's filled to the brim with kitchen gadgets. I examine the pizza cutter and garlic press. I determine the odd silver contraption is an automatic jar opener.

"It's called A Day Off," Jack explains excitedly. "And look, it's got a tomato press." Jack demonstrates where the tomatoes are inserted. "You like to make homemade sauce."

"Thank you, Jack." I say, in a careful voice, flicker a fake smile, but cannot manage the hug. Inside I'm thinking *what a careless, thoughtless gift,* and restraining the anger filling me like a pool.

He can't be that dense. Watch any sixties sitcom, and there's a theme on kitchen gadgets women don't want on birthdays and holidays.

For the last several years Jack has spoiled me with simple, thoughtful gift baskets. Theme baskets put together with love and affection. Last Christmas my gold-sprayed basket was filled with chocolate roses, floating candles, two sets of earrings, and fuzzy snowflake pajamas. A warm afghan, a classical CD, and a love note written in amateur calligraphy topped off the creative gift.

I pull golf clubs with a big red ribbon out of the closet with a sloppy tug. They cost much more than I usually spend on Jack's gift. After spotting them and smiling wide, he walks over to me and gives me a warm hug, the most intimate hug of the morning.

"These beauties sure beat the old ones I'm using."

He pulls out a club and practices with it. Puts a lampshade on his head and says, "What do you think, girls? Do I look like a pro?"

And they laugh and say, "Oh, Daddy."

"How about breakfast?" he suggests, as he puts the clubs away. "All that wrapping has me starved. Eggs Benedict, blueberry muffins, fresh fruit, espresso. The usual." He laughs jolly. "You can use your new egg poacher."

I'm having trouble here!

"At least let the girls finish opening—"

"Wait. We have presents," Faiths announces, as she throws down her new doll. She and Hope walk through a sea of used paper and retrieve presents concealed behind the tree. They hand us homemade pillows. Blue corduroy for Jack, pink and lace for me.

"Those will look beautiful on our bed. Don't you think, Jack?"

"Sure," he smiles.

Then they hand us tiny hand-painted boxes. Jack opens his to find tie clips. He hugs the girls. I open mine, and gasp to emphasize my delight.

"Just what I wanted."

Hope clasps my necklace from the back, and Faith kisses my cheek.

Still mulling over Jack's thoughtlessness, I shoot a look of disdain, hoping he will understand without me having to say it in front of the girls.

Jack catches the obvious glare, but obviously misunderstands.

"Hold on. Hold on, Karan," he says as he stands up. "I'll be right back."

He walks backward out of the living room like he's scared I'm going to shoot him in the back. I was upset, but now I'm livid—but I'm trying to pretend that I'm not for the sake of the girls who are opening the last of their gifts.

Jack comes back waving a check like a banner of surrender.

"I know those golf clubs must have cost at least $1,500, and your present … well, it was a little less than that."

The clubs cost $1,200 on sale, but I'm not telling.

"Spend it as you wish, madame. You can buy a lot of paint or a top of the line digital with that green."

He hands me a check for a thousand dollars. I hand it back.

"I don't want it, Jack. It's not about the money."

"Take it; take it. *I* can afford it."

"I said I don't want it."

"Take it, Karan," he says. "It will make me feel better."

"Thank you," I say, and peck him on the cheek. Then put my feelings aside again.

I won't ruin Christmas for the girls. They deserve normalcy, though nothing of this holiday is normal. Last year they got a tenth this much, and were just as happy.

The last gift the girls open, the first that Jack wrapped and I haven't seen, are hand-painted wildlife statues. Faith's are humpback whales; Hope's is a polar bear. Both are arctic scenes of the same collection they get every Christmas. And for once today I am pleased with Jack. He remembered, and I could care less if he forgets me for the rest of my life as long as he remembers the girls.

Little eyes well and leak and drip, and then the girls are bawling. Jack asks why. "Are they cracked? The wrong ones? What?"

But I don't have to ask.

"Don't you get it, Jack?" I say, holding the girls near and comforting them. "They miss Alaska. We all miss Alaska."

"Do you girls? Do you?"

They look up and nod twin nods, but are crying so hard they cannot speak. They sob and shake in uncontrolled bursts of emotion.

You'd think he'd be touched; in the least bit touched.

"Well, this beats all. I give the most fabulous Christmas ever. Buy presents most kids would fight over. Even do the shopping on my own. And this is the thanks I get?"

"You still don't get it, Jack."

"What I get is that the female species is complicated."

He folds his arms tight over his chest. The girls are now laid out on the floor bawling, for their grief is one that has been held too long, and the river is flowing and won't be stopped. It has to take its course.

I knew it. I knew they were too brave.

Jack has a look, like he's going to solve the problem.

"I forgot to tell you guys; we're going to Disneyland tomorrow. I'm taking the day off, and we're doing a family excursion to 'the Happiest Place on Earth.'"

I sigh. They cry. Jack continues.

"Goofy, Cinderella, Snoopy."

"Snoopy is Knott's Berry Farm, Jack."

"Okay, we'll go there too; some other time. And the zoo," he says. "The San Diego Zoo. They have koalas and animals that wouldn't last a day in Alaska, and snakes like the ones in Louisiana."

He plays his hand like a snake and pretends to bite the girls, but they are bawling.

Happiness can't be bought, and this is something everybody knows—everybody except Jack.

16

*D*isneyland didn't cure all the woes or heal all the hurts, but it did distract.

Mickey Mouse was precious, Space Mountain was wild, and Pirates of the Caribbean was the best.

The girls have stopped crying; I have stopped nagging (temporarily); but Jack has not stopped spending.

Every week it seems he buys himself a new toy. The week after Christmas he bought a guitar. An expensive Martin guitar. He plunked it a couple of times, and since then it's been in the closet. Last week he bought a handheld computer. He was intrigued with it for a few days.

And then two days ago Jack casually mentioned that he'd love to own a Ferrari.

I didn't agree or object; I just nodded dumbly. How did I know what he was thinking?

It's Saturday, and I hear this roar in front of the house. An accelerated press on the gas pedal.

Jack told me he was going to the bakery to read the newspaper.

I stand in front of what looks to be a very fast and expensive red car.

"Climb in," he says from the driver's seat.

"What are you doing, Jack? Whose car is that?"

"Mine, I hope."

This is the stuff you read about in magazines. How men come home with cars they can't afford, choosing them over family and common sense. Foolishly displaying their expensive toys so the world will notice their success.

"I saw an ad in the paper, and the guy who owns it is letting me take it for a test drive."

"Is the business doing that well, Jack?"

"It's used, Karan, a 1970-something model."

"Then it's a classic, Jack. How much does it cost?"

"I'm sure it's negotiable."

He's going to do what he wants anyway.

"You're a big boy, Jack. You make your own decisions."

"Then I'll take that as a yes."

He smiles, blasts the stereo, waves, and speeds away.

I'm sure you will, Jack. I'm sure you will.

Prefabricated steel building may be the rage, and maybe they can hardly keep up with the demand. But for how long? What if things go bad a few years from now … or a few days from now? What if the competition gets stiff, or Bradford doesn't know how to handle the business? What do we really know about Bradford's business practices? I heard going into business with relatives is on the top of the "things not to do if you want to be smart" list.

One night, three days after the red Ferrari sits in our garage looking untouchable, Jack comes home from work early. I find this odd.

He looks pale, like he did on the boat that day at Prince

William Sound. Stands for about thirty seconds looking dysfunctional and melts into the blue velvet chair with a huge sigh.

"Bad news?" I ask.

"The gig is up."

"I don't know what 'gig' you're talking about."

"Bradford's company is going under, Karan. This new company just down the street is underselling us. He's been acting like everything was fine, but the Meyers job ended today, and he said that was it. There isn't any more work."

My woman's intuition was right. And for once I am sorry for it.

I don't say anything. Just watch his shoulders slump, and his head bow low, and think how small he looks.

"He's closing up shop and might even have to file bankruptcy. Can you believe it?" he says in a soft, croaked voice.

I want to say yes; instead I say no.

I play with his corn-silk curls and, for the first time in ages, feel sorry for him.

"So what now, Jack?"

He pulls his head away, and I take the hint.

"McDonalds, DeMarco's Pizza … Wal-Mart, maybe. I'm practicing the greeter's wave."

"Joking, right?"

"No." He pauses. "Well sort of."

"You can get another job. You have college."

"*Some* college." He pauses in disappointment. "I would have finished my degree like you if I hadn't been busy building our house."

"Look, I know you're frustrated, Jack, but don't pull that. *You* made the choice to drop out."

His head falls in his hands. He lifts it slowly with a groan.

I move to the couch and lay my feet across the coffee table and think as Jack ruminates over his ruin.

"You can get another job as project manager for another construction company; I don't see the problem."

"I worked for twenty-one months in that field ages ago. That's not experience for around here. Bradford hired me because I'm family. Nobody else is going hire me at that level. Nobody."

"What about your other skills?"

"Outfitting?" He rolls his eyes. "'California Beach Outfitters: Grunion hunting in the high tide surf under a full moon. We help you catch!' Come on, Karan, be realistic."

"Let's move back, Jack. Oh please, let's move back. This may be God's mercy in the end."

"No way. Besides, the professor has a lease."

"Well, at least that house is paid for, and we have the rental income."

"That might pay the van note and the minimum balances on the credit cards … and maybe the new car note," he adds sheepishly.

"I don't remember applying for any credit cards. Don't we just have the one?"

"That credit card was maxed-out with the move and the plane tickets."

"I thought Bradford was giving you an advance."

"It didn't quite work out that way."

"So then you're telling me we have more than one credit card?"

"I had to apply for a couple more. For the furniture and stuff."

"I wrote a check for that stuff."

"Where do you think the money came from? Cash advances that I had deposited into the checking account, Karan."

"A couple more credit cards?" I am floored.

"And the business credit card. I'm sure Bradford will take care of that."

"Oh my gosh!" I sink in the couch. "What have you done, Jack?"

No reply.

I gather my senses.

"We'll have to live on the rest of our funds for now, that's all," I say. "How much is left?"

Jack looks like he needs CPR.

"Answer me, Jack; you're scaring me."

"Nothing. Not a penny."

"There was over $170,000 in there!"

"I know. But most of it went for the down payment and the Yukon," he says innocently.

And the rest I don't need to ask about. Toys! It went to buy toys and useless things like gold watches that sit in drawers and expensive clothes that get dirty at construction sites; it went for overpriced cologne he knows gives me a headache, and guilt presents for the girls. And a souped-up Yukon with an amplified car stereo system, subwoofers, and a radar to avoid speeding tickets. And now he'll want to fix up that stupid Ferrari.

I tell myself to breathe until it comes to me naturally.

"Where's the money George Cavanaugh gave you toward the business? The dogs, the boat, and all your outfitting gear and equipment?"

"He hasn't been able to pay me yet."

"He'll never pay you, Jack. The man lives in a shack."

"He's trying."

"You should have insisted he get a loan to pay you. If you had tried, you could have gotten a qualified buyer. You spent years building up your clientele, and he's going to run your business in the ground."

"What do I care what he does? It's his business now."

This whole mess is two dreams past a nightmare!

17

I'm looking around at the strange fabrics and fashions in this teenybopper shop called the Bee Hive in the corner of the mall. It's a cute shop with a yellow and black color scheme and retro hippie jewelry hanging on steel racks. Shoes with unrealistic heels are the predominant footwear, and the mannequins in the window look wildly dressed and commonly bored.

Two girls walk in wearing big pants, army boots, and cut-off socks around their wrists, looking like non-conformist clones.

"Oh, sweet," the blonde one says as she picks up a pair of earrings, a massacre of steel and glitter that could ruin a good outfit.

"Can I help you?" I ask in my most pleasant trying-to-make-a-sale voice.

The taller one stares at me with an appraising look.

"Thanks, but no thanks," the blonde says, as she looks at her friend amused.

The manager pulls me aside. "Karan, if you're going to work here, you're going to have to dress a little … " She pauses and feels the fabric of my peasant flowered blouse, the nearest thing to cool that I own ..."a little more fashionable. Fun and funky is our motto, and, frankly, you don't look very fun. I'll have Kelsie come over later and give you some tips."

What am I doing here?

After weeks of sending out resumes and receiving form rejection letters, short of interviews, things aren't looking good for Jack.

Now I don't know if Jack was serious when he said he was going to apply at DeMarco's Pizza, but I do know that a woman's pride is less easily wounded than a man's. We can endure almost anything for the sake of family. Even baking pizzas and flipping burgers. And so I took it upon myself to look for a job.

I must admit I was confident that my degree in English literature would land me a job, because the bulk of the jobs I applied for called for non-specific bachelor's degrees. But I guess my lack of job experience hurt me, because I didn't land even one job out of the ten places I applied. Out of those ten, I received two callbacks for an interview; and out of those two, one called me back for a second interview, and that one hired my competitor and told me that I should feel very good about it because I was their second choice. Sort of like being second runner-up in a beauty pageant. They pretend it's such an honor, but then they shuffle you off stage where you promptly go to the cry room to retrieve a Kleenex.

Cindy and I were shopping at the Bee Hive the other day. She bought an outfit that was a little funky for me, but she could get away it with because she's younger and cuter. As we were walking out, she pointed out the help wanted sign by the cash register and then started making these indiscriminate hand motions like I was supposed to get her drift, which I didn't.

Frustrated with my failure to understand sign language, she grabbed five shirts off the rack and pulled me into the dressing room.

"You have to apply here!"

"Have you gone mad?" I wrinkled my forehead in displeasure.

"You'd be great here!"

"And you are basing this on … "

"The fact that you're a punk princess just dying to get out."

And we both knew it was a very bad joke.

"Okay, you need the job, that's why."

So I filled out an application, with no intention of actually getting the job, just to pacify Cindy and tell Jack I had applied for another job, because now he is suddenly overly enthusiastic at the idea of me working.

Truthfully, I was shocked when the manager, Katrina, called me. She said she didn't usually hire over the phone, but she was in a jam and could I come in tomorrow?

"I guess I could."

And then she asked my age, which is against the law, but I gave it to her anyway.

"Hmmm." And then silence. "Well, I'm thirty myself, so I think we can make this work."

It's only temporary, I tell myself. *Until I find a real job.*

So here I am, Christina Aguilera's powerhouse voice playing in the background, feeling absolutely ancient at thirty-four, and hoping nobody from church sees me. But on the other hand, what's wrong with selling clothes? After all, this isn't a "goth" shop with spikes and chains. Maybe a little extreme. But not over the cliff.

And the shop has zippy dresses and preppy tees and big yellow beads like my grandmother used to wear.

When I get home I expect a happy homecoming. The smell of a decent dinner cooking, a table set for four, maybe even classical music in the background—if Jack thinks of it. After all, nearly every day of our marriage I have dutifully and cheerfully performed the chore. Jack should be more than happy to sub for me, especially since I've been on my feet all day and am slightly grumpy.

I turn the knob and walk in the tiled entryway knowing I am not a beautiful creature to behold for the wear and tear of the working world and thinking I should take a quick shower to freshen up for Jack.

Am I off base! Food is on the table, but the smell of it is unfamiliar to me. Frankly it's something closer to roadkill than dinner.

Aunt Candy walks up to me dressed in a dark blue Hawaiian print, her hair in a bun.

"How was your day, Karan?"

"Aunt Candy, what are you doing here?"

I try to smile, but feel my mouth go crooked. She doesn't notice my concealed horror. She tends to be in her own happy little world most of the time.

"I'm fixing dinner for the girls: miso, baked tofu, rice, and temphi salad," as though this is perfectly normal and accepted family fare.

"Where's Jack?"

"Same place he's been all day."

"Where's that?"

"Driving his Ferrari. He's working out the kinks."

"How long has he been gone?"

"Since ten o'clock this morning." she says, thinking hard.

"Then who picked up the girls at the bus stop?"

"I think they walked. I couldn't get over here until four-fifteen."

She turns her mouth inside out.

"But, they're fine. They're playing in their room."

"Okay." Baffled look undetected by Aunt Candy. "I'll freshen up and be out in ten minutes."

Calm down. Calm down. I tell myself. I look in the mirror. I am red to the eyeballs and mottled in anger.

The girls take two bites and say they aren't hungry. They ask if they may be excused. I don't want to torture the poor things because they are good little girls. I know they would eat the temphi with the cabbage and vinegar and seaweed, and whatever other inedible ingredients are in the dishes. In fact, they would down every bite of it in obedience, though Faith would make faces, and it could take all night.

I can always microwave something for them later.

As for me, I am an adult and, therefore, must make a choice whether to offend someone unnecessarily or suffer silently. I choose to suffer, because I have grown to love Aunt Candy and would not hurt her for the world.

"They really do eat big lunches at school, Aunt Candy." I make the excuse.

"Well, they did have an ice cream bar. I think that might have spoiled their dinner."

That was easy.

But not so easy is my task. I keep a glass of water handy; Aunt Candy drinks mango juice.

She gobbles the muddle of chaos like it is the *crème de la crème* of health food.

I choke down my dinner and ask a lot of questions about Hawaii, since this is the only subject Aunt Candy knows anything about other than health food and bad marriages.

I am overwhelmed with relief when she apologizes for no dessert.

"Sure, I'm disappointed, Aunt Candy. But I think with a meal like that, dessert would be too much anyway."

"Next time I'll make some vegetarian gelatin."

Now Aunt Candy is a great cook, but health food in its purest form is something I eat only when my doctor makes me.

"Light and refreshing. And it comes in tangy fruit flavors," she adds.

She almost makes it sound good, but I know that plant-derived gelatin even smothered with whipped cream cannot compare to standard junk desserts. Oh well, I would have felt guilty eating dessert anyway after having two candy bars for lunch.

The whole time, since two minutes after Aunt Candy greeted me with her beautiful wide-eyed smile, I am waiting for Jack to come in the door so I can ream him royally like the bitter, nagging wife I feel tonight.

At 7:05, five minutes after Aunt Candy gathered her flowery handbag and said, "Aloha," Jack walks in wearing a foreign hat and looking like he's been naughty.

"Okay, Jack. I will try to ask this nicely. What on earth was going through your mind that you would leave Aunt Candy to do *your* work?"

"What? She wanted to."

"As nice as your aunt is, I will not have my family eating things that ferment for ages to taste like cardboard drenched in discolored substances."

"Can't a man take a drive in his new car?"

He turns away before I answer. I can see this is going to be a one-sided conversation.

"Turn your back to me, Jack. That works well."

"I'm taking a bath." He pulls off his squirrelly looking driving shoes and walks away.

As surprising as it might be to Jack, I understand his fascination with the vintage car. The leather interior calls him; he's captivated by the rev of the engine, drawn to the highway where he can test his driving skills and local law enforcement. It's called escape.

But the thing I don't understand is what Jack is escaping from? He's got a working wife who loves him, and beautiful, obedient children who adore him.

Go figure.

18

Brown eyes with purple glitter, a nose ring, and a half-naked blue fairy tattooed on her right forearm, Kelsie, sixteen years my junior, is giving me fashion advice.

She holds a denim halter tie dress to my skin that looks ages too young for me, and makes me look ages too old to be working here.

"Wow! You've got an Audrey Hepburn body!" Kelsie exclaims.

"How do you know Audrey Hepburn?"

"*Roman Holiday* is like my favorite movie in the whole world!"

"I would never have guessed it."

"She was so fragile, so real," she says with expression, like she's imagining the icon on the silver screen in a *Breakfast at Tiffany's* gown, gloriously charming.

"Anyway with that body, Karan, you can get away with wearing capris and sleeveless dresses when you're eighty."

"Thanks, Kelsie. I'll take that as a compliment."

I'm feeling like a dinosaur again. She's practically got me

in the grave. And I don't think Audrey Hepburn would have shopped here if the clothes had been free.

Imagine my look of shock, the blood draining from my face, when Delilah, wigless, and wearing trace makeup, walks in the door.

"Delilah, is that you?"

"Karan!"

Her diamond is noticeably smaller. Jack told me Bradford was going to hawk her four-carat wedding ring to keep the Mercedes. This one could be cubic zirconium. Who can tell?

She hides her hand.

To a woman like me, a diamond is a rock; to a woman like Delilah it means more than it should.

"So what are you doing here?"

"Just passing by. Candy told me you got a job here."

Her whole style has changed; her demeanor is more relaxed. I think I like her better in the disaster of ruin. She looks better for sure, less plastic.

We talk about things that actually matter. She says she's soul searching. Cooking less, sewing more.

"I didn't know you sewed."

"I made my own prom dress."

She gains my respect. I tried sewing an apron once and accidentally pinned the pieces to the carpet. I realize there is something more to her than what I have seen before. But that's true of everybody, I guess.

I pull a fuchsia stretch cotton shirt off the rack, the mildest thing I can find in the store, and hold it up to her face. It goes with her blue eyes.

"Sorry, I can't afford it."

She's got that look, like she did the day she talked about her unfortunate childhood. Only more genuine.

I feel tremendously sorry for her and wish I had the money to buy the shirt for her, but her pride would be hurt anyway. Besides, Jack says Aunt Candy could afford to bail Bradford out if she wanted to. Apparently, she had a son who died, Bradford's older brother. She gave him everything he asked for. Regrettably, he ended up drunk one night in Cabo San Lucas, fell off a yacht and drowned. So she tells Bradford he can have her money when she's in the grave, and not a penny sooner.

I invite Delilah to church.

She says she'll come.

When she leaves, I sing.

When I walk in the door, I am expecting to see Jack donning an apron and sipping a chef's spoon. After the trouble I gave him last night, he has to be making something yummy. Jack is a fantastic cook when he wants to be. Gumbo, jambalaya and bread pudding are his specialties.

There's no one here, and so I figure he took the girls out to dinner. But, no … there's a note in kid print that reads, "Over at Cindy's house."

I am fuming, positively fuming.

Jack must be escaping reality again. The job … it occurs to me. That's why he's escaping. Well, maybe.

What is it about men and jobs? They work too hard, and they need to escape; they're unemployed, and they need to escape. Can't they get it that work is a place you go to earn money to live. Why is it such a defining thing to them? It seems to be tied up with their masculinity, or identity for sure.

You can't shirk your responsibility just because the boss quits signing the check. Women can't stop—not ever—or the kids would starve and be taken away by the state.

Jack refuses to sell the Yukon or the Ferrari, and I find this absurd. He says it makes perfect sense to him. Now the state of our financial matters is something Jack is keeping hidden from me these days, like I'm the janitor and he's the president of this operation. As alpha male, and the only male, he insists on taking on the role of head of the Department of the Treasury of LaRue Financial Affairs, of which there is little cash flow to manage.

Previously, I handled the money and our business books—all of it. But now I am suddenly incapable of understanding our simple budget.

I wonder what mess he's gotten us into? My measly little no-account check might pay for the food and a few necessities of life.

Day after day I walk in the door to find a vacant house and a penciled note, sometimes with a piece of candy or a flower taped to it. The note is always from the girls who I barely see these days except over schoolbooks, in towels after their baths, and later under the covers. The notes of explanation are never from Jack. However, he did write me a note with his dirty laundry: "Don't know how to work the washing machine. Help!"

Jack gets home when it's nearly dark, says he's eaten, and heads for the bathroom to take a bath. Then he comes out in his robe and reads awhile in his study, then heads to the kitchen and pours a glass of milk. He takes ten humongous gulps and goes directly to bed. Every day I pray that things will change.

I have finally caught on that Cindy is watching the girls after school. Jack pays her five dollars an hour, but it's a game. He pays her in an envelope, and we get the envelope back. Every day the same money passes between them. I find it in the planters, taped to the door, and once in my breakfast cereal bowl.

*F*ebruary doesn't seem like an optimum time to take up surfing, but finding a surfboard leaning against the wall, a wetsuit, and some board wax, I surmise Jack is planning to "catch some waves."

He doesn't ask my opinion. I realize he's going through another phase, and I wonder how long this can last. I'm not looking forward to years of waiting for him to grow up.

I used to be cute and funny, but now I look in the mirror and feel old and out of touch, like I'm no longer even trying to reach for anything. Just surviving.

Now it's a matter of who cracks first and whether the other has the strength or the will to peel their partner off the floor.

The surfing kick lasted a week and wasted money we don't have. I'm glad it's over, because Jack was wearing some stinky gook in his hair that smelled up the bedroom and stuck to the pillows.

I heard from Cindy who heard from Steve that Jack was clamoring for space with the other ancients and got into a confrontation that gained him a slug in the gut, which explains why he was walking hunched over for a couple of days.

Apparently, Jack thought since he could snowboard, that surfing would be no challenge. But he surfed "goofyfooted" (whatever that is) and fell a lot. And then on day number seven of his seven-day surfing experience, overcome with unexplained frustration, he threw the surfboard into the waves and told some beach bum he could have it if he could swim. Throwing our hard-earned money to the sea. "Seven times seventy" I repeat twenty times.

And so he's taken up biking. He bought this shiny red bike. A mountain bike with lots of gears I don't think he needs. Of course, he needed all the garb that goes with it: helmet, eyewear, knee and elbow pads, gloves, water bottle, and cool biking shorts so he won't look like a "bike geek."

I guess I should be happy he didn't buy a Harley.

He didn't say where he got the money for the bike, so I assume we'll be receiving a bill in one form or another. And here I am feeling guilty about ordering a latte after noon.

Our story only gets more hysterical, or maddening, depending on whether you want to survive or not, at which point you call it hysterical so you can laugh about it and move on.

A few days later when the house was quiet I decided to open the mail, which I hadn't done in a while. There was a notice from the mortgage company that we were ninety days behind in our payments and that late fees were accumulating. I realize that bills don't just go away, but I didn't realize Jack hadn't paid the mortgage payment in three months, and we could eventually lose the house.

When Jack finally got home and was in the garage putting his bike away, I confronted him about it.

"Yeah, I meant to tell you about that."

After a lot of words and vigorous arm waving, Jack finally agreed to sell the Yukon to pay the back house payments and three of the maxed-out credit cards (he finally admitted there were four).

Aunt Candy generously bought the SUV. I say generously, because I know Aunt Candy has no intention of driving it. She shrieked when Jack demonstrated the stereo's capability.

But the biggie was that Jack agreed to return the Ferrari to the private party he bought it from, forfeiting $1,200 of his down payment. That day was like the death of Kennedy.

"I'm a prisoner. A virtual prisoner," Jack whined.

I had no sympathy.

"You've got a bike. Start pedaling."

And he stomped his feet. Actually stomped his feet.

*M*om, I'm worn to dirt. Beyond myself. We're on the brink of destruction. I'm wearing huge platform shoes that are so uncomfortable I could cry just so I can get more sales."

I pick at my neglected fingernails, lamenting my future.

"You have to get Jack back in church," she counsels. "Without God in the equation, you're going to stay at zero."

"Zero?"

"The lowest point, dear."

"Oh Mom, I miss you so much and Alaska and the dogs. Everything! Why did things have to change?"

"Change is a necessary part of life. When we make changes we welcome them, but when they're not our idea, we resist. Remember Mary Engelbreit's quote about changing your thinking?"

"Why do you think we resist, Mom?"

"We want to be in control of our own lives, and that's natural. But control is an illusion."

"What do you mean?"

"In truth, we control very little about our lives. Sickness, natural disaster, financial ruin. None of these things are under our control."

"Jack is loving whatever control he still has."

"Don't give up on him, Karan; he'll come around. You see, once you know truth, giving it up makes for a very hard and miserable life."

"I'm not sure if Jack is miserable. In fact, he seems to be having fun."

"Are you up for a challenge?"

"My middle name."

"Tonight you pray that God will allow anything it takes to come into his life in order to help him see where he's wrong."

"That's it?"

"It can be a powerful prayer. And scary."

"You mean like he could get some disease or something?"

"Not that. It's just that sometimes people have to hit rock bottom before they wake up."

"I'll do it. Will you pray too, Mom?"

"I will, dear. I'll pray that God will take control of the situation."

"Okay, Mom. Thanks."

"One thing, before I go."

"Yes?"

"Your middle name is not 'Challenge.' It's Marie, and it's a beautiful name. Names hold a great deal of meaning to a mother, you know."

"Yes, Mom."

"Goodnight, Karan Marie."

"Goodnight, my beautiful mother who gave me a blessed name."

19

I don't plan on working here forever; I choose not to entertain such an enormous thought. But I am feeling better about it. I don't think God wants us locked up in closets or only working at the church office ministering to our own kind.

What I'm seeing is that the girls who come into the Bee Hive looking all tough with tongue and eyebrow rings, sporting punk hair, and reclaiming the ghetto with their dress, have never lived in the ghetto; they know nothing of the ghetto experience.

They are affluent, spoiled children, driving expensive cars and owning colorful cell phones, whose daddies pay their credit card bills. They've never had a rat in their house, have never paid for anything in food stamps, would die if they had to drive an old Chevy Impala that didn't start half the time.

They aren't worried about getting beat up or dodging bullets. When they look out their windows, they don't see police cars at their curb. Yet they want to glorify this prison life they know nothing of so they can have something to identify with.

They are scared little girls using clothes as security blankets. Playing dress up and hoping the world will notice them:

"Look at me; I'm different." When actually they are much the same.

The outrageous, funky clothes they wear are merely tents. Sometimes scrawny little tents that expose too much skin for my taste, and probably most of their parents' taste; sometimes baggy tents that hide what's underneath. Either way, a covering.

That's how I see it.

They're asking questions like Jack is asking questions: "Who am I? Why am I here?" And they are hoping somebody will tell them, even if that means telling them harshly, or with a look of disdain, "You're nothing. Worth nothing." Even with their defiant attitude and lack of respect, deep down they believe they are nothing.

Kelsie is from a broken home. She showed me a bruise cleverly administered by her father who she is forced to visit every other weekend and on odd holidays until she turns eighteen in a month. The mark is on her side where it won't show.

"Daddy beats me," she says, shame marking her eyes. And I wonder how she can call him that. Maybe Father or Dad. But Daddy. I can't understand that kind of love.

We have a heart-to-heart about men, marriage, and children. She says she wants them all some day, but right now she can't imagine a future. It's enough to keep her head together for today.

I would have used Jack as a shining example of knighthood, but he's off his horse right now, and his armor needs buffing up.

I tell her about Jesus, which is better than flesh. How he

loves everybody and died on the cross for her. How he ate with sinners and healed people.

"I need healing."

"I know," I say. And I give her a hug.

We pray. I promise her a Bible.

*I*t's now three days after our talk—a Friday. Kelsie is smiling big and hanging a new shipment of shirts that look like old men's bowling shirts. No kidding—in black, aqua, and some with yellow stripes in the middle.

I am in the window display trying to make the mannequins look more relaxed. Arms up, arms down. Nothing seems to be working.

"You have a phone call, Karan," Katrina calls from the office. "Line Two."

Probably the girls.

"This is Karan."

"Karan, this is Sonia Maxwell from the *Independent Daily Sun*. I hope you don't mind me bothering you at work. Your husband insisted it would be fine."

"Not a problem."

"You applied at our newspaper previously. I'm sorry that job didn't work out for you. The competition is stiff in this business."

"That's alright; I understand. I don't have a lot of work experience."

"But you left some examples of your writing."

"I remember," I say, embarrassed. A couple of articles I wrote for the university paper ages ago and some old poetry from my bureau I copied to disguise the smell of lavender oil.

"We have another position you may be interested in if you'd like to come in to discuss it."

"Whenever you say."

"Ten o'clock, here, Tuesday morning?"

"That would be fine."

"Good. See you then, Karan."

"Thanks. See you then."

"What's that about?" Kelsie asks, one second after I hang up the phone.

"A job. But don't mention it to Katrina yet."

"That's awesome!"

"Probably the mailroom." I say, resigned to small imagination.

*K*elsie is right, Karan," Cindy says that night as we rummage through my closet.

"That I don't have any decent clothes?"

"No, that you're a dead ringer for Audrey Hepburn … or you would be if you cut the tresses."

She turns my hair under and pushes me to the mirror.

"Dead ringer," I exclaim. "You said that on purpose." I see the reflection of her eyes dancing in the mirror. "That's a scene right out of *Roman Holiday*; the photographer guy from *Green Acres* that spills all over himself says that."

"I know. And she cuts her hair too. Remember? Before she meets Gregory Peck on the street."

She stares at me with lengthy examination and arranges my hair like she's a professional hair stylist.

"We have to rent that movie," I say, nostalgically. "I haven't seen it in forever."

"You have to cut your hair, Karan. Short and blunt. But not the Audrey bangs."

She pulls me into the living room, despite my resistance.

"Jack, oh, Jack … "

"What?" He looks up from his biking magazine.

"Watch the girls for your wife tomorrow, will ya? She's about to make a drastic change."

I nudge Cindy with my elbow and whisper. "Stop. He'll say no. He'll say a woman's hair is her crown."

"What are you two youngsters gumming about? What is this drastic change?"

"She wants to cut her hair, Jack. But for some strange reason, she wants your approval."

"Look." She turns my hair under again to demonstrate. "Beautiful, huh?"

"Yeah, Gorgeous George."

"So she can?"

"Dreadlocks, pink, multicolored. Whatever you want is fine, Karan."

He goes back to reading his magazine.

Those nights under moonlight when you said my hair was a gleam of shine and made me promise not to cut it—not ever. Never let anyone touch it but you with your trimming scissors …

Thank God for my blue suit; my old reliable dress of sleeveless linen and matching blazer. Simple, classic, never out of style. Perfect interview dress.

I glance in the mirror and arrange my hair. *I do look like Audrey Hepburn with this haircut. I never noticed I had such a sleek neckline. Oh, I hope they don't think I'm trying to be a vintage queen.*

I panic momentarily.

Lord, you are in control. I pray for your will.

I know God is with me, but I'm still nervous. And I have no idea what the job is.

"Karan, can we skip the formalities?" Sonia Maxwell asks, smiling from behind her desk.

I smile back, unsure of what this means.

"I'll be straight with you. Our poet, Zeya Maung, is on maternity leave, and the three poets I considered for this position … well, let's just say they were second rate and leave it at that."

"I see." I try to shift in a comfortable standing position, but I feel like the mannequins in the Bee Hive window display.

"Sit down and make yourself comfortable."

"Thank you." Her friendly manner eases my nerves somewhat.

"Have you read Zeya's poetry? She's an award-winning poet."

"I'm sorry. I really haven't read your newspaper, or any newspaper lately."

"Top sheet, Section C."

She hands me a paper.

In the top corner right, a black-and-white of a woman, maybe thirty-five. Looks nice. And a poem entitled "Indigo Sky."

"Go ahead, read it."

The poem is about a little girl picking flowers under an indigo sky. Not very original.

"Do you think you could write something similar?"

"Not similar. But I think I could write something. It's been a long time since I've been dedicated to the art, but it doesn't really ever leave you."

"I don't mean to put you on the spot, Karan. But can you show me?"

"Now?"

"Yes. Something simple. A few lines."

"About what?"

"Anything you want. Whatever strikes you."

"Well … alright."

I look around the office for inspiration and see basic, ergonomic-style furniture and plain dark blue blinds. A no-nonsense woman. No help to me.

"I'll get us some coffee. Cream? Sugar?"

"Cream, please."

She grabs her mug and leaves me to my thoughts.

Smoggy sky outside today.

God, help, please.

"Ghetto Song." The title pops in my head and then as fast as I can write the words come in this beat. My feet dance in step to the words.

> *Banging my feet down the urban streets,*
> *I'm a wannabe ghetto queen.*
> *Cause no one seems to notice me.*
> *Little girl lost under big clothes and chains.*
> *I'm nothing that I want to be.*
> *So I'll just pretend for you.*
> *And hope that you think I'm cool.*
> *I'm a wannabe ghetto queen.*

Sonia is back with coffee. "If you need some privacy, I can come back in fifteen minutes."

"No, that's fine. Here's what I have; I don't know if it's any good. I could make it longer if you want. But you said a few lines."

Surprise on her face.

"Zeya Maung can't write that fast." She laughs.

She arranges her red spectacles and reads the poem. I am hoping my reckless handwriting is not a turnoff, but when you write you aren't thinking of being neat.

I sip my coffee too fast and burn my throat.

I should have rewritten it. I should have.

Her face is indecipherable.

"This is … "

I gasp for air.

"This is good, Karan. Definitely edgy. I think that's what the people want though. I'll show you to your cubicle."

"Just like that?"

"I'm sorry. I didn't mention the salary. It's $40,000 to start; a pay raise after two weeks, depending on the response. And it's temporary—until Zeya is ready to come back. Could be nine months."

I leave the mug of coffee on her desk and follow her navy blue pumps.

She continues talking as we walk through the busy newspaper office. Phones are ringing, people are in tremendous hurries. I think I'm going to like the excitement.

Someone runs from behind and hands copy off to Sonia.

"Weed abatement hearing," the gawky teen says.

"Thank you," Sonia replies, not missing a step.

"Over in that cubicle to the right with all the posters is our sports editor."

"I see."

"And this is Rammie, one of our reporters."

"Hi," she says, in a rusty greeting, as she fills her cup with coffee—coffee I found much too strong, possibly to keep tired reporters awake.

"Hello," I say back, as we continue walking.

"Most of this job is PR, you know," Sonia says, and takes a deep breath for our hectic pace.

"You mean, public relations?" I ask.

"That's right. Answering letters, comforting souls. There are a lot of lonely people out there, Karan. Some buy the paper for the poetry and crossword puzzles alone."

"I love crossword puzzles myself."

"Don't tell the reporters, but they are the lead-in band," she says softer, as distant eyes watch our every step. "Your little corner, front page, Section C, is the big band. The one that makes their heart sing. Makes them think deep thoughts they can't come up with on their own."

"I never thought of it that way."

"I was an English major myself, Karan. Just never had the talent to go along with the love of it."

What do I say? So I say nothing, just keep up with her.

"God given, Karan. God has blessed you with a gift."

"You're a Christian? So am I."

She stops for a moment and looks at me.

"I know." She winks.

I wonder how she knows.

"Do you have to give notice, Karan?" she asks as we reach my cubicle.

"I don't think so, but I'll ask."

"We'll work it out."

She introduces me to my new office. "Here it is."

The cubicle has ergonomic furniture like hers. A simple setup of computer, pen and pencil holder, paper clips, and a stapler. But a window. Thank God, a window. And sky, however bleak today. Writing while staring at walls is severe.

The mail girl drops a stack of letters.

"First order of business. Answer these letters," Sonia says with gusto.

"What do I say?"

"Tell them it's not so bad. That there's somebody worse off than them. Tell them to leave the laundry and take a bubble bath instead. Tell them we're all making a difference, whether we're sitting behind a desk, washing twelve-story windows, or wiping snotty noses."

I drop my posture at the thought of the responsibility.

"Tell them whatever God tells you to tell them." She winks again. "But don't mention his name. It's not allowed. It's strictly not allowed."

20

Katrina says two weeks' notice is not necessary. In fact, no notice is necessary. I don't think she minds losing me. Old ladies are bad for business.

As I'm leaving, I stop at the window display to say goodbye to the mannequins. "You guys behave, and relax a little; you look too stiff."

A teenager walks in, giving me an odd look that questions what I'm doing in this store and why I'm talking to mannequins.

She's dressed in a zebra minidress with black seam panty hose and red boots higher than her knees. Her hair has one of those falls that they weave into your own hair.

"Katrina?" she asks, spotting the manager. "I'm Claudia, but people call me Stonee."

"Radical," says Katrina, like she's never said to me.

And when did she have a chance to call in my replacement since I just told her I was leaving three minutes ago? She must be Kelsie's replacement. Doesn't matter; I'm glad to be out of what is definitely not my element.

I'll keep in touch with Kelsie. Cindy and I made her over into this shiny, little girl with the purest face ever.

The nose ring left a tiny hole, but by wearing short sleeves instead of going sleeveless she can cover the tattoo easily enough. And they loved her at the Christian bookstore. She starts in two weeks. Katrina wanted the notice in her case. That says it all.

Jack didn't say much about my new job, but the girls are excited.

"We're going to hang your newspapers on our walls, Mommy, and show our friends."

They go around the house, playing reporter.

"So when did you find out that somebody killed the bear out of season?" Faith asks in a deep voice, wrapped in my blue blazer to look like a reporter.

"The blood trailed all the way to his truck," Hope replies into a pretend microphone.

"Here, hold this, Hope," says Faith. "I mean Forest Ranger person," and hands her a red brush.

She takes a pencil and pad of paper out of the blazer pocket and writes something down.

*T*he sound of the old lawn mower is tame compared to the powerful riding mower I'm used to. I breathe the exhaust fumes of my proud garage sale find, pushing crooked paths with one arm and wiping evidence of hard work off my face with the back of my other hand.

Cindy crosses the street looking ready for a workout in a black spandex outfit and Nike tennis shoes.

She mouths words I cannot hear.

I shrug my shoulders and turn off the mower.

The sound settles.

"What are you doing, poetry lady?"

I take a sip from the water bottle hanging off my shoulder before I speak. I squirt it over my face and hair and in my mouth.

"I'm getting better acquainted with the grass," I say, short breathed.

"Did you ever think you'd be mowing a lawn in March?"

"Never. In Alaska the snow is still falling."

The exhaust dissipates, and the fresh grass smell lingers in the hot air as the sun is sinking low. I imagine the cool of the falling snow, the beauty of the snow blanketing the landscape.

"It's not like this every year, Karan. We're having a heat wave. Hey, that's a song."

She dances to an imaginary beat.

"The lawn had to be mowed. I'm going to leave this patch I didn't get to and see if Jack notices it."

"You should make him mow the lawn."

"Are you kidding? He never sees the place in daylight. He's out of the house at six o'clock, and gets home … " I look at my watch. " … well, just about anytime now. He's training for some bike race in May. He's up to twenty-seven miles a day."

"Impressive."

"He probably thinks we still have a gardener."

"Yeah, what happened to your gardener?"

I run my fingers through my wet, short hair with a light and breezy feel. I hardly remember the weight of my thick, long hair.

"I'm not wasting my hard-earned money on a gardener."

"So, are you famous yet?"

"Well, there was a lady in the bakery the other day who actually recognized me from that warped picture of mine."

"Really?"

"I think it makes me look like a gopher."

I make a scrunched face.

"Not exactly a gopher. Maybe a prairie dog." Cindy laughs and tosses her shoulder-length, two-toned hair.

"They're practically the same thing."

"Not at all. Prairie dogs are cuter, Karan."

"Prairie dogs can be diseased."

"I know, my girls wanted one."

"They're illegal in California," I say, wondering how I know.

Cindy sits down on the fresh-cut grass. I lie down with my grubby tennis shoes pointed upward. I watch the sky. A dull blue today from the heat and smog combination.

"You'll like this, Cindy. The lady in the bakery told me I looked like Audrey Hepburn. I thought of you when she said that."

"You do, for sure."

"Hmmm."

"Who was your fan?" Cindy asks as she drowns her hair with water from my plastic bottle.

"Well, she was an older lady, recently widowed. She had to tell me her whole life story—1929 to present. It was a very bad year, you know, except that 'Blue Skies' came out that year."

"Blue skies smilin' at me," Cindy sings off key. "Irving Berlin. My grandmother loved that song."

I continue over her tune. "But I didn't mind her stories. She was a lonely lady who just needed to talk. She said my poems inspired her, and she was going to write the editor and tell *him* so."

"You *are* poetic, Karan. I read your poem today called 'In Strange Measure,' but I only understood it to the fourth line."

"Four years of English lit. Something had to come from sitting through those boring lectures: Sir Gawain, Marlowe, Milton … "

"Whoever those dead guys are."

"Critical to literature."

I sit up. Cindy pulls her shoes and socks off and wiggles her painted toes. "Like I told you that day, Karan, when you gave me the half heart. You had to find what was in there."

She points to my heart with her long French-manicure fingernails shining in the last of the light.

"I've got a deep well to draw from, that's for sure. I wouldn't have said that a year ago. It was actually almost a year ago," I say dreamily, "when Jack came in heavy footed and slammed his body in the chair and began the sad saga … withering wife."

I throw grass in the air, like Jack that long summer night I've thought of all too often.

"But look at all the good that's come out of it."

Cindy throws grass too.

"I don't know about the good. I do know that's when I started making concessions."

"Everybody makes concessions, Karan. From the time you're six, and you want the cherry lollipop, and the teacher says you have to have orange."

"Nobody wants the orange," I say, remembering.

"I know. I know. Why do they even make them? My kids get radical flavors like bubblegum, marshmallow, and mango." Cindy licks her lips.

"But moving almost 3,500 miles away with Canada in between. That's a concession and a half, Cindy … and becoming the new title of my life, I'm afraid."

Cindy stands up and pulls my lagging body.

"The title of my life would be 'untitled,' because I have no clue whatsoever about what is going to happen one day to the next."

"Why do women make more concessions than men?" I ask.

"You can always say no to things you don't want."

She demonstrates with my mouth and makes me speak it.

"Nooo!" I say.

"Very good. You'll learn."

I take another sip of water.

"And I don't think women make more concessions, Karan. It's just that the guys don't know when they make concessions, because we don't let them know."

"May be true."

"It is true."

"By the way, my new Bee Hive wardrobe is a bomb. I have no idea what to wear anymore."

"How about Ann Taylor, Nordstroms. Something fitted, sophisticated. You'd look beautiful, Karan."

"Beauty is marred these days," I say thoughtfully. "In this golden Mecca of beautification, it's like clothes and hair are all that beauty is. It's in your face, twenty-four-seven. Sometimes you forget the soul."

"Save that thought for your next poem, Karan. Really. The poetry lady is ruining you."

"They actually dress pretty casual at the newspaper."

"Well then, I guess your black silk dress is out."

I stretch, let my head roll forward and to every side in a slow circle. Cindy does Pilate stretches on the grass.

The girls ride up on their matching Christmas bikes, already clogged with dirt.

"Mommy. Mommy. Can we ride to the park?"

"I don't let my girls ride to the park," says Cindy, standing up.

"No, you may not!"

"Okay," they say without argument.

"Easy girls, Karan. If mine were so easy."

"Yours are wonderful."

She glows in pride.

"Hope, what did you name your bike, anyway?"

I turn to Cindy. "Hope likes to name things." I almost mention Pickles, but catch myself, remembering she belongs to the professor now. The guy is probably sleeping in my bed as we speak. I correct my thinking. No, he's probably using my shower. Alaska is only an hour later than California.

"I didn't think of a name," Hope says, dejected.

"How about … Red Fury."

"She doesn't name things anymore, Mommy."

"What do you mean, Faith?"

They put their bikes down on the lawn.

"Tell me, girls … what you mean."

They are silent, but their eyes are telling stories. Hope is biting her nails.

"Are you still feeling like you did at Christmas? Would you want to move back home? If you could, that is?"

They don't want to say.

"Tell me true. No Pinocchio."

"We miss Grandma and the dogs and winter and the Northern Lights," says Faith, jumping up and down in release.

"And church and halibut tacos," adds Hope. And then with a sigh. "But mostly Daddy."

"What do you mean about Daddy? What do you mean?"

"We don't want Daddy to die," says Hope.

"Die?"

"Daddy told Grandma LaRue on the phone that he was dying in Alaska, and now he's better," Faith says as fast as a rocket.

Cindy hugs me sideways. I feel my heart sinking with the sun, but maintain a placid look.

"That's a figure of speech, and you can't take it seriously, girls."

"What's that?" Faith asks.

"A figure of speech is like if I were to say that you have so much dirt on you that I'd have to bulldoze it off."

"Funny, Mommy," says Hope.

"Thank you."

I hug them both.

"It's getting dark, so why don't you put your bikes away and take a bath. I'll make you a snack."

"Can we have a fire and make 'smores?" Faith asks, dirty streaks of sweat dripping.

"Can we have cocoa?" Hope asks, face shiny and excited.

I wish I could say yes.

"Please! Please! Please!" They extend their lips in the most adorable, pitiful look. They must practice in the mirror, or maybe I taught them ... yeah, I taught them.

"Girls, it's summer weather. We would roast before the marshmallows."

They walk away disappointed.

"Put your bikes away."

They change directions and grab their bikes.

"As soon as it gets colder, we'll cozy up around the fire with cocoa."

"It won't ever get that cold," moans Faith.

They ride to the garage.

"Cindy, I'm not a good mother anymore."

"What? You're supposed to control the weather? How goofy is that?"

"I used to be the perfect mother. Do all the right things."

"There is no such thing as a perfect mother."

"My mother was close to it. She got up in the dark to heat a water bottle so my feet would be warm when I got up."

She holds my face in her hands and squeezes.

"I am not my mother! I am not my mother! Say it!"

I remove her hands, gently, not in the mood for play, and release my heavy breath.

"I feel all disconnected with my girls. Like I've been rewired. Know any good electricians?"

"I heard some good advice once, Karan. Sometimes you have to be a 'good enough mother.'"

"I don't want to be a 'good enough mother'; I want to be better than good enough. I want to be fantastic. The kind of mom my mother was."

"You told me your mom didn't work."

"She didn't."

"So, good enough will have to do. You can't do it all. Nobody can."

"I'm not so sure."

"And the truth is, neither could your mother, or my mother, or even June Cleaver. June Cleaver once made Beaver eat his brussels sprouts in a restaurant. What kind of substandard mothering is that?"

I laugh, because I know it's true.

21

As Jack tells the story, ten miles into his thirty-mile biking trek the road folded in front of him as a friendly dog settled onto the pavement and refused to move. He swerved and braked to avoid the mass of fur and hanging tongue, shot in the air like a cannon, hit the pavement, and skidded ten feet. Whereupon a muscular Saint Bernard with a massive head—brown and white with huge black circles under his droopy eyes—besieged him with slobber.

"*Canis deformis*," Jack called him.

Latin for disgusting dog. This Latin I know, not because I paid attention in Latin class, but Jack frequently used this term for our dogs with large affection.

When he recovered his senses, an ugly man with a Jimmy Durante nose and Fabio hair, who insisted he was a world-class cyclist himself, offered to give him a ride to the emergency room in the back of his truck, which was filled with construction equipment. His own dog, a yappy Terrier, occupied the front seat.

After positioning Jack on the long bed of the truck with the help of a passing biker who wished him "the best" and continued on his way, the Durante/Fabio character jumped in the unreliable-looking truck and accelerated to full speed. He turned to Jack through the open window and started telling him about his biking accident in China with a vegetable cart and how his bones jutted out and blood was spurting everywhere, not considering that Jack was bleeding profusely over himself and his own piece of canvas.

The driver went on in his thunderous voice about how it took him forever to get medical attention and how the facilities in China are inadequate for the people, especially the rural poor. He shared the useful news that his aunt gives to this world health organization because she is into overseas humanitarian causes, speaks Greek, and makes phyllo dough things that he has to taste sometime.

Finally, he gets Jack to the hospital. After x-rays, it is determined there are no broken bones. They stitch him up, sixteen stitches in the knee, give him pain pills and antibiotics, and send him home with an instruction sheet and lots of bruises and scrapes.

Only after the character drops Jack off and takes the twenty dollars he offers him for his trouble, does Jack realize he doesn't have the bike. So he sends Bradford to find it.

Bradford reports back on his cell phone that the bike is gone. Vanished.

"Jack, you can't just sit there and stare at the wall," I say.

"Put on ESPN for me, will ya?"

Sorriest words ever spoken.

See, Jack never was one for watching sports, except for the Super Bowl or world-class soccer—something big like that.

And now he sits in the velvet chair all day staring at the tube. Watching football, basketball, golf. All the majors.

Two days later he's channel surfing the less prestigious sports: horse racing, wrestling, bowling. Anything that moves. And he never does—move that is.

The only reason I know his mouth still works is that he cheers every time someone scores, makes grunting noises from time to time, and calls out for pizza.

Other than that he says "goodbye" when I leave for work and "hello" when I return. And, every once in awhile, calls an order from his chair. "Have you loaded those dishes in the dishwasher, girls?" or "Bring Daddy a snack; will you, honey?"

He knows better than to ask me.

"Jack," I say, several days into his sports marathon, knee mostly healed and bruises diminished, "you need a new hobby."

The man is driving me nuts!

Now this suggestion scares me, because Jack has acquired a taste for expensive hobbies. But scarier is the fact that he's lost to this underworld, this subculture of machismo.

Jack says, "Uh huh," which is one of those expressions you could take either way.

So I write this poem for my poetry page called "Sports Junkie," and break the record on public response. "More letters than ever," Sonia says.

The letters are mostly from frustrated women. They tell me how their husbands and boyfriends would rather watch a game than go out with them; how they spend too much money on sports memorabilia and sporting events; how they ignore them and yell at them when they stand in front of the TV. One woman's husband built a TV room, put a lock on the door, and kept the key.

No matter what I suggest to get him out of that chair, Jack doesn't budge. I even buy him a muscle magazine with buffed guys for motivation. I tell him I'll work overtime to pay for a Gold's gym membership.

"Rats, I missed the score with you gabbing."

He's got this thing growing on his chin that might be a beard, but Jack never could grow a full beard. *He'll never get a job with that stubble,* I think. I'm beginning to understand why one of my readers poured hot oil on her husband's lap.

I am getting desperate. But things tend to turn out better in life when you let God work. Because I truly believe God cares about the small things in life. In fact, everything is small to him.

*S*aturday, 10:00 AM, and the April morning is warm. Jack stands in the kitchen with his eyes barely open, his cup held out. I pour French Quarter coffee and present a tray of fresh-fried beignets, which I made special for him because he is about to blow his top.

He stuffs the beignet in his mouth and heads toward his familiar cushion, coffee swishing dangerously. He plops in the chair, reaches for the remote, and starts flipping channels like pancakes—the way he does every day.

"What's going on here? Where are my channels?"

He's shaking the remote.

"I meant to tell you, Jack; they turned off the cable first thing this morning. We only have the regular channels now."

"Turned off the cable? They have hardly any sports on regular TV. Couldn't they have turned something else off?"

"Like what? The phone?" I say too happily. "You must have forgotten to pay the bill."

Some mumbling, an exasperated sigh. Nothing close to rage like I expected.

And that is the end of it.

Jack is back to sitting in the chair staring at the wall and occasionally reading the want ads, but doing nothing about it. He's eating the remainder of his biker bars since he knows we can't afford a new bike.

*A*re all those groceries for us?" Jack asks, his first discernible sentence in days.

I'm worried about the man. He's obviously depressed and getting round in the front. Immobility and junk food can do that.

"Nope. We're having a barbecue, Jack. You'd better take a bath and shave."

"I don't want company," he says, disheveled hair, grungy beard, and wrinkled clothes tainting his good looks.

"They're already invited; they'll be here in an hour."

"Shucks," he says, like I am his mother.

This role reversal is twisted. Where's my spiritual leader, the lovable control freak?

"I guess I better," he says a second later, like the kid of a mother who doesn't want to clean his room.

I want to tell him to do his laundry that is nearing the ceiling, since he's actually listening. I won't do it since he's home all day. But I'm just happy he's not throwing a bigger fit about the party.

I have a full-time job; he sits in the chair. I cook dinner; he sits in a chair. I help the girls with their homework; he sits in a chair. Something is wrong with this picture. Why isn't it obvious to him?

Jack appears from the back looking more like himself, minus the fuzz and grime. Aunt Candy greets him with a hug and a Hawaiian phrase.

"Jack, you're looking 'Olu'olu,'" which she says means cool, or some variation thereof.

I wouldn't trust Aunt Candy to translate for me at the Hawaiian grocery store down the street. The clerk, a true Hawaiian, told me (while Aunt Candy was shaking macadamia nuts to see if they were crunchy) that her Hawaiian is bad. Very bad. So bad that it's a disgrace to his culture.

I just smiled.

Jack is raring to go. Grinning and moving his shoulders in circles like a fighter ready for a bout, all set for a good time. Amazing how a man dead to himself an hour ago can suddenly perk up when he wants to.

Before more is said, the rest of the group arrives, and we gather in the back.

Jack fires up the barbecue.

"Hey, let's play golf Sunday," Steve suggests.

And for some reason Jack is not excited about it. Could it be that he is as rotten at the game as Cindy suggested? Even with Steve giving him a generous handicap?

Soon Jack is looking depressed again. I don't get it!

Now, I made it clear to Delilah, who was supposed to make it clear to Bradford, that we are not to let Jack know that this is a "cheer him up party." But Bradford, foot-in-his-mouth kinda guy that he is, says, "I brought some reading to cheer you up, Jack."

"It's X-Men and Spiderman comics."

I don't know if it's intended to be a joke or if Bradford actually reads on that level.

You see, Bradford is one of those types that is either genius or brainless, and it's hard telling which one. At age four, Aunt Candy tells me they thought he was brilliant. He would build Lego towers to the sky and could recite the preamble to the Constitution. At eight he was demoted to average, based on the fact that he couldn't read—at all. At twelve he was considered academically weak. But in high school and through college, he regained his genius status.

Now, my theory is that the coaches might have had some influence over his grades because he was an all-star football player who knocked over linebackers like bowling pins.

"Cindy, what do you make of Jack?"

"I don't know. He's your man, not mine."

"I think we need a vacation. A change of scenery. But we don't have a penny to spend."

"Then pray, girl. Pray hard."

22

I'm happy today, especially happy for a Monday. The weather is actually cold, and I plan on building the girls a fire tonight, which with my gas fireplace means turning the knob.

I walk in the office to find Sonia in my cubicle.

"I'm not late, am I?"

"Of course not. I wanted to warn you that there might be some changes coming up."

"Changes? I knew it. How could I think that my amateur poetry—"

"It has nothing to do with your poetry, Karan."

Sonia pats my back.

"Your poetry is honest. People love your poetry because it's truth, not because you're an award-winning poet with perfect technique."

"Phew." I put down my purse.

"The changes I am referring to are related to management, and I can't talk about it yet. In fact, I shouldn't have even brought it up."

"Oh."

"Anyway, I have something I want to ask you, and it's good."

My face relaxes.

"My husband and I rented a house in Big Bear this week and … well, his mother is coming into town from Wyoming, and the last thing she wants is snow. We can't use it and can't get our money back. Would you like to use it?"

"When?"

"Tomorrow through Sunday. And don't worry about taking the time off. We'll just reprint your most requested poems."

"It's an answer to prayer, Sonia. I didn't even have a chance to pray twice."

She hands me a map and a key.

ig Bear is a little town in the San Bernardino Mountains. "California's best-kept secret," one travel magazine called it. News flash! This place is no secret.

As I told Jack that day back in our living room in Alaska as he was rooting for the California team, and Alaska was down by at least seven, Big Bear is one of the most congested places in the world. And here on this winding road with traffic like Macy's Thanksgiving Day Parade, traveling at minus five miles per hour, my position is reaffirmed.

People who live in semi-arid climates obviously don't know how to drive on icy roads. They brake at every turn in the road.

Jack is *trying* to hold his temper because he knows I was right. I see his white knuckles clenching the steering wheel, and his eyes bulging out of his skull.

I suppress my delight. *Life is going on here, Jack,* I want to say to him. *Isn't that what you wanted?* I am such a sinner.

By the time we arrive in the charming village, because

"charming" is the buzz world on quaint villages, we are starving peasants and would eat anything. The air is stuffy from the blasting heater, and we are spent.

I open the car door and breathe deep.

"Real air."

We stop for a bite to eat. Of course, a charming little town has to have a charming little coffee shop, and this is it. The hostess seats us at a table so close to the others that if we stretched our arms too far, we could be eating off our neighbor's plate.

But the conversation is lively and the atmosphere aesthetically pleasing.

You can learn a lot by listening to the locals; they are the eyes and ears of the community. You ask the business owners, or the chamber of commerce, or consult the newspaper, and you get the chocolate-covered-cherry version of town living. The locals know "where it's at."

"They want to make us Arrowhead," one leather-skinned local says, before he bites into an oversized sandwich. I have the feeling this is his daily conversation. He barely swallows, then expounds on his interesting philosophy.

From what I can surmise, Big Bear is a town with an identity crisis playing dress up for its tourists, kind of like my ghetto girl. In terms of people, Big Bear would be a teenager, and the tourists would be her picky friends. So, here you have this teenager constantly arguing with herself on how to please the tourists, who visit and spend money—money she needs—while maintaining her individuality.

"I think we need a new outfit," the teenager says to herself. "No, I think the vintage dress we have is fine," she says back to herself.

Take the theater, for instance. Fifty-cent popcorn, and you'd think everybody would be happy. But, no, they have to remake the old practical place into fancier separate theaters. That's what the man with the greasy face at the counter is saying, possibly the town mechanic making a quarter-million off new brakes for the people who brake at every winding turn.

After a fairly decent and ridiculously expensive lunch, we arrive at the lakeside house. Of course, it is also charming, but too close to the other houses to be called a retreat.

"Never look a gift horse in the mouth" was one of my daddy's favorite sayings. Usually he used this expression when someone gave us something that didn't work. The ice cream maker with the burned-out motor, the broken-down lawn mower …

You see, people were always leaving Alaska in a hurry and leaving useless junk behind. But Daddy was a handyman, and he could fix the stuff.

Getting a better look, the atmosphere is just what the doctor ordered. Me, being the doctor. There's nobody in the houses next door. Rich people can afford two, maybe three houses.

Serenity at last. Peace and freedom and all those good things.

I stand on the deck and sing loud, high operatic notes because I can.

In two seconds flat the girls are enjoying themselves. Down below they are making a game out of sticks and rocks.

Jack plops in an oversized leather recliner in the living room with a picturesque view of the lake, leans back, and arranges his feet comfortably on the footstool. He stares out the window with a half scowl. Even before unloading the car, he is in a regrettable mood. If Jack were a computer, his screen would read, "Can't open this page."

I decide that I will not let his sorry boy behavior ruin my week.

Mom, perfect mother that she is, sent me two hundred dollars, so the girls and I are going to have fun. And we do.

We eat out, go to the movies, shop, and play. By Saturday night we are exhausted.

Jack is exhausted too. Tell me how! He hasn't moved as far as I can tell, except to finally take the luggage in. There's no TV, and no reading material other than Danielle Steele novels. I haven't fixed him a bite of food. Guess he's been living off our doggy bags.

"Goodnight, Daddy," the girls say and hug him. He smiles for them.

"Goodnight, my princesses. Pleasant dreams."

Then he closes his eyes. He's going to sleep in the chair again without even saying goodnight to me. I don't believe it, but he is.

My dream, condensed ...

The girls and I, in summer clothes, are standing on the shore of a shining blue lake. It begins to snow, soft big flakes. We are laughing. Playing as we do. It's so real I can feel the cold, but it is a pleasant sensation.

Jack, also dressed in summer clothes, is on the other shore under falling snow, a lake between us, but at the same time, right next to us. One of those things that can only happen in dreams.

I can almost touch him, but there is an invisible barrier of some sort separating us. He is far away. Unreachable. The division is exasperating.

Strangely, the snow stops on his side, but not ours.

Sunshine, translucent rays from heaven pour over him. It is beautiful. But he just stands there, no life in him. As though the beauty doesn't phase him. A deadness in his eyes. A numbness in his body. His limbs hang limp as he stares, just stares.

We beckon him to join us, but he cannot or will not hear our cries.

And then an awful thud.

"Daddy, Daddy," Hope calls. "A bird has fallen from the sky. Please, Daddy, fix her!"

Faith picks up the wounded creature, struggling for life.

"Daddy, help or she will die!" Faith calls to him with a look of terror in her eyes.

And then I plead, "Jack, we need your help! Jack! Please, Jack! Please!"

He stares ahead.

The snow stops and begins to melt fast and washes into the lake. We sink our feet deep in the sand to keep our balance for the deluge of water rushing over us.

It starts to snow heavily on Jack's side of the lake. In seconds the landscape is covered in high snow. It is up to his knees, and then to his chest, but he does not seem to notice.

And the bird is dying. And we are calling. And the snow keeps falling on Jack, and he is still staring into nowhere.

I awake to find myself caught up in a tangle of sheets, sweating, heart racing thirty beats faster than normal.

I do not understand the dream; I am not inclined toward interpretation. I only know that it speaks of the deadness of Jack's spirit. I only know that I am frightened and feel an urgency, a pull in my spirit. We have come to a crossroads of Jack's life. I will gain him or lose him.

I check on Jack. He is sound asleep in the leather chair. I touch him to be sure.

I amble groggily toward the bedroom, still in a dreamy state. Knees on the hardwood floor and face on the bed, I pray. I pray from such a deep and wounded place. I pray all the words that I have until they are gone, and, when they are, I pray with no words. For God knows my silent prayer. The dull, remote pain throbbing inside me. He knows me, he knows Jack and the girls and the sky and all the answers to all the questions ever asked before they're even asked.

I don't know how long it is that I pray. Sleep comes in between. But when I lift my head to read the clock, it is 5:00 AM, and my body is stiff.

Without being fully cognizant, I go to the kitchen and turn on a small light. I find a large steel bowl in the cupboard and fill it with warm water from the sink. I gather a towel, a washcloth, and soap, and take it into the living room where Jack is staring into darkness. For how long I don't know.

He looks at me, wondering what I am doing, but does not speak.

I place the bowl down, without saying anything. I take his right foot and place it gently in the basin. I begin to wash the dirt off his chaffed, neglected feet I used to care for so much. Feet I used to rub at night; using cream around the hard skin to soften the cuticles.

I don't know why I'm doing this any more than I understand the dream. Just that I'm supposed to.

I take a washcloth and scrub gently. At first some resistance, but then I feel Jack relaxing to the soothing comfort of the warm water and gentle lather.

Then I hear a sound. A cry in the dimly lit room. A small, controlled cry.

Why is it men always cry in the shadows and never in broad daylight? I guess because it's safer and hidden.

The cry expands, like it can't be held back, until Jack is weeping uncontrollably, like the girls on Christmas.

I don't stop. I continue washing his feet. I dry the first and position his left foot in the soapy, dirty water.

Perhaps having your feet washed is humility in its fullness. I think of Jesus washing the disciples' feet. God washing the stinky, dirty feet of humans, and how that speaks of his love and servanthood.

Jack's cry is softer now. His spirit is breaking, like huge pieces of icebergs falling into the sea—"calving" they call it.

Jack's weeping calms to a suppressed sob.

I leave him to himself. I put the things away and go back to bed. I leave the rest to God.

In the late morning the girls wake me with kisses and the smell of dry roasted coffee in a dainty flowered cup they say they made themselves. I taste it; it is bitter. I smile and tell them it is wonderful and it was kind of them to think of me.

They tear from my presence. Always going somewhere.

I stand at the window in my soft flannel pajamas. This week is the first time they've been worn since our move to California.

Jack is walking the lake. He stops at regular intervals and picks up rocks from the melting patches of snow. The girls come up behind him, and he gathers them in his arms. They walk together and pick up rocks. It's the first time I've seen them in their old way since we left Alaska.

I want to believe that things will change. That Jack will change. But doubt has become a pattern with me. I push the hopeful thoughts from my mind.

The rest of the day talk is small and unengaging.

We head down the mountain in traffic, the same as we came up in, the same cars it seems. Same poky drivers who ride their brakes.

I sleep most of the way home. I sleep until we pull in the driveway.

I unpack, shower, and sleep through the night, awaking once or twice to watch Jack sleeping as sound as ever.

23

The infallible proof that my coveted position as poetry lady is in imminent danger is sitting in my office. She is older than her picture, rounder, and lacking the ruddy glow one might expect of a new mother. In fact, she is positively purple, and, unless I am reading her wrong, she would like to hire a hit man to "off me."

"What do you want me to do with this thing? It doesn't go with my décor," she says, displaying the homemade snow globe Hope made me for Mother's Day two years back.

"Uh, hand it to me."

She throws it up in the air.

"Oooops," she says, like Cruella DeVil.

It lands on the floor. I inspect it for cracks. Thankfully, there are none. I am a lion when it comes to my cubs.

"The rest of your stuff is on top of *my* filing cabinet."

She points her red-nailed finger and stares through me. Her eyes are badly in need of eyedrops, and her dark dyed hair hardens her already hard appearance.

"Take it and leave my office!"

One of ugliest plagues of mankind is ego. Tragedy has

befallen many men and women because of it. More, perhaps, than any other form of human vice or weakness.

Because I am not as clever with comebacks as I am in prose, and, more important, because I am a Christian and therefore am to love unceasingly, I grab my scant belongings and walk away to avoid further incident, in the direction of Sonia's office like "everything is just fine, thank you" and looking straight ahead to avoid wandering eyes begging for a story.

Sonia's door is open, and she is expecting me. I drop my box and close the door.

"So you met Zeya?"

"Met her? More like collided with her."

"She used her option. Came back early after hearing your office was vacant for a few days."

"Why would she come back early?"

"Two stars, one sky. Word around the office is that you are making her look bad. The copy editors call you 'golden fingers,' and her 'silver pinkie.'"

I remember David and the people's hero chant, "Saul has slain his thousands, but David his ten thousands." I imagine a spear being hurled in my direction as I leave the parking lot.

"Do you mean, Sonia, that she's going to sacrifice the time with her newborn baby because of a few lines of poetry?"

"She doesn't have God in her life, Karan."

"Yeah, I guess."

"And now I have some news. You remember what I wanted to tell you the other day."

I fidget with the buttons on my cotton blouse.

"I'm being transferred to the mailroom; I knew it."

"No, Karan. You don't give yourself any credit."

Sonia looks tired and used up; there are deep lines in her

face I never noticed before, and her movements are slower, heavier.

"I'm being fired, Karan. Technically my position is being eliminated. They offered me a lower position for the same pay, but I declined."

"They're eliminating the editor? That's not too bright."

"They'll just reclassify the position, give it some other title. It will be the same job."

"Yuk."

"It's alright, Karan. It happens in this business. Anyway, my husband is retiring next month. We may move to Wyoming. He likes to hunt."

"Who's taking over?" I ask, but feel guilty. I should be talking about her life instead of thinking about mine.

"Andrew Russell is taking over. He's from the *Chicago News-Mirror,* which, as you know, owns this paper. And he's good friends with guess who."

"I see … so few run the world, don't they?"

I plunk in a chair, hoping for something to sink into. My body meets a thin cushion that offers little comfort. Sonia is staring out the window, thoughtlessly swinging her spectacles. She walks over to her desk and sits in her ergonomic chair. Flings her glasses across the shiny desktop. Her neat pile of papers scatter.

"I spent the bulk of last week acquainting him with the position," she says. "He read your poetry page and loves it. He thinks your picture looks like Audrey Hepburn."

"Really?" I act like I never heard it.

"But apparently Zeya caught wind of Mr. Russell's interest in you and threatened, through the pipeline, to sue the paper's pants off for race discrimination if anybody messed with her poetry page. Andrew Russell happened to be in my office when Julie Langton splashed the story. She didn't realize who he was."

"Why, that's surprising, Sonia." My face is a sarcastic eddy.

"Funny thing about it is, this place is a rainbow of races."

"Any more diversity, and we'd be the Tower of Babel," I say, in a feeble attempt at adding lightheartedness to what must be a shocking turn of events to Sonia.

"We don't know or care what her origin is, or anybody else's origin," she says straightening her papers.

"I know where she came from." A look of satisfaction.

"You do?" Sonia asks, laying her arms across the table and stretching her neck in interest.

"She was hatched from the planet of Mean." I catch myself. "Not nice. Sorry."

"That's fine. You're doing well with this, Karan."

"What is going to happen to me then?"

I clear my throat and feel my eye twitching in a sporadic pulse.

"Before I'm out of here, I'm putting you in a reporter spot. You can write and even take your own pictures if the situation calls for it."

"Reporter?" I reflect on my lack of experience, my naivete of journalist duties. "I don't know if I'm up to it."

"Give it a try. The reporters' cubicles are on opposite sides of the building from Zeya's," she says encouraging me.

"That's an incentive. Plus I need the work."

"I want one last poem out of you for tomorrow's paper."

"Won't Zeya object?"

"I'm still the editor, *today*."

"Alright."

"Go to a bakery somewhere. You can take my laptop."

She walks over to me. I stand up. We hug; we laugh; we cry.

A Place to Ponder is one of my favorite places to be. A great place for a poet to start the morning. It's nostalgic of a Beatnik coffeehouse with its artsy décor and shabby chic furniture. But you won't find any tightpanted, turtle-necked, beret-wearing, bongo-beaters here. Just guys in ties and gals in pumps.

When you walk in, your nose is overtaken with fresh bean and bakery smells. A liberal assortment of classic literature lying on dark wood shelves calls you to greatness. It's small enough to be cozy and large enough to be nameless.

I sip on a foamy grande caramel macchiato, outrageously daring for me. Normally, I'm a single, low-fat latte, no foam, no flavor kind of gal.

I look at all the intelligent people, sipping between thoughts, talking between sips.

Let's see … I've written poems on greed, fashion, abuse, flowers, fish bowls. That just about covers it.

What to write? What to write?

I chew a bagel. I sip my coffee. I wait for inspiration.

Leaves. Too boring.

I haven't written about death. Too morbid.

I could write about a two-faced woman who throws children's snow globes around.

Too obvious

I could do a thank you letter to my readers.

No. Sonia wants a poem.

Give up, Karan.

No. Zeya would love it if I conceded to the enemy.

This is the worst day of my life so far.

I drop my bagel, and it lands cream cheese face down on the floor, which is where I leave it.

This whole thing is Jack's fault in the first place. I'm tired of making concessions. Having what I love ripped away from me and allowing it.

I missile my frustrations toward ground zero. The title of my life—you go girl!

And it bursts forth into a mosaic of weedy emotion:

Concessions

I feel like you tore my heart out of my chest and tossed it on the ground.

Feel like I'm making concessions for you every time I turn around.

Tuba player blows deep down notes, like a funeral is coming to town.

And little girls dressed up all in black aren't allowed to make a sound.

See, a man can't see the forest through the trees when he's only seeing himself.

And the things we used to do together you tell me to "do-it-yourself."

I don't know how a man can live when he forgets those he says he loves.

You definitely need a stronger prescription when you call a vulture a dove.

Daddy's sure having lots of fun, but he's causing us a lot of pain.

But I suppose that I should be happy that the man still knows my name.

To top off my list of grievances, the man's not even aware.

Cause he just sits there staring at the wall in a comfortable easy chair.

While I make the concessions.

Too many to mention.

his is raw, Karan. Purposely obscure, yet explicit. Not personal experience, I hope," Sonia adds with a hesitant expression.

"Not my fault, Sonia. Blame your computer."

"Are you sure you want me to print it?"

"I'm sure, Sonia. I'm sure."

"By the way, Karan, everybody makes concessions. From the time you're four and want the red balloon the other kid wants."

"I know, Sonia. I know."

24

I walk in the door feeling sick, like the day I packed my life in boxes. But it's a different kind of sick. Stomach churning, stole a candy bar and got caught kind of sick.

We all make mistakes. We do. But I think I just made a biggie. *Why didn't I rip up that stupid poem?* And it's already gone to print.

Regret: to feel sorry, remorseful, ashamed, to want to hide in a dark closet and never come out again.

Jack is whistling in the bathtub. He hasn't whistled in nearly a year. What's up with this?

"Hey, Jack," I call from the bedroom, pulling off my black flats and squeezing my toes in relief. "Where are the girls?"

"They're having dinner at Cindy's."

I wait for more I know must be coming.

"I got a job," he shouts over the splash of water in the sunken tub.

"You got a job?" I ask excitedly.

My thoughts cease for a moment, considering the possibilities.

He emerges from the bathroom in a towel, not properly dried. Dripping on the carpet, he looks pleased with himself.

"Share the details."

"Blossom Tires down the street. So close I can walk."

"Well … maybe not what you expected. But that's good."

"That's what I think too," he says.

I plop backward on our bed atop a soft blue comforter completely exhausted, which is how I feel most of the time. I know I should be more enthusiastic, but I'm not sure how excited I can get about such a menial job. I never pictured Jack working at a tire shop.

"What about the girls?"

"Aunt Candy is going to watch them at our house after school. Since they don't have lessons anymore, she'll just be picking them up, not carting them around."

He lies down next to me, soaking the bed like a seal. The feel of his skin against mine is strange; it's been so long since he's made a point to be near me.

"I don't know, Jack. She'll feed them tofu dogs and that fermented bean paste soup again. And poi. Oh my gosh, have you tasted that stuff? It's some kind of plant, but it's nasty, Jack, and the girls aren't eating it."

"I had a talk with her, and she's going to cook from your menu. I told her the girls needed balanced meals."

"And what did she say to that?"

"She said health food was balanced. Then I explained that children need different vitamins than adults, or something like that, and she was fine with it."

"Your aunt is a wonderful person, Jack, and I've grown to love her dearly, but I'm also concerned about her religious influence on the girls. She's into that Huna religion. Last week she told them she has Ti plants bordering her property to ward off evil spirits and bring good luck."

Jack gets up and dries off in the bathroom. I sit up and fold my feet under me.

"I told her no telling the girls strange tales, and she agreed," he calls. "And I also told her straight out what we believe in case she didn't already know."

"Well. I don't know, Jack. What did she say about it?"

He comes out looking gorgeous in a white robe, wet hair rubbed a mess. It's been so long since I've noticed.

"She said she doesn't object to any religion as long as it doesn't harm anyone."

"Maybe the girls can have an effect on her," I reason.

Jack sits down next to me again, rubs my shoulders and kisses the edges of my ear.

His attentiveness is bothering me. I can't help but be suspicious. He's had a few waves of niceness since we moved here, but like waves they swell and melt away like they never happened.

"Guess what, Jack?"

"What?"

"You are looking at five-star reporter."

"Naw."

"Okay, one-star, but a reporter, no less."

"More money?"

"I'm not sure."

"How did that happen?"

"Zeya's back, and I look like Audrey Hepburn."

"Well … okay," he says, massaging the back of my neck, along the sides of my head to my scalp. It feels so good.

"I'm too drained to go into it now. Maybe after dinner.

But I will tell you that it could be more hours and a lot more stressful."

"We'll work it out," he says, in a most pleasant way.

He's being so nice tonight. Maybe he's changing. Maybe.

I turn to him and smile, reserving a part of myself.

He beams back, soft blue eyes holding me like they used to.

"What are you thinking?"

Gulp. "Nothing ... nothing."

"In case I haven't told you lately, Karan. I appreciate you."

I grit my teeth to form a smile.

"And I love your hair."

"Thank you for saying that."

"Audrey Hepburn," he says, eyebrows furrowed in thought. "Wasn't she in a movie with Spencer Tracey?"

"No, that was Katherine Hepburn."

"Well, anyway, you're more beautiful than both of them."

"Especially since they're both dead," I say.

He laughs, a deep, soulful laugh I thought I'd never hear again.

So flattering tonight, I think. I wonder what looms on the horizon. Sophocles, the great tragic poet once said, "If you are out of trouble, watch for danger."

I asked Aunt Candy to please, please hide the newspaper when it came today. I had to leave before our habitually late newspaper boy's misdirected delivery in the bushes. She said she would.

Judging by Jack's hurt expression, however, somehow she failed to execute this simple plan.

"Hi."

"Hi," he says, newspaper lying on the floor next to him, pain manifested in his face.

"How was your first day of work?"

No answer.

"One thing I have to know, and I have to know it honestly, Karan. Is this me in here?"

He picks up the newspaper and waves it in his hand. "This monster of a man who doesn't see past the trees."

"I didn't say anything about monsters."

"Is it me?" he asks.

"It's about a lot of men. Everything I write is about a lot of people, never one person. Experiences are universal. That's why it's appealing. People can relate."

"But it is me too, then?"

"When I write, I don't think about it. Poetry is exaggerated expression. It just comes, and I allow it, or don't. I allowed it to come and what it was is what it is."

"So you wanted me to know the pain that I've put you through?"

"I didn't think you ever read my column; you never mention it." I rub my eyes, wishing I could rub away the moment. "You weren't supposed to see it."

"Just the world, but not me?"

"Not the world. It's a small readership. Not the world."

He drops the paper. I sit on the edge of the chair and look into his eyes the way I did the night he began his descent.

"The terrible thing about it is that I know every word of it is true, Karan."

He will not look at me. He looks at his fingertips, outside the window, but not at me.

"How could I have done that to you and the girls? I saw it; I knew it. Yet I did it, knowing the pain it would cause."

"Nobody is going to think it's you, Jack," I say analyzing away my regret.

"Well, maybe you're right," he says, hanging his head low. "Aunt Candy read it, and she didn't connect it with me."

"Imagine that," I say.

"She was reading it when I walked in the door and then gasped and said I wasn't supposed to see the paper today. I asked why. She said 'bad news probably.'"

We laugh at Aunt Candy's sweet simplemindedness, and then for a moment nothing is said.

I rub the back of Jack's neck, a simple gesture meant to comfort the pain of realization he must be feeling. Just an hour before I would have wanted him to endure it at its full measure.

"What can I do?" he asks. "What can I do to make it up to you? Short of Alaska," he adds quickly.

He touches my cheek tenderly.

"One thing would solve it."

"One thing?"

"Aunt Candy could figure it out."

"Love?"

"Sorta. Very close."

"Something we need?"

"Something we both already have—definitely. And the girls too. But not Aunt Candy. Not yet."

"God?"

"Yes, Jack. Invite God back as Captain, and your seas will be smoother. Is that simple or what?" I am hoping he can relate to the nautical analogy I heard on the radio this morning.

"I must admit I've been under the knife of conviction lately."

"Please come back to church with us. Pastor Abraham is wonderful. He's not Pastor Davies, but he's good. And Easter is on Sunday. You could invite the whole family. Delilah's been coming, and she likes it."

"Well, since my life has basically been in the pit since I quit going to church. Maybe—just maybe—I should listen to your advice."

Bright man, my Jack. Maybe a bit late. But bright as a shiny penny under murky Louisiana water, as his mother always says of him when she's proud.

The night I cried myself to sleep, before my nose matched my face and my Audrey Hepburn body took shape, when I was still a gangly teenager with pimples and braces, my father told me, "Karan, things don't change overnight. They just don't."

But in this case, things have changed overnight, or nearly so. Mom said it would happen. Mom always knows best. Jack is not the same man.

If I were the conniving type, like Cindy, precious soul that she is, I might have thought up some effective plans to snap Jack out of his unrealized misery. But I look at it this way. I could have thought up all the strategies and executed them, to shock and to hurt and just for revenge. I could have whined and stamped my feet and spent money and even pierced my belly button. Whatever. But, you can't force a person to change.

But, God, well … he has his ways. I remember the night back in Alaska when I asked God to give Jack a little nudge and wake him from his rainbow dream.

At that time I couldn't have imagined my mild-mannered Jack a reckless horse at full gallop, seeking Solomon's crooked road to fulfillment (except for the women, thank God).

But God has a knack, like I said. Sure Jacob tried to wrestle him. But one touch, and he was down. And maybe on the ground looking up isn't a bad place to be when you're trying to figure things out.

So here we are. Me and Jack. The beach. A sunset. Who needs Paris?

There were times I tried to convince myself that it wasn't as good as I remembered it, that I wasn't missing so much.

But now that he is my life again, and I remember how generous love is, I can say it is every bit as good as I remember, and even better for the loss of it.

It brings to mind the day I lost my wedding ring. I couldn't find it anywhere. I fretted all day long, and when I found my 0.4-carat diamond, it was like finding the biggest diamond ever.

And, no, this isn't Alaska. And we're not standing on our own property with the trees we planted and the northern sky that held our eyes a thousand nights. This isn't our "house that Jack built" while I poured gallons of lemonade.

So be it. God still rules.

"How about the Italian place?" Jack asks.

I nod a joyful, yes.

25

astor Abraham, the epitome of pastoral elegance, is shining from the pulpit this Easter Sunday. The worship is glorious, but it could be ordinary and it wouldn't matter with Jack at my side, his beautiful tenor filling my ears with song. I stop singing, for I'd rather listen to a voice engaged in worship after a long, starved drought than to my own that I hear all the time.

Eleven of us sit in one pew. Jack, me, and our girls; Aunt Candy; Bradford and Delilah; Cindy and their girls, with Steve, making his spring holiday appearance and looking as bored as a peanut.

It is a more ceremonious church fashion than Pastor Davies presents, and a larger congregation, but the message is clear, simple, and appropriate for Easter. I am praying that one of these lost souls will make today their second birthday.

When it happens, it is so unexpected that breath escapes me. Pastor Abraham has given an invitation, and then I see the woman moving down the isle. Tall, curved Delilah in lemon shoes and dress is walking purposefully toward the front of the church with the humblest face ever.

I eye Bradford casually. He's got this shocked expression on his face, mixed with the countenance of conviction.

Jack squeezes my hand. In the old days that meant, "Pray." And we do, the both of us send Federal Express prayers to heaven. Because who knows if we'll ever get Bradford back in church again.

Aunt Candy is looking expectedly confused.

Bradford's body inches forward and then backwards again. Like the devil is toying with his soul. Again, he lurches forward. It appears he's going to stand up, but doesn't.

Two people follow Delilah and are standing next to her facing Pastor Abraham. The music is still playing softly. Pastor Abraham asks, "Anyone else?"

Delilah turns around and looks at Bradford, her eyes red by now, tears trickling a wet gleam from the sun shining in through the windows.

Bradford breaks for the front. No reserve, close to a trot. He holds her hand in both of his.

Jack and I hold hands too, and the girls release this restful sigh.

I can hear my Grandmother Plummer telling me as a little girl about the angels singing, and I wonder whether glorified mortals are allowed to join in the heavenly chorus.

I remember the day my name was written in the Lamb's Book of Life. I was only five, and it was cold. The smell of gingerbread cookies permeated Grandma's house, which was down the road from ours. She was in her bedroom rocking, tinted blue-gray hair in a bun, praying from this inner well that sprang from within her.

There were times she didn't leave her room for days if she was praying for something specific. She was a prayer warrior to her last breath. Whenever I was around her, I felt the presence of God, and such peace.

On this particular day, while listening to her whispering praise and prayer, I was overcome with emotion. She pulled me off the braided rug on the hardwood floor, onto her lap and asked me why I was crying.

"It's just so beautiful, Grandma."

"It is, isn't it? To be close to the One who made you and knows how many hairs you have on your head."

"But when you go away, the feeling goes away. I want to stay by you so I can feel it forever."

"Why, we can solve that real easy, Karan," she said. "The reason you don't have Jesus with you always is you haven't asked, and we're gonna ask right now, child. Because I won't be around forever, and you don't need me anyway."

She held my tiny hands together and told me what to pray. When we were done with my salvation prayer, my child heart felt clean and free.

I jumped off her lap and did a little jig of joy. Grandma laughed and said the angels up in heaven were dancing too.

"That joy and peace you're feeling is yours to stay with you now, whether I'm here or gone," she said, a magnificent smile overtaking her.

It's as beautiful a remembrance as I have.

I figure I've been spared a lot of hurt by knowing God so young. Before my demanding adult emotions had a voice.

After church we eat sandwiches. Delilah and Bradford hold hands and smile. I see questions stirring in their eyes, being thought out. Like the first time you learn about death, only they're learning about life.

Since I was so young when I accepted Jesus, I didn't have

the questions about God that new adult believers may have. I remember wondering what God's house looked like after hearing how big our mansions were going to be.

The first question that comes out of Bradford's mouth is, "How can I be a better husband?"

Not wanting to be nosy, I gather dishes from the table.

Jack moves into this beautiful explanation, about how God's design is for the man to be the spiritual leader of the home.

I move into the living room to give them their private moment.

Aunt Candy is sitting on the blue velvet chair, once again looking confused. I think she's been hurt by too many men—her father and, later, her husbands. And it strikes me that perhaps she is thinking in her unhinged way that God is a man, and, therefore, cannot be trusted.

"You know, Aunt Candy, that people fail us."

"I know that, Karan."

"But God doesn't—not ever."

Cynical unbelief plagues her face, diminishing her beauty.

"What is God but energy and light?"

"Do you prefer to look at God as impersonal?"

"I prefer to look at all of us as free," she says in a deeper, distant voice.

"Aunt Candy, if you refuse to look at him as a being, as Jesus come to earth, you can keep your distance. Isn't that true?"

"I prefer not to think at all … and take whatever comes my way."

"Because you won't get hurt?"

"Because I can't get hurt," she says, her eyes looking suddenly frightened.

I hug her and realize how much she means to me. There's been enough heavy talk for one day.

"Let me get you some mango juice."

"Thank you, Karan," she says, and shivers as though a cold wind has touched her.

*A*ndrew Russell has a weaker chin than one might expect a managing editor to have, but a good name. He is a big, graying man, late fifties—at least—with a soft body that wobbles when he walks. His eyes are restless, and his nose is too small for his plump face.

The first day he took over the new position, he alienated half his staff with his intimidating manner. He told Julie Langton, who does the health and fitness page and can't be over 125 pounds dripping wet, that she needed to go to the fat farm; Gary Austin, the sports writer, that he was too scrawny to know anything about sports; and Bill Sanders, features writer, that he needed to interview more stupid people for his article on mental disabilities.

Add to that intimidating manner, a dreadful temper, and frequent use of derogatory language, and you have a thoughtless, bully of a man who belongs in a less-enlightened century.

His giving no thought to his overt violations makes me wonder why he was so concerned about Zeya's cry-wolf threat of race discrimination.

Now, I don't know where Mr. Russell got his journalism degree, or if he even has one, but it seems to me that a man in his position should have some judgment. Common sense would tell you that if you want to achieve your objective (which in this case is running a newspaper), it's best to avoid presenting an offensive manner and creating a hostile working environment.

The reason I have escaped his harassment may be because I have only been in the presence of the man for about thirty seconds in the lunchroom. During this time, he ogled me.

I am walking toward the "jungle" now, aka Mr. Russell's office, where I have been summoned to discuss the seven articles I have written to date. Two city council meetings (a bore), three animals stories (a bore), a reunion story (less of a bore), and an article on proposed annexation of lands for the Sanitation District, which came with a tour of the facilities (the biggest bore of all, and the smelliest).

On my way to his office, Julie Langton grabs me. She's standing in this peculiar posture. Stomach in, chest out, shoulders back to the extreme. It occurs to me that she's trying to look skinner after Mr. Russell's comments.

"I found out why Russell's childhood friend landed King Arrogance the position here," she says as we walk. "There were and still may be complaints filed by angry employees at his former newspaper, and they wanted to get him out of there."

"That's why he was nervous about Zeya."

"Well, he should be nervous about all of us," she whispers.

I wave her off as I reach Mr. Russell's office. He catches the signal.

"Flies, Audrey?"

He called me Audrey. I am taken aback.

"Sit down," he says.

I do, in a new leather chair.

In the short time he's been here, he's managed to take

Sonia's neat office and turn it into a bonfire of a desk: a disorganized jumble of papers, pens, and pencils, lying about.

"I like what you've written about Waldo and the happy reunion of that family with the oversized ears."

"Thank you."

Rude man. Very rude man.

"I have a couple of new assignments I've written down," he says, cheek full of tobacco.

I nod.

"Are you hearing impaired, or something?"

"No, I'm not, Mr. Russell, but I may be related to someone that is."

"I doubt that."

I cross my legs and hold my pen in position in case he says something important.

"That's it. Here's your assignments." He hands me a coffee-dripped piece of paper with messy writing.

"You have what it takes, the heart of reporting," he says. "I'm putting you up a rung. Let's see how you do."

"Thank you."

I stand up hesitatingly, not sure if our meeting is concluded.

"You can go, Audrey."

I would like to say, "My name is not Audrey," but that would involve conversation, which may lead to me speaking my mind, which may lead to me being fired.

"Nice legs," he says, as I walk out the door.

I turn around, eyes spitting fire.

"On the table over there in the corner. It's new."

"Uh huh," I mutter under my breath.

Could this be the result of a brain aneurysm, or is this Dickens character for real?

26

Mid-May moon a beautiful glow. How I love the moon. In Alaska for months the moon is lost in daylight.

Imagine a huge mass of rock and metal covered with meteor dust hanging in the sky with other moons belonging to other planets, and moons and planets yet to be discovered. Mind boggling to earthly beings.

I wonder about so many things above. Is quiet in space quieter than quiet on earth? I consider our human frailty and wonder why God bothers with us when he has such beautiful things as space to manage. I guess I'm not such an original thinker, because King David thought that too.

Jack will be joining me on the patio after his bath and saying goodnight to the girls. As long as I've known him he's preferred baths to showers, and I've never asked him why.

Tiny goosebumps rise on my arms even with a sweater. A chilly night tonight, but then California nights can be like that.

Jack will come out in a robe, fresh and smelling of Lava soap. I miss Jack in khaki, as strange as it is. I miss the scent of what I call "real man." The smell of the earth. I miss him dripping in the mudroom donned in a feathered fisherman's hat and rubber hip boots, grinning ear to ear with his catch of the day dangling in his dirty fingers, like he's done something really important and wants my praise.

Jack is back to his old self. A bit more serious, more meek. Maybe he had to go through it, and that's just the way it is. Maybe some people—men or women, young or old—need to discover for themselves what they knew all along. That's how they give themselves permission to accept things as they are, only after they've convinced themselves things are the way they are for a reason. And the reason is a good one.

I am not the same myself. I have also changed. I am now a journalist, and that title has redefined me. I understand why people are curious about the position. There you are, some woman in her cubicle, influencing all these people with your words. And there's power in that position, satisfaction.

But not so satisfying are the long hours and deadlines; chasing a breaking story and then writing it furiously only to be called out on another breaking story; tracking down a dead end; perfecting a line of questioning only to watch it fall like a bad soufflé.

All in all, a newspaper article is read once and appreciated once, and unless highly newsworthy, those well-thought-out opinions, however eloquently stated, will be recycled, ending up in someone's wastebasket, later to be lifted by the hydraulic arm of a robotic garbage truck and compacted along with the rest of the trash and be renamed debris and buried to slowly decompose into dirt.

Jack comes out, and we sway under a dark sky. We don't say much these nights. All our words are spent at our jobs. It's enough to be together holding hands, casting dreamy smiles, and enjoying undistracted attention.

I don't want to talk about the little girl in the children's hospital oncology unit I saw today, her mother's face more wounded than hers. She reminded me of Hope, but with her blue eyes sunken in her sockets and the grayish tint of death approaching. An Anaheim Angel player brought her a baseball cap while I was there and said really nice things. That's when you know there's not much time.

I don't want to share about the teacher arrested on allegations of inappropriate touching, and the girl who stuttered when she spoke; I don't want to talk about the poor care the elderly are receiving in the nursing home I visited, and the woman who begged me to get her out of there; or the author who's writing a book called *Effective Technique* that teaches people how to con others without their knowing they're being conned.

"Audrey, Audrey, come here."

I am stumped because Mr. Russell is looking directly at me as I pass his office, but calling someone else's name.

"What's wrong with you?"

I realize he's talking to me. Calling me Audrey again. Even though his secretary has told him three times my name is Karan with an "a."

"You called me Audrey, Mr. Russell," I say boldly.

"Well, anyway ... " He tugs at his weak chin. "Sit down."

Guess I better get used to it. Comfy chair anyway, more forgiving than Sonia's, I must admit.

"That article you did on the beating last Tuesday."

"Yes?"

"Too fluffy."

"Fluffy?"

Sounds like a rabbit.

"Needed more drama." He looks around the room, out the window, on the floor, as he tends to do when he's talking to people.

"The boy was beaten and left for dead in an alley, Mr. Russell. He's in the hospital in a coma. That's pretty dramatic in and of itself."

"Is he going to live?"

"They think so."

He looks almost disappointed.

"In the future, there's got to be more to the story. A grabber. Something that doesn't happen every day. In Chicago, beatings are as common as Starbucks."

"Beatings are never common."

"Put on your thinking cap. What could have been your grabber?"

I pretend to be thinking, and I am, but not about the article. I'm thinking that my boss needs a good psychiatrist. But I have to say something.

"I could give him hypothermia complications in addition to his coma."

Since Mr. Russell is from Chicago, he has to think a minute before he realizes that California and hypothermia do not go together, like Phoenix and Delilah's frozen fingers do not go together.

"I get it, Audrey. It's a joke. Let me do the jokes, okay. You're rotten at them."

Karan. My name is Karan.

"I write truth, Mr. Russell, not fiction."

"Newspapers don't sell facts. If that's all there were to it, we wouldn't need reporters, just typists. Embellishment, Audrey. There are ways to do it and maintain your credibility."

"I'm not good at embellishing if it means calling vanilla ice cream New York Super Fudge Chunk."

"You've got it. Flavoring, Audrey, flavoring."

Chocolate, fudge, nuts … I am fantasizing.

He stamps his fist on his desk for emphasis.

Back to reality.

"I don't think I can do that, Mr. Russell."

"The *Orange County Register* outsells us three to one."

"They're a huge newspaper."

"That's the point, we need to work harder to get there."

I command myself not to roll my eyes. I want to do so badly.

"You like weddings, Karan?"

"Yes, of course; doesn't everybody?"

"You like writing about socialite weddings and taking your own photos? I hear you're a photographer."

I'm trying to understand, and I think he called me Karan.

"And what about car wash openings and Girl Scout awards and obituaries. You like to write obituaries, Audrey? Cause I'm sure the redhead with the skinny legs would love to switch places with you."

"Just what are you trying to say, Mr. Russell?"

"You're cute, Audrey. Cute."

Cute? Sexual harassment fireworks go off in my mind. This man can't last another day.

"But cute doesn't cut it," he says with a sly, uneven grin, and then he looks away.

I try to put the flash of scare in his eyes with my expression of alarm, but he doesn't notice. He's looking at his framed poster on the wall. A can of Campbell's tomato soup. He told me last week that the artist was Andy Warhol, like I should be impressed. But to me it looks like a can of tomato soup. I'm sure I'm missing something.

He looks at me again and gives an intimidating stare.

"Headlines are what people remember, and the disastrous details, not the nice ones."

"I agree that stories need to be interesting, Mr. Russell. But I also believe responsible, concise reporting is what the people want, and that's what sells papers."

"If that were the case, then tell me why tabloid sales are through the roof while our sales are average."

I don't have an answer.

"Here, Audrey, I made some notes."

Mr. Russell loves notes. His secretary says that by looking at the notes on his desk she can tell everything he is going to do and say.

He points his arthritic finger.

"Instead of 'hitting him' like you had in the article, how about 'they pummeled him to the ground and kicked him mercilessly.'"

"I don't know that they did."

"And take this 'left him bleeding in the alley.' How about 'blood drained from him like a river, making a grotesque scene.' And maybe even add, 'the color of the red rose' to give it a poetic edge."

"And what's the scoop on his family? I'm sure there's a sob story in there."

I lean over his desk trying to read his notes.

"What do you think?"

"Honestly, Mr. Russell?"

"Yes, honestly."

"Not much."

"Here take it anyway."

The paper stinks like tobacco.

"You like your paycheck, Audrey?"

"Yeah, so do my bill collectors."

I think of our remaining credit card debt.

"It seems we don't have a meeting of the minds, so starting tomorrow you're on nine-one-one."

"Nine-one-one?"

"Ambulance chasers. Broken glass and mangled steel, fires, choking babies. Emergency room drama. I want you to cut your teeth on it. It will help you understand drama and how to write it well."

I am flabbergasted.

"Porter comes with the job," he adds.

I've heard about Porter. He's that hairy guy with the caterpillar eyebrows that people take extreme detours to avoid. For some reason they can't fire the guy, so the bottom of the barrel end up with him, and I guess that's where I'm going.

"I'm going to be blunt, Audrey. Drama, and lots of it. Women crying, tragic loss, blood and gore. Lots of blood and gore. Then we'll see about returning you to the more preferred stories."

"And what if there isn't enough blood and gore?"

"Off the record, Audrey, make it up. But I didn't say that," he adds posthaste.

27

"Keep up the gumption," was veteran reporter Thermon Jameson's advice to me about Porter. "And don't let that Neanderthal get to you. He may make you rethink your position on evolution, but he's harmless, basically stupid, and a good photographer."

So here I am in a news van with this creepy, hairy guy. Protruding forehead, hunching stature.

Now I've never been one to judge people by their looks. I was the playground avenger of the weak and beauty challenged. I couldn't care less what people look like. I've met some less than fabulous looking people who were queens and kings in personality, and some absolute visions who lost their allure the moment they opened their mouths.

But Porter's looks are hard to ignore, mostly because his personality is also Neanderthal. He burps a lot, stuffs whole sandwiches in his mouth, and wipes his bushy beard with his shirt.

"You don't mind me driving, do you?" he asks in a voice to match.

"No, it's fine."

"I like to be in control," he says, a peculiar gleam in his eye.

As we're going down the street we spot this ambulance, and instead of pulling over Porter starts chasing it full speed.

"Porter, are you nuts?"

"I want to get there before the *Register*."

I think I am going to die because Porter has no regard for stoplights, other cars, or concrete dividers. Somehow we land behind the ambulance before the police arrive.

Porter grabs his camera.

"Grab your notebook and come on. Put on your reporter's badge, and they won't care."

I do what he says, feeling queasy.

Porter's on an adrenaline rush. I can tell he's devoted to tragedy.

It's a bike accident. I see the mangled blue steel off to the side. The police arrive and start directing traffic.

What am I supposed to write?

On the asphalt, there's this blond little boy spread out on the road without a helmet. I think of Jack and how God protected him in his biking accident. I confess to God that at the time I didn't realize the grace of the situation.

The emergency workers are caring for the child, and this lady sitting on the curb is all shook up. Blood is trickling down her forehead, and kids are screaming in the back of her car and yelling something to her in Spanish.

All I can think of is that she's going to live the rest of her life knowing she mangled or even killed some mother's kid and having flashbacks and wretched guilt which she'll transfer to her own children, and they'll grow up not understanding what happened to them.

Fumes are choking me, the June heat is suffocating, I'm wearing the wrong shoes, and I don't know who to ask what.

Porter is having a blast snapping pictures. Apparently film is no object. He seems to be appreciating the experience as a normal person might appreciate a Monet oil painting, but I'd like to vomit.

Accident scene investigators show up, taking their own pictures and drawing lines in chalk. It starts to rain. Rain is not in the forecast, but it pours. The cool drops feel good but are a nuisance.

All these people are off to the side. Seven people are huddled under some guy's black umbrella.

"I'm a reporter for the *Independent Daily Sun*." I show my badge, feeling soggy.

"Did any of you witness the accident?"

"I saw it," an older man with baggy eyes says, one of the seven under the umbrella. "She ran the kid down like she didn't see him."

I don't bother taking notes; my paper is useless.

I walk back to the ambulance. The emergency crew is doing CPR on the boy, but he's not responding. They load him into the ambulance and drive away. The siren blasts, and traffic merges to the right.

I'm getting wobbly-kneed thinking about his mother now. Two families will be ruined. I'm thinking how he was probably on his way to school. Maybe he just got the bike, because the chrome is still shiny. His family will be devastated forever. His siblings will have to share in the price tag. Or maybe he's his mother's only child; she's a single mom, and he's her hope.

Porter comes over. "Got some great shots. I think the kid's dead."

I am on the verge of spilling tears.

"Hey, you'll get used to it, Karan. Pretty soon you'll be loving it," he says, his first smile of the day.

His words are vile, contemptible. Can anyone love such things?

*M*y thoughts as an aging reporter after my first day on my new beat:

Write notes on blood and gore accident this AM on dead boy while eating a Subway sandwich, watching Porter stuff his whole and failing to wipe the Mountain Dew dribble off his beard. Bang off notes in article form and hand to copy editor.

To the scene of accident two. Hysterical woman, unconcerned man. Minor injuries. Drunk driving suspected by hysterical woman. Not newsworthy.

Accident three. Freeway pileup. Boring.

Check e-mail and in-box. Say goodbye to young man whose official title I am not aware of and whose name nobody knows because everyone calls him, "Here you go." Leave newsroom completely deflated. Drive home in bumper-to-bumper traffic, fantasizing about old life.

Punch holes in Styrofoam cups; fill with potting soil; press seeds into soil.

Oh, how I long to be home playing with dirt.

Drive to 586 Castle Lane. Park in driveway so girls can wash car because cars in California are shiny, the girls need a project, and I refuse to pay more to have my car washed than for lunch.

Scan the neighborhood with my roving reporter eyes, because I never do.

Neighbor to the left drives a black Saab. Has two kids, a

gardener, a maid, and a wife who drives an Audi and only waves when looking the opposite direction.

Neighbor to the right, single. Works for The Irvine Company. Owns an airplane.

Neighbor in the middle, unhappy camper. On the verge of emotional breakdown. Never wanting to view another accident in her life.

I open the door feeling like I've been through a war, and this is my bomb shelter.

The girls are sitting too close to the big-screen TV watching cartoons, speakers so unnecessarily loud hearing loss is imminent.

"Hi, Mommy."

They look exhausted between adrenaline rushes, which is what they seem to run on these days. And candy, lots of candy, which I don't have the heart to tell them will rot their teeth. The working-mother syndrome. Don't want to be the "bad guy" and take away their fun.

The girls don't read much anymore; they say they have too much required reading. Don't go outside and play as much; too much PE (but I'm not so sure about that).

I want to tell them, "Let's do something together like we used to," but then I'd actually have to follow through, and I don't know if I, feeling as robotic as I do, could fake the motherly glow. I never do anything fun anymore.

I remember one day in Alaska we cut pieces of cellophane, different colors, and made these neat glasses. We went around everywhere with them, looking at the world through colored glasses. It was a great day.

One winter, we spent an entire day watching the ants in our ant farm. It's fascinating the way they tunnel and move like city people. We read ant facts off the Internet. How a million ants can lift one elephant. How if a man could run as fast as an ant for his size, he'd beat a racehorse.

We read at night, with Jack, the classics: *Moby Dick, Little Women, Pilgrim's Progress*. We baked, we hiked, we made daisy chains in the summer. They were growing up to be well-rounded little girls.

The last time they begged for a story, I made one up for being so tired.

Once upon a time there was a little girl, and this little girl had big thoughts …

And, of course, I ended it that she had a prince of a husband and two beautiful daughters who always behaved, ate their spinach, lived in a beautiful house, and spent every precious moment of their lives together.

But life is not a fairy tale.

*T*wo weeks later, but ages in my mind.
No fun, no play, I wanna quit. Hey.
I'm talking to myself in rhyme. Cindy was right. The poetry lady has ruined me. Truth is, I want to be back in my cubicle writing deeply moving prose. Affecting people's lives.

But here we are at a stranger's house. This lady is weeping because her baby just drowned. The ambulance has just taken him away, and the police aren't here yet. Porter is snapping pictures, and she's talking to me. I find this unbelievable.

The woman's hands are an earthquake, and her hair is beauty parlor perfect.

"I left him for no more than one minute. To grab the phone off the bed. He's such a big boy. I never imagined … "

I want to tell her that God loves her anyway, but I can't. Not allowed.

"We'll take you to the hospital," I say, and touch her shoulder.

She tries to get up, but falls face down on the bed wailing.

"Will they charge me?" she screams.

And here I am taking notes.

I don't believe it, Jack. Look at my article on the accidental drowning. I didn't put this in here, and I know it wasn't the copy editor."

Jack reads. "I hope you didn't write this."

"A 29-year old woman admits negligence in her 18-month-old son's drowning … "

"Andrew Russell, then?" he asks.

"Can he do that? Lie like that?"

"I don't know, Karan; he's the editor."

"Not for long—I hope. The man is Napoleonic. He can't get away with the stuff he does."

"I have to go." Jack gets up. I notice he is wearing his work shirt.

"But it's Saturday, Jack. We were going to do laundry together." I protrude my lip as far out as I can.

"They switched my schedule on me." He dusts hair off his face. "I'm a prisoner to that place. And they really push us to sell their products. You know how I hate sales."

Jack is as tired as I've ever seen him. His face is drawn, his posture is sagging, and he seems to be virtually comatose. I feel more sorry for him than I do for myself.

"Another job will come up."

"After months of looking, nobody wants me. Stale goods.

I've applied for dozens of other jobs, Karan. Who wants a guy who worked for a company a few months and then it went bad? It's like having Enron on my resume. I think I've been too honest about the business failure."

"Bradford got a job."

"Yeah, he works the graveyard shift for a service company. Restoration repairs, water damage, and stuff like that."

"We only have the one credit card to pay off now. Soon we can get another car, and you can be more aggressive in your employment search."

"Maybe I can get a paper route." He practices a newspaper boy throw.

*O*n Sunday, Jack sleeps in, and I can't blame him. At 12:45 PM, when we return from church, he's still dragging. Indoor life for an outdoorsman is incarceration. A forty-hour work week can tire a person like Jack more than sixty hours outdoors in his natural element.

Now may be the time to ask about Alaska—again.

"Jack, can we go back home to Alaska? What have we got to lose?" I ask as he pours himself a cup of cold coffee.

"The house," he says, and puts his mug down. "Real estate is hot in California, but, I have to be honest with you; this house has major problems."

"I don't get it."

"Pauline advised me to get an inspection by a qualified home inspector, but I thought I could do it myself. She also advised me to get a home warranty, which I also didn't do. I was in such a hurry to buy the house; I didn't think it was necessary."

At least he's admitting it.

"So what's wrong?"

"You're aware of the plumbing problems."

"Well … yeah. Those are fairly obvious."

"The roof is at the end of its life, and the water heater is about to go anytime."

"Ouch." I bite my finger for emphasis. "That's going to cost thousands of dollars we don't have."

He pulls me outside. I see I need to water the flowers.

"See those cracks in the driveway and over here in the corners of the stucco?"

"Yes," I say, not noticing the extent of it before. "Pauline called that normal settling. Cindy has cracks in her driveway too."

"In our case, it's defective."

I follow him into the house, and he points to the wall.

"If you look close, you can see where the former owner plastered the cracks in almost every room in this house. And in my study, the wall is actually buckling."

He walks over to the fireplace and runs my finger over clear bonding.

"See this, Karan? Where the cracks have been sealed? This is indicative of foundation problems."

"Shouldn't Pauline have disclosed all this?"

"I don't think she knew. You can't always tell with a visual inspection. But it would have shown up with the home inspection."

"So that's why this house was on the market so long? Cindy told me three people tried to buy it, and the deal always fell through."

"The only good news is that we don't have termites. The termite inspection was required."

"Good. Those things can fly, you know."

He looks tortured. Enormously tortured.

"Imagine, Jack, a termite magnified a hundred times. Those ugly mandibles with teeth on the big screen chewing at thirty bites a minute. We could write a screenplay called 'Termite Invasion.' It would be a hit."

One of the reporters just did an article on termites, and so I am well versed in termite anatomy. My joke does not amuse Jack. Nothing can amuse a man whose self-esteem is in danger of extinction.

"We've got $120,000 tied up in this house," he says in a voice sounding distant. "The girls' education; our future. No thought for my own family. You know that saying about men being pigs. What kind of pig was I?"

"A clean pig, a pig who knew well enough to get out of the mud. Pigs are clean, you know, Jack. And smart. They've been given a bad rap. If people knew how intelligent they were, they wouldn't be so quick to eat their feet."

Still no hint of levity on his face.

"So basically we're stuck in this mud hole, Karan."

Jack is calling this paradise—royal beaches; unbelievable shopping; endless entertainment; perfect weather; beautiful people, houses, and cars; and, oh yeah, Trader Joe's, the "kahuna" of specialty grocery stores, as Aunt Candy would say—a mud hole. He must miss Alaska. I struggle for hope.

28

*I*t is the first day of summer, and the weather is gloomy and gray. No matter, we are celebrating tonight with a midnight barbecue under tiki lights, courtesy of Aunt Candy.

I call Mom from the news van on my cell phone.

"Where will you be at 4:00 AM tomorrow, Mom?"

"At the Eskimo Cafe, of course."

"Alone?"

"No, Margo is going to join me. But, it won't be the same as having you."

"We're having a celebration here. But, Mom, it won't be the same as having you."

Long sigh on the other end.

"I'm sorry you won't have the girls tonight. I know how you used to look forward to that."

"I won't lie, Karan; it's not an easy time for me."

"I'm still hoping and praying to come home, Mom."

"Home is wherever your husband is."

"I know, Mom. I know."

Porter is gobbling, absolutely gobbling, a Subway sandwich. I finally figured out that he's on a Subway diet. He eats sandwiches for breakfast, lunch, and dinner. The news van smells of mustard and rotting meat.

But wonderful news, Mr. Russell is being transferred next week to the *Bismark Daily News*, also owned by the Chicago newspaper that owns us. Sonia will be coming back!

You see, it doesn't matter who you know when you insult the mayor's wife, two times. The big guy gets a call, and that's when his affections flip. Because the bottom line is money in this business, not knowing some guy from childhood.

No more lists. No more lists. Mr. Russell will not be missed.

The typed list I have in front of me now titled "preferred terms," was in my in-box with a memo from Mr. Russell stating that I need to use stronger adjectives in my articles. Instead of "unhappy," he suggests "despondent"; "concerned" would be replaced with "alarmed"; "assumed" would be defined "certain"; and the list goes on.

No one would believe it. I rip the list in pieces and stuff it in Porter's Subway bag.

"Ever notice how those little dust particles flying around look like some kinda fairies?" Porter asks, as he stares into space.

Intelligent conversation for a one-celled amoeba.

First order of business when Sonia gets back: "Get me out of this van with this maniac photographer. I can take my own pictures."

Porter's cell phone rings as he starts the car. He mumbles something about a residential fire.

My uncle was in a fire when he was six. He still remembers the Texas cowboy boots he lost in the flames. I suppose you never forget something that terrible.

"Fire. Sweet. I haven't had a fire in too long," Porter says. "I'll take a fire over crushed glass and mangled steel any day."

"We're talking about someone's life here, Porter. Doesn't that bother you in the least?"

His mouth is full of salami as he's driving fanatically. So I guess the answer is no.

"Where is the fire?"

"Not far. Castle Lane by Safeway."

"That's my street."

"No way. What are the chances? Like one in two billion?"

"Shut up, Porter. Just shut up and drive."

The days of putting up burst like Niagara Falls. I'm contemplating punching him out and taking over the wheel. But praying may be a better option.

Oh God. Please keep my family safe!

It could be the neighbor's house. I spoke to Aunt Candy twenty minutes ago, and she said everything was fine. She was putting up decorations and everyone was coming, including some girl named Kelsie "who sounds very nice."

But then again, that could be my house burning. My family could be in there.

It's not hard to follow fire, the cloud of billowing smoke rising. Fire draws crowds quicker than free corn dogs. A crowd is gathered in front of a house, and it is my house.

"Sorry, Karan," says Porter as he hits the curb, and he may mean it; I'm not sure. He jumps out of the van and starts clicking the camera. I guess not.

I am contemplating having Jack punch him out this time, if I can find Jack. I pray and look for Jack at the same time. I'm trying to find the girls and Aunt Candy. Anyone familiar in this mass of looky loos. I see my neighbor, Pam, in the distance. She waves like my house burns down every day.

The smell of fire overwhelms me, but it is a good smell. I feel bad that I think so.

The siren is singing, but I am unaware of what it means. Sort of like waking up from a dream. Cut that. Nightmare.

An ambulance stops in front of the house, and I try to get to it, but I can't see through the crowd. I wing my elbow in some older woman's ribs and don't apologize. I gasp. Aunt Candy is lying on the ground, but it is not Aunt Candy's face. It is something different. A breathing apparatus is covering most of it, but I can see that her condition is bad. Her skin is charred.

"Jack! Oh, Jack!" I scream as his precious face comes into vision. He holds me close. "Where are the girls?" The kind of question any mother would ask first.

"Across the street with Cindy."

I cough from the mass of smoke. The thickness of it makes it impossible to see Cindy's house clearly.

"I hope they're not watching out the window."

Too much in too short a time. Flames are engulfing the house, and firefighters in shiny red hats and yellow jackets are watering the neighbors' roofs, trying to keep the flames from spreading. Our house must be too far gone to save.

"There was no time to get anything out," Jack laments. "Not a thing."

"Who cares about things? I just want Aunt Candy to be okay."

And maybe that's the kind of thing everybody would say, what everybody should say. Because when it comes down to it, people really don't care about anything else but family at a time like that. Later, I don't know.

"She's not okay, Karan. She's not."

"I know, Jack. But we can pray."

"That's all I've been doing."

His face is soot covered, his hair darkened by ash.

We watch the emergency workers administer first aid to Aunt Candy on a stretcher as the smoke overwhelms us, and we feel the wall of intense heat. She is not moving.

Porter comes over, snapping pictures with his rapid finger.

"Porter, get that camera out of my face! You tell them 'no reporters.' Do you hear me?"

"Well, excuse me for living."

"See those huge flames crackling and roaring like the MGM lion you think is so pretty? Somebody's life is being affected, Porter. Don't you ever get it?"

"Karan, that's enough," says Jack. He touches my face in comfort.

I fall on the ground, weeping uncontrollably and coughing up a storm.

"We need to move farther back, Karan."

Jack pulls at me.

I don't budge. I want to sink into the earth.

"Porter, you better go."

"No problem, man. I guess woman are more emotional, dude."

"Now, Porter. Now!"

The next day we stand in front of what no longer exists. Jack holds a fistful of ash and releases it to the earth. The girls are buried in my chest, and I hold them near and tell them Aunt Candy will be fine. My lungs are still stinging.

We watch the heap of charred remains, a holocaust surrounded by perfect houses like some memorial. Neighbors are watching from their windows, and I can feel their compassionate stares. They've offered to feed us and bed us. Neighbors, who never said hello before, offering clothes and blankets, even money. I wonder why we couldn't say hello before.

Cindy, especially, insists that we stay with them. I explain that Aunt Candy is in the hospital, and we're staying at her house. "But thank you for asking."

It's gone. Every bit of it gone. Why, God, why?

I forgot to ask before. I forgot to ask because I was busy explaining to the girls that stuff happens, but God still loves us.

Jack says the firefighters suspect the water heater exploded, and so does he. Or it could have been Aunt Candy's candles, or the tiki torches. Who knows? He was at work at the time, saw the fire, and ran all the way home.

"The investigators will be out to determine the cause."

Do we care? Aunt Candy is in the hospital in Intensive Care. Do we care about the cause?

"My Mom always told me things are best started from scratch, so that's where we'll start, Jack."

I cough. Jack coughs. The girls stay close.

"We don't have a choice, do we?"

"No, we don't."

He swallows me in his arms. We stand in utter disbelief.

Cindy comes over with hugs and a newspaper.

"Why don't you girls go see Meagan and Samantha. They've been begging to come out, and I told them no."

"Yes!" they yell, and fly across the street.

"They'll be okay, you know," Cindy says.

"Hope mentioned her stuffed dog; that was it." I say.

"And Faith asked about everything," says Jack, amused.

"Look here." Cindy shows the newspaper.

"Front page bottom."

"You're joking, I hope."

"Would I joke at a time like this?" she says, her eyes welled to overflowing.

"Poetry Lady's house burns to the ground!" in bold headlines.

"So I'm the newspaper's new poster child?"

"There's nothing derogatory in here. But won't Zeya flip? They're calling you the Poetry Lady."

"I'm not even going to analyze the motive."

"I see Porter got his fire picture in." Cindy points to a close-up of our house in flames.

"Well, at least it's just the house. I'm surprised he didn't get me clawing the ground."

Jack holds my hand. I raise his fingers to my lips and kiss them tenderly and repeatedly.

Cindy examines the destruction.

"I'm not reading the article, Jack. In fact I think I'll burn it."

"Symbolic gesture, huh?"

"Over here, you guys," calls Cindy.

"Get out of there, Cindy. You'll ruin your shoes."

"You just lost everything you own. I could lose a pair of shoes."

Lying in the ashes are the springs of the blue velvet chair. The most overused, adored chair in the world.

"Oh my gosh," we cry in amazement as we walk over to the charred box of springs.

"Odd how this happens in a fire," I say. "How one thing is left intact. I remember reading *Little House on the Prairie* to the girls. When Laura Ingalls' house burned down, all that was left was a serving plate."

"Hope never named this chair," says Jack.

"Go ahead. Name it."

"Springy," Cindy suggests.

"Will we ever find a chair so comfortable anywhere?" I ask.

"Maybe in Alaska," Jack says.

And I want to ask, but I don't, because taking one more spoonful of disappointment at this time might kill me. I talk to God instead.

Oh, God please ... Use your strong arm!

29

Aunt Candy ... beautiful Aunt Candy ... is lying in a raised hospital bed in a room full of monitoring equipment. She is covered head to toe in bandages, and unrecognizable. Her eyes, swollen and smothered with ointment, are the clearest blue, like Jack's. But there is nothing else about her that would tell who she was. Her fingers are nubs hidden under wrap. The nurse in the hall told us that her ears are partial ears.

"I asked you all here because I wanted us to be together," she says in a cracked voice.

Bradford, Delilah, Jack, and I are all standing around her in disposable gowns and gloves. We are in shock. Crushed in sadness. Disbelieving that days ago she was living fully and breathing regularly, and today she is hardly human. Her breath is labored, and she has a strange smell about her.

We look at her tenderly, almost pitifully.

"I have things to say and not much energy."

"No problem, Ma," Bradford says with effort.

"For the past couple of days you must have worried, not being able to see me. The fire was nobody's fault but mine. I left candles burning and forgot about them."

"We don't know that, Aunt Candy," says Jack. "It may have been the water heater."

"No one should feel the least bit guilty," I say, the Cleopatra of guilt queens.

"I just had to get that off my chest. I don't remember the fire, and I'm glad I don't," says Aunt Candy.

"We don't care how it happened. Honestly," I say.

"Jack and Karan, I'm truly sorry about your house and things."

"They're things, Aunt Candy. Things that can be replaced." Jack says.

"I'm glad you feel that way." Her body leans, and she utters a moan. She speaks slowly. "Anyway, my nurse in Intensive Care was named June, like the month. This month, in fact. She's from Hawaii. Imagine that ... and she's a Christian."

I feel an overwhelming sense of excitement as I already sense the change.

"She prayed over me the whole time I was in her care and stayed past her hours to be with me. And to make it short, we prayed together, and I'm clean inside like your snow, Jack. White as snow," she says.

We look at each other and smile, huge smiles. My primary thought is *we'll be together forever!*

"Over two-thirds of my body is burned to a crisp, kids. The doctor says two-thirds of the world is ocean, so that's a lot of burn. Even with surgeries, my prognosis is poor."

She coughs a deep barking cough I know must be painful.

"No, Ma, no. We'll take you to another burn center," says Bradford, extending his arms out as if thinking he could hold her. He then draws them back to his chest.

"This is the best right here, and they've done good, son. The doctor will explain more to you later."

She takes a breath and coughs some more. A highway of tubes dangle about.

"First off, Jack, I want you to have the Yukon you sold me with all those crazy gadgets I can't figure out. I haven't titled it in my name yet—procrastinator that I am. It's yours."

"Thank you, Aunt Candy," Jack says.

We want to touch her in appreciation, but there is nowhere on her entire body that can be touched.

"Bradford and Delilah, you know the house was paid for years ago. I hope that one day it will be filled with the sounds of children."

Delilah smiles; Bradford beams.

"She's pregnant, Ma. We were going to announce it the night of the fire."

Aunt Candy's eye gleam a turquoise glint. I am surprised at the news. I remember Delilah's bold insistence that they never wanted children; but God can change hearts, because the two of them are obviously thrilled.

"I can't tell you how good I feel about that. I'd like to hug you, but that's impossible right now."

In normal times, the day would have been spent discussing the details of the pregnancy and contemplating the gift of new life, but death's timeline is more hurried.

"Anyway, Bradford, your father left me a decent amount of money when he died, and my stockbroker invested well in the eighties. It's been down recently, but the last statement I received it was still more than $300,000."

Bradford smiles, but not as big as one might think.

Delilah's look is sadness. These are changed people. Billy Graham kind of changed.

"You look tired, Candy. Should we come back?" Delilah asks, swallowing hard.

"I am so tired … " her voice dies on the last word.

"Rest, Ma, rest."

"I can't rest until I finish. Pray for me, please."

Bradford does. For strength. For wisdom. But not for healing.

"Thank you. I feel stronger already." Her breath is easier.

"I have life insurance, Bradford. My attorney and friend, Dave Landon, will take care of the details, so you don't have to worry about any of it. He also has my burial instructions. I'm to be cremated."

For some reason the talk of death is not strange to me. When someone feels right about it, when they're about to be scooped up in the Savior's arms and spared a whole lot of hurting, who are we to keep them here unwillingly?

"Now, for the part you won't want to hear. I don't want a funeral."

Bradford gasps.

"I knew you would be shocked by that," says Aunt Candy, eyes directed at Bradford. She might laugh if she could. "I want you to go to Maui. All of you to go to Maui, including the girls."

"Maui?" Bradford asks.

"You stay at a fancy hotel and do anything that costs a lot of money. Spend at least thirty thousand dollars. No less. Go snorkeling, and see the sights; rent a limo, and dine at the fanciest places you can find. Do all the things I did, and all the things I wanted to do."

We look at each other with blank expressions.

"And don't ask if I'm thinking clearly," she says, as if knowing our thoughts.

"It's a wonderful thought, Candy," Delilah says.

"Karan, you take lots of pictures. Have the girls buy a shell, one that sounds far away. Sometimes they can listen to it and think of their crazy Aunt Candy."

We nod in acknowledgment.

"I want a simple ceremony on the beach. Don't go on about my life and how great it was, because the only thing that really mattered in my sixty-four years is the last few days, as bad as they were. And, Karan, you write a poem about heaven."

She stops for a moment. My mind is working overtime. I'm thinking this woman in front of me is about to know a mystery no mortal is privy to.

"Jack, all these years you told me about Jesus, and I never listened ... truth in my face, but I wouldn't listen."

"Aunt Candy—"

"I remember your mama took me to church with her when you were a boy, and you sang a solo about the old rugged cross. What a beautiful voice you have, Jack. I should have listened better."

"Please, Aunt Candy."

"Yes, Jack, that is the only thing I'm sorry for. You sing that song. And when I get my strength up tomorrow, we'll call your mama and tell her about all this."

"Alright," says Jack, to keep it short.

"Bradford, you read a passage from the Bible."

"I will, Ma."

She moans and repositions herself.

"I can't go much longer because the painkillers are wearing off. Delilah, you take care of my son."

"I will, Candy. I'll do my very best. Almost as good as you."

A quiet moment, and then the birds outside the window start in a song that softens the harsh reality. We listen for a moment.

"I'll call the nurse," says Bradford.

"No, she'll be in soon."

Then we start weeping. Even the men, in broad daylight. All of us, except Aunt Candy. A river of tranquility is flowing from her, and the room is lit with the brilliance of peace. The struggle of pain is yielding, like a storm wind sweeping toward the heavens.

Aunt Candy's eyes wander upward and hold their position. We look at each other, drawing strength.

*T*wo days later ... a beautiful day. The kind of day when flowers bloom plentifully and grass grows faster. Aunt Candy is gone; her last uneven breath was drawn. And the earth should be sorrowing, because she was one of those souls who made life lighter by her simplicity and gladness.

No one was with her, and I think that is often the case. Bradford went for a cup of coffee, and now blames himself for not being there.

I told him I thought it was purposeful, and that people who know God never die alone.

My mom's friend, Margo, is a nurse who's seen a lot of death. She once told me that remarkable words are seldom shared on the deathbed; it's during the days and hours preceding death that the dying share their hearts and minds. She also told me that as loved ones make the transition to a perfect place, they are less aware of things and those around them and more aware of their ultimate destination. People can be disappointed at how easy it is for the dying to leave them, but that is how it should be.

We are travelers on a journey, and our footpath leads upward, not on level ground.

When Aunt Candy's doctor saw the picture of her we showed him, he literally gasped for breath. She was that beautiful. He said it was a blessing that she died when she did, that it would have taken a lifetime of surgeries to restore her face and body, and it wouldn't be anything like she was. It would have been a long, excruciating recovery with skin grafts, physical therapy, and respiratory complications. We were comforted by that thought.

"Celebrate me; don't mourn me," Aunt Candy told us, as we left the room to her and Bradford that day at her bedside.

I am reaching for the celebratory mood. For a Christian, death means entering heaven's glory. Overcoming. "Oh death, where is your sting?" Paul said. And I understand that saying in my head, but my heart is still receiving the message.

Next week we fly to Maui.

Diamonds and Maui, as Cindy once suggested. But this wasn't the way I expected. Delilah gave me one of Aunt Candy's diamonds. She said to think of it as nothing, because Aunt Candy had a treasure chest full.

I wonder what colors the jewels are that Candy is seeing now in heaven. Colors never seen by human eyes.

30

Cindy:

In case you're wondering how I got a computer, Bradford gave me his laptop.

We landed, unpacked, and had a simple service for Aunt Candy on the beach, just as she requested. Then all six of us piled into a limo to attend an authentic Hawaiian luau. We thought by doing something so completely different we could get our minds off the details of death and be able to honor Aunt Candy's wishes to celebrate big.

Celebrate we did, with an eighteen-course buffet. I had the Lomi Lomi Salmon, Mochiko Chicken, Kalua pig, Macadamia Nut Shrimp, salads, and fruit (papaya, my favorite). And for dessert, Haupia pudding and coconut banana cake. I tried everything else too. Everything but the poi.

And then, bursting at the seams, we were expected to get up and learn to do the hula. I declined. Delilah, however, did rather well with the hip motions. The rest of us just watched and laughed.

The afternoon ended with a demonstration of some wild native dance.

Oh yeah, all this took place in a tropical lagoon with a waterfall like in your dreams.

Our limo took us back to the hotel where I am now enjoying my ocean view and thinking sweet thoughts of Aunt Candy, which I find hard yet to classify as memories. The girls are asking me to swim in the whale pool, so I have to go.

Don't expect an e-mail from me for a couple of days.
Love, Karan

July 1
sonia@worldspan

Sonia:
You asked for the poem I wrote for Aunt Candy, and here it is. Short, simple, and sweet like she was. But for your eyes only, please.

> *The sky is gray today*
> *Though sunshine pours magnificently from the sky*
> *I only see the dreary cast of gloom*
>
> *On earth we mourn today*
> *While yesterday you spoke and laughed*
> *Today your body is absent of your beautiful spirit*
>
> *Heaven is happy today*
> *You meet God who knew you first*
> *And wholeness is now your covering*

Blessings, Karan

July 2
Letter via U.S. postal service

Dear Mom:

Telephone rates being what they are from Maui to Alaska, and knowing how we gab, I am sending a real stamped letter via post office delivery. Yes, I know the last letter you received from me was when I went to camp whatever it was called and got homesick and begged you in a letter (which you received four days after I came home) to pick me up. But, honestly, Mom, the food was terrible, we got one skinny blanket, and could only take a shower every three days. What can I say? Being the perfect mother, you spoiled me!

Did I ever imagine Maui? Not even in my dreams. Was I unimaginative or what? This place is so olu'olu, as Aunt Candy loved to say. Translation: cool, neat.

Mom, I'm sorry you never met Aunt Candy. She was like no one you know in Alaska. I told you the story and all. Did you ever refill your Kleenex box?

Speaking of stories to tell, Sonia, my friend and former editor, had one of her own. Get this: Zeya (the poetry lady) had a nervous breakdown, which she is blaming me for. Here I am in Maui, and I am the cause of her nervous breakdown. Just lost my house and all my worldly possessions, lost Aunt Candy, and I am scheming for her job.

Sonia said that after pearls and diamonds, meaning my poetry, Zeya's poetry was garage-sale imitation, and that rip came from one of her readers. Unfortunately, Zeya had to answer the letters. I'd like to read one of her responses some day.

I know, Mom. She's a lost soul. I'll pray for her healing and salvation.

As for your question the other day as to whether return-ing to Alaska is a possibility, my answer is yes! Not only yes, but for certain. Now Mom. Stop at this point. Put down the letter. Pick it back up. Are you breathing well? Good.

Now for how Jack, gifted visionary that he is, presented me with this happy news. While we were having dinner alone last night (Delilah was watching the girls), I asked him for the hundredth-plus time since we arrived in Hawaii about the possibility of moving back to Alaska. And, no sur-prise to me, he said "When pigs fly!" which is one of his favorite sayings, as you know.

I was annoyed and throwing a temper fit, until the waiter brought me this really olu'olu Mahi Mahi and other equally delightful delicacies that caused me to forget my grievances temporarily.

The next morning on my room service tray along with eggs Benedict, crunchy potatoes with blue cheese, crepes, blueberry muffins—the whole works—was a skinny newspa-per, and you will flip at the headlines—"When pigs fly!"

Now, Mom, since I have been in Hawaii I have seen birds fly and dolphins fly and even people fly (they call it parasail-ing, and it looks scary), but not pigs. I've seen pigs lying on tables with an apple in their mouth. But no flying pigs.

Anyway, pigs flying are apparently very common. Let me tell you how I know this. The front page of this paper had various headlines: When Pigs Fly CD, featuring the Oak Ridge Boys and Don Ho (strange combination); When Pigs Fly screensavers, rubber stamps, clubs, even a restaurant that bears the name. Jack went to a lot of trouble to get these true and fun facts together. He said there were something like 87,000 hits on the Internet.

On the second page, which is actually the back of this fake newspaper, was the booty, the mother lode: "LaRue clan returns to Alaska!" That's right, Mom. And then this cute little article Jack wrote I'll let you read when we get HOME.

So we will drive almost 3,500 miles in Gold Dust (so named by Hope) with no possessions, because we don't have any, except the shopping we did here courtesy of Bradford and Delilah in memory of Aunt Candy. Very flowery, very Hawaiian.

I could go on and on, but this letter is too long already. I will call you before I put my purse down and share the beautiful details.

Love, Karan

July 2

diamondinrough@quickmail

Cindy:

Just saw a pig fly by—we're moving back to Alaska!
Love, Karan

July 2

diamondinrough@quickmail

Cindy:

In reply to your quick response, you will too live without me. The human spirit is indomitable.

Delilah and I have gotten to know each other better, and I feel bad for having judged her so harshly. You know the thing about the mittens in Phoenix? Turns out she lived in Prescott, Arizona, too. And it snows there. Her father worked in construction, thus the steel-toed shoes.

We are so quick to judge, are we not?

When I get back, we'll sit on the beach and talk about everything.

I still don't have any secrets to share. Do you? I do have a lot of other fun stuff to share, but for now I'm still doing it. Love, Karan

July 2
sonia@worldspan

Sonia:

If the job is available from Alaska, I will take it. But how will that work?

The big guy finally fired Porter, huh? The man was a drug-crazed maniac. He was always staring at air dust particles.

Your fill-in poem was great. Whoever told you that you were not a brilliant poet was wrong. Three hours on a poem is not outrageous, but if you do that every day, you won't get anything done.

Tell me the subject; I'll e-mail you a poem. God bless, Karan

July 2
Letter via U.S. Postal Service

Dear Kelsie:

It was nice receiving your letter in Maui at the time I needed it most. You must have sent it before we even left. Thank you for your beautiful thoughts.

I'm glad you prefer the Christian book store to the Bee Hive. It is a more uplifting environment.

Josh sounds like a great guy, but what does "mutually exclusive" mean in a relationship? I'm old. Very old. Hey, since he goes to seminary, you could become a pastor's wife.

You asked about your tattoo again; I say don't worry about it. It will serve as a testimony to some. I once knew a pastor's wife with a tattoo on her ankle. She never wore sandals, and I thought it sad, actually. Because it should have been no big deal.

I told you it wouldn't be easy being a Christian, Kelsie. When you don't have anything to believe in, it's easier.

As for your dad, you can love him from a safe distance, but you don't have to put up with him down-talking you anymore. I don't care what Bible verse that lady quoted.

Maui is awesome, as expected.

Love, Karan

July 3
diamondinrough@quickmail

Cindy:

Regarding my comment that the human spirit is indomitable, and your comment asking what it means. "Indomitable" means unconquerable, determined. You need a thesaurus. I would lend you mine, but it ashed in the burn. But I know you own a dictionary.

I'm learning Hawaiian slang, drinking fruity drinks, and finding out that I don't look good in a bikini. My one-piece works well though.

Love, Karan

July 3
sonia@worldspan

Sonia:

That's wild about the readers sending us money.

Curious why you picked the subject of Alzheimer's for my

poem. But it was not a problem. I believe the spirit shines through no matter the mind's deterioration.

I am attaching it as a separate document.

Blessings, Karan

July 3
diamondinrough@quickmail

Cindy:

I can't believe Pam watered our flowers and that there was anything to water. Like the charcoaled remains of a structure isn't going to be an eyesore, regardless. Yes, we have insurance, and, yes, it will replenish the girls' college fund (and our retirement). And, no, we cannot send your girls to Harvard. As for the house, I have no idea what will happen to it. We're not rebuilding; that's all I know.

You won't believe this, but people actually sent cash money to the newspaper c/o the Poetry Lady—$1,200 or something, Sonia told me. That will help pay for our trip.

After this, no one will ever be able to say that I haven't been anywhere!

Love, Karan

July 4
sonia@worldspan

Sonia:

Not sure you're working today since it's a holiday.

I am so happy my poem was a personal hope for you. I didn't know about your mother.

Today's poem was inspired by watching the "surfer dudes" at the beach "catching waves and soaking rays."

Nothing deep about it—except the water. But I think that is my point.

Precious thoughts, Karan

July 4
diamondinrough@quickmail

Cindy:

Happy Independence Day! I don't know what kind of celebration we can look forward to today on the island. I only know I'm not too enthralled with fireworks or anything to do with fire right now. I'm looking at it as Aunt Candy's independence day.

As you know, Aunt Candy wanted us to spend big, and we are. The guys are golfing (or trying to, in Jack's case) and taking windsurfing lessons; the girls are taking part in the numerous kid programs. We are planning to enjoy every tourist attraction imaginable the next few days, and I am taking pictures with your camera. Thank you very much for the loan.

In our spare time, Delilah and I are having all the treatments: scalp and hair treatments, facials, manicures, pedicures.

They even waxed my toes. I didn't know I had hairy toes.

I was introduced to aromatherapy. Wrapped in grape seed oil, lavender flowers, and some other sweet-smelling stuff. I was surprised I wasn't attacked by a legion of bees.

The best was the deep tissue massage. I have determined that if I were rich, I would rather have a masseuse than a maid.

By the way, I passed on the acupuncture. Delilah elected to be a pincushion. The lady asked me if I wanted to watch.

"No thank you," I said politely, and went to get a tropical drink—blue with lots of ice.

Guess what. I'm getting over my guilt complex, or is that obvious? I told myself I deserve this. Aunt Candy wanted me to enjoy myself, and I am. Massively.

By the way, did you know that Hawaii doesn't have any native land reptiles or amphibians and only two native mammals: the horay bat and the monk seal?

Didn't think so.

I probably won't be able to write you again from Hawaii because we're going to be so busy, but I'll call as soon as I get back.

Love, Karan

July 8
Postcard via U.S. Postal Service
Dear Mom:

Leaving tomorrow. I can't wait to see you. A week or two to get everything in order—and then, Alaska here we come! Isn't that supposed to be California here we come?

Since I'm sure you prefer solid chocolate to liquid, I'm sending your chocolate covered macadamia nuts by mail.

It's going to take a million words to tell you everything, but we'll have a lot of time together. If you see a smear on this note, it's my tear, and I have shed many in our time here.

I hope the dogs know us. The girls talk about you endlessly now that they know we're going HOME.

Your loving daughter,
Karan Marie LaRue

31

For most of us, life is not high spending on an exotic island. It's cooking dinner, taking out the garbage, and tucking the kids in at night. I think it's meant to be that way. It would be easy to lose sight of the fact that this life is a precursor to another more glorious dimension with such alluring distractions as deep tissue massages and views that have you staring out the window all day. Besides, we'd all weigh more than we want if every day was vacation.

Back on the mainland, Beethoven in the background, I allow my mind to float. In the tropical paradise that was Aunt Candy's backyard are orchids, ginger, aroids, and heliconias that smell of Hawaii. And now I understand why she loved it. I am, however, hoping Delilah has a green thumb, because exotic flowers require special care. Ah, but they can afford a gardener now.

To have someone here, and then suddenly be gone, is unfathomable: to know that Aunt Candy's laughter will never be heard, that she will never leave a footprint or cut a flower, that she will never have another worldly thought.

To me it reaffirms that earthly life in its brevity is negligible compared to the unseen world above, which will be ours to discover one fine day.

Delilah, showing the early signs of pregnancy, steps out on the patio wearing a backward baseball cap. Her face is ridden in dirt and she is wearing rubber gloves. What a change from the red-carpet woman I first met.

"Are you sure I can't help you, Delilah?"

"I'm sure. It's my house now, and mine to clean. You have only a couple of days more here, and I want you to enjoy yourself. The guys sure are."

"Well, it's been wonderful."

"Karan, should we go out for dinner?"

I am happy for the suggestion because as much as Delilah has changed, her cooking has not.

"Sounds great. If we can pull the girls away from their Surfs Up game."

"I was thinking McDonalds."

"For the girls!" we say together.

Delilah has decided that not only does she like children; she adores them. Every minute she is not cleaning, she is spending with the girls.

"How many McDonalds do you think there are between here and Alaska?" I ask, gritting my teeth.

"About 100,000."

"To tell you the truth, Delilah, I think I can handle retrieving my own condiments for a while. The pampering and attention was incredible, but a bit much for me. Too many cords, not enough outlets. Extreme overload!"

"I don't know, for me sometimes the world becomes too much and having someone else massage your face with the wonderful smells, it ... it ... "

"Fortifies your soul?"

"Yeah."

*S*o, did you get your pics developed?" Cindy asks in a sorrow-tinted voice, as I wiggle my toes in the sand.

I pull them out of my beach bag.

"This is us snorkeling, and here we are on the road to Hana."

"I heard that's a dangerous road."

"It is."

"This picture is our new yacht."

"And I would like to sell you a bridge," Cindy says handing me a piece of her licorice, which I eat despite my dislike of licorice.

"So I fibbed. But it was our yacht for the day. The undersea life was incredible."

I turn the photos.

"You went on a helicopter?"

"Fantastic view of Haleakala's crater from up there. The girls loved it."

"Where's this?"

"The lobby of our posh hotel. The flowers were always fresh. And the hotel buffet—I've never had so much fantastic food."

"And you had no guilt about the desserts?"

"I think you can tell that by looking at me."

The experience is already a memory, just as me sitting here with Cindy on the rise of the sandy cliffs overlooking the Laguna blue will be a memory tomorrow.

"Tomorrow's the day. I bet you can't wait to get back to your old life."

"It won't be my old life; it can't be."

"What do you mean?"

"I'm not the same person. There's no going back to exactly who you were."

"Is that bad?"

"No. Change is necessary to personal growth. I didn't think that was something I would ever say. I've been resistant to change. Why fix it if it ain't broke kinda thing."

"Well, why?"

"Why what?"

"Fix it when it doesn't need fixing."

"Because sometimes it's not our choice. That's why. And we all need some minor tweaking, whether we're aware of it or not."

"Sounds reasonable."

A flock of seagulls descends near us. Their caws seem a lost cry.

"Through every experience is the chance for expanded creativity."

"I'm not creative like you, Karan."

"Creativity: imagination, inspiration, ingenuity, resourcefulness."

"You are such a dictionary," Cindy says, pushing sand into a misshapen castle.

"You're not going to tell me you're not creative, Cindy. I've seen you talk your entrepreneur husband into things so against his logic—"

"I don't think that's much to be proud of."

"So take that resourcefulness and use it in a more positive way."

"You mean like going back to school?"

"Not necessarily. Find out what you love and pursue it."

"Fashion. I love putting outfits together and color coordinating."

"There you go."

"Maybe I can work at a clothing store."

"Everything begins with a starting point. Wasn't my thing, but could be yours."

"Yeah, I'm tired of living an invisible life. Being my children's mother, and that's it. The world needs my opinions."

"My biography was pretty short before coming here. But let me tell you being my children's mother is 'boss.' That's surfer talk, by the way."

"I know surfer talk, Karan."

She looks around.

"Do you see a polling booth around here?"

"A polling booth in July?"

"I don't want you to go, Karan. I think I should have a vote in this."

"You want me to be happy, I know."

"Yes, I do—unfortunately."

"We need to appreciate the time we had together. And I'm sure I'll be back from time to time since I'll be freelancing for the *Sun*."

"Are you happy about it?"

"Extremely. I love California. Who wouldn't? But my heart is somewhere else, and that's something I can't change."

"Then I'll try to be mature about it." Cindy stands up and kicks her castle.

"We better go. We told the boys two hours." I help kick her sand pile to its destruction.

The inevitable moment of parting. Tears, hugs. Thoughts that overwhelm.

"Best friends, remember?" I say, telling myself in the background to hold my emotions.

We press our gold hearts together.

"Send me pictures of your Northern Sky," says Cindy.

"Send me your innermost thoughts over e-mail."

And the seagulls fly away.

We're ready to go, you guys," the words come easier than expected. I'm ready to go home.

"Sixty-nine hours of driving, huh?" Bradford considers our arduous journey as Jack packs the last of our meager belongings in Gold Dust.

"It's 3,363 miles according to AAA."

Bradford smiles big, holding Delilah close to him.

"You've been great to us," says Jack.

"It was what Ma wanted," Bradford tears.

"You come visit us in Alaska," I say.

"We will," Delilah replies. "All three of us," She pats her belly.

It is with mixed feelings that I leave California. I never expected to love the place. To find and love a best friend, and gap-toothed Bradford, and high-strung Delilah. I never expected to love Aunt Candy and to have to say goodbye too soon.

The girls run out of the house, half excited, half something else. Delilah holds them in her arms until they tug away.

I hug Bradford and Delilah, and we all load into the car, looking out the windows. The girls press their hands on the glass. Delilah matches hers on the other side.

"Got the map?"

"Yup."

"Got your wallet?"

"Yup."

"Cousin Delilah," Hope calls through an open window.

"Yes, Hope."

"I think you should name Aunt Candy's car Happy Bug Lady."

"That's a good name," Delilah says through tears.

"Thank you!"

Hope sits up satisfied, and I know that she's going to be okay. We're all going to be okay.

32

On the morning of the fifth day we arrive in Dawson Creek, British Columbia, the site of Jack London's original log cabin. A huge sign reads, "You are now entering the world famous Alaska highway." The Alaska Highway, two well-traveled lanes winding over rolling hills in view of lush green forests.

"Mile marker zero. Approximately 1,500 miles to home," Jack announces. "Like starting over again." But I am the only one awake to hear him.

"How about breakfast at Smitty's?" he asks.

"Not unless you want to."

"Naw. It's too early. I just liked the name."

The girls, visions of loveliness, are in the back seat sleeping as sound as babies. When they were babies, a car ride would cure them of their crying. I watch their faces and think of the months I've missed with them.

Hope is ten now, and model beautiful. I hope she never gives up naming things or loving the powerful way she does it. Faith, nine, may be more of a challenge, but a delightful one. I'll have to strike a delicate balance between keeping her free spirit in check and not breaking it.

They are so excited to be going home.

Though it was our intention to get to know all those little dots on the map Jack once made reference to, we are basically stopping for gas, to eat, to sleep, and to gawk at some major point of interest. Many of these monuments are highly over-rated, especially the tower made out of bottles and tires that Jack said may be a violation of the Department of Environmental Quality.

I've come to appreciate waitresses and truck drivers more and have gained a healthy respect for wild animals. Like the skunk in the bathroom at the rest stop.

Jack and I take turns driving. He drives, I sleep; I drive, he sleeps. We've managed a lot of miles that way, but also have managed to miss some beautiful countryside.

We took an inordinate amount of pictures along the way. When all your belongings are burned, and there is nothing to show for your children's lost teeth and birthday cake smiles, you try to make up for it with ten pictures of your daughters standing by a tree.

Among the many places we have been, we recall especially: Crescent City, California, where the coast was lit by a lighthouse and pelicans tried to eat our food; Eugene, Oregon, where there are a lot of health food stores that Aunt Candy would have loved, and nobody uses an umbrella; and Seattle, Washington, where the coffee is supreme, and the city is as busy as Toronto.

As we passed through the towns and the cities, I thought that people are much the same everywhere. Somewhere a husband is discontented, and a wife is not, or vice versa. Somewhere a child is crying in his pillow unbeknownst to his parents. Somewhere a family is enjoying a board game or reading the Bible before bed. Maybe no words at all at another house, perhaps occupied by a lonely spinster with the TV blaring to shut out her solitary thoughts.

"Imagine, Jack, we will never know anything about these people whose houses we watch from a distance."

"Karan, you think way too much."

So I tried real hard not to think.

But when we passed a house at 2:00 AM with the lights on and people inside waving their arms, it was Jack who commented, "Do you suppose he lost his job, or she had an affair?"

"I don't know," I say. "Never think of such things."

He laughed and said, "I've decided I like it better when you think. It's boring when you don't make thoughtful comments."

And so I resumed thinking.

Jack chokes on the price of the gas here in Dawson. We talk about staying at one of those quaint bed and breakfasts tonight, because we need a good pampered night's sleep and the feel of bare skin on fresh sheets.

"And a bath," I note.

"And a bath," he agrees.

At Watson Lake is a signpost forest with signs of every kind. Road signs, hometown signs, signs from all over the world. The tradition started in 1942 when a homesick GI put up a sign pointing to his hometown. And now any tourist type who is able to do so stops here and adds his or her own sign. "Over 60,000 of them," one man said, though I'm not sure who does the counting.

"We don't have a sign," Hope says sadly.

"I have a sticker," says Faith, and plants it on a sign that says Stevensville, Montana.

We never stop at a bed and breakfast. We drive all day because we're too anxious to get home. Jack has been driving for hours and is drinking coffee by the gallons and listening to Don Ho, the only CD we now own. Our long-owned CD collection was lost in the fire, and Jack's questionable CDs we burned by choice, after he realized that lyrics about how you should hate authority figures for their excessive rules, no matter how good they sound, are simply not edifying.

We agree to stop when we reach Whitehorse. I get some sleep. I dream about Don Ho in a parka having a concert at an igloo village.

I look up drowsily. I am missing some terrific scenery, Jack says. I go back to sleep.

A burst of fresh Yukon air fills my nostrils. Clear blue lakes, forested mountains, and caribou abound. The girls look for bears.

We finally stop in Whitehorse around midnight, exhausted. It's a standard motel with antiquated plumbing and beds of rock.

Back in the SUV the next evening after a day at a museum and some pizza, I zonk as soon as I hear the doors close.

Jack's voice wakes me somewhere down the road.

"Did you notice we almost hit a bull moose back there?"

I open my eyes to light.

"No, I didn't notice."

"It was huge, Mommy!"

"And you say I sleep sound," Jack teases, in a good way.

"It was Don Ho, Jack. He was amazing," I tease back.

It's dark when we enter Alaska. The girls are asleep, and

we're tired of listening to Don Ho, and the radio stations aren't coming in. The silence begs for words.

"If I ask you something straight out, will you get mad, Jack?"

"No, I was expecting it."

"Expecting what?" I ask.

"Female talk."

"What's that?"

"About my inner feelings and all."

"Jack, how do I know you won't feel trapped again? That you won't want to escape when winter is four months into its gray?"

I sigh in relief of the words reaching the air.

"Because, Karan, it wasn't the winter, or the cold, or the gray. I was looking for a richer experience than the one I thought I had."

"And what experience was that?"

"I guess I thought there were things I needed to do, but after I did them they weren't what I thought."

"We all feel trapped from time to time." I say, and sigh again.

Jack echoes my sigh. "What I found is that working was the same trap, only a worse one. When I got home, I didn't want to do anything but block out the world."

"You did that very well."

I put my hand on his knee.

"It's like having your foot stuck in the mud. Slogging through a duck marsh."

"I'm glad you're unstuck."

"It's natural to equate value with success. But if success were the measuring stick of life, Alexander the Great would have died without any unfulfilled expectations. There's always something more out there we think belongs to us," Jack says wisely.

"In truth, nothing belongs to us," I say.

"I was the one holding myself captive, because I didn't think I had options." He tightens his grip on the wheel.

"I never wanted to stand in your way."

"I had to blame someone, Karan. You just happened to be there."

"It's all about perspective," I say, as I tear open a bag of Cornnuts.

"It's all about knowing God and trusting that he has the best plan," Jack says, putting his hand out for a taste.

"Do you want me to drive?" I ask.

"No, you sleep. We're almost to the end of the line."

Sleep? I can't sleep. The last miles of a journey are anticipatory, possibly anxious. And my thoughts turn toward home. Not the general home. The specific home, like how the hay smells and how the water tastes.

*G*old Dust is a mud bath, barely recognizable when we reach Mom's house.

The dogs bark like they know it's us.

"Ah … " Jack sighs. "You can never have too many dogs or too much sky."

"Are we really home, you guys? Or is this a fantastic dream?" I ask.

The girls jump out and twirl. "We're home! We're home!"

Mom greets us in a bathrobe and curlers under a floral shower cap.

The girls kiss her heatedly and then proceed to the back

yard to envelop Max and Martha with their long-held affections.

Jack hugs my mother and then follows them like a tornado. I have to laugh.

The first words out of Mom's mouth are, "Guess I won't be doing any reclining mid-February."

"You never know, Mom. You never know," I say.

"Maybe next time you go, I'll go with you."

"No question about it."

"I'm glad you're here to enjoy the last of the daisy ring days," my mother says picking one and handing it to me. "Winter will come soon."

"I'm glad I'm in time for my August dream. And I can't wait for winter."

And then a scene of celebrity glee.

We walk in the house hand in hand. It smells of early morning cooking. I hug Mom so tight and so long. I am a little girl again, consumed in her arms. I feel safe, like the world could be crashing, but Mom is here.

Her face is dusted with powdered sugar, and I wipe it off.

"You've been making crepes," I say excitedly.

"Picked the raspberries off the vine this morning."

"My favorite, Mom."

"Oh, course, dear. Did you expect anything but?"

After breakfast and endless chatter, Mom, hair fixed and dressed in complimentary blue, asks us to sit on the couch for a surprise and leaves the room.

"I wonder what—"

Jack's expression gives away too much.

"You're in on this, aren't you?"

The girls are smiling too wide, also.

"You guys, too?"

"Close your eyes," Mom calls from the other room.

I do.

I hear activity and have no idea what the surprise could be.

"Open your eyes."

A vision far beyond the Northern Lights sits on the coffee table. Six scrapbooks of pictures: the prettiest, laciest gems you ever saw.

"Your life condensed," Mom announces proudly.

"This is impossible," I say, with tears streaming down my face.

Jack hugs me. The girls hug me. I hug Mom.

"I borrowed all your photographs before you left. It was to be a Christmas surprise, but it took me longer than I expected."

"We worried you would actually look in those boxes marked photos in the attic and find them full of crunched paper," Jack says.

"We wanted to tell you, Mommy. Especially when you were so sad after the fire. But Daddy said not to," Faith says.

"This is unbelievable."

I feel inexpressible joy.

"And our trip to Prince William Sound, too," Hope says, examining an album.

"Mom, we can go to any craft shop or garage sale in the country, and I won't ever say another word; I promise. You wonderful scrapbook queen!"

"Cool," says Faith. "Look at these stickers!"

I am in such shock I cannot decide which one to pick up first.

Mom pulls the most precious from the pile.

"Here, darling."

I open it slowly and catch my failing breath.

"Baby pictures. And lost tooth and birthday cake smiles I thought were gone forever." I say in a voice barely above a whisper, catching my tears with my sleeve.

33

It is ten o'clock, the last of day, and a sky of brilliance looms before me. It is the sky of my childhood dreams; the sky of my adolescent introspection; it is the sky of my wildest imaginations; the sky I sometimes share with my family, but more often share with God.

It's good to be back under my sky, in the company of my seasonable companion.

The happiest of my news is cuddled at my feet. Max and Martha are once again the audience of my thoughts.

The saddest news is the other half. George Cavanaugh won't give up the Illustrious Seven, which are now the Illustrious Six. Jack's favorite, and the leader he called Moose Chaser, died. I know that Cavanaugh overworked him. I'll be filing an animal cruelty complaint if it will help.

Stories do have happy endings, but not perfect endings.

The sound of footsteps breaks my thoughts. Faith steps into the Igloo and wipes her tired eyes.

"Faith, what are you doing out here?"

"I can't sleep. Tomorrow, Mommy, I want to clean up the kennel for Daddy's new snow dogs."

"Who said anything about snow dogs?"

"Daddy's whistling, Mommy, and that means snow dogs."

I chuckle at her perception. I believe it's true. I found a mushing magazine under Jack's pillow.

Hope slips in.

"Hope, you too?"

"I could feel that Faith was gone."

"Well, here I am," Faith laughs, and they cuddle with the sleeping dogs.

"And I wanted to see the Big Dipper in a green glow."

"Sorry, not tonight, angel. But look at that band of colors."

And for a moment we gaze in silence.

"Mommy, Hope and I were talking and—"

"Uh oh," I say, with a worried face.

"Since we're getting a new computer, we want to start our own Web site," says Hope.

"And where did you two learn about Web sites?"

"At school, of course." Faith says.

"We want to set up our own Web site and call it Alaskaiscool dot something," Hope says with determination.

"And what would it say?"

"Like one hundred, million, zillion reasons we love Alaska," Faith says.

"And you could take pictures, and we could put them on the Internet for the whole world to see," Hope adds.

"That's a wonderful idea, girls."

"We know," says Faith.

I turn on a small light and grab a pad of paper and pen. I write something down.

"What are you doing, Mommy?" Hope asks, petting Martha.

"I'm writing your father a letter."

"Why don't you just tell him?" asks Faith.

"I do that too, but letters are words thought out better."

Another patter of footsteps.

"Join the party, Jack."

I put my pad of paper down.

He sits in front of me on a beanbag, our poor replacement for the blue velvet chair, aka Springy.

"This is like old times, and it feels good," he says.

We huddle together, all of us.

"I thought you were watching TV, Jack."

"No, I've been reading my Bible."

I smile.

"I haven't seen that shirt on you in forever." I sniff him. He smells of the earth.

"Probably because I haven't worn it in forever. I found it hanging in the mudroom."

"What is it that you're writing?" Jack asks.

I turn the paper over.

"Not for you to see—yet."

"Hmmm."

I change the subject.

"What did you think of what the professor did to the schoolroom?"

Jack turns his profile to me. "He told me it was supposed to be a symphony of the Northern Lights."

"It looks like a ghastly intrusion of disconcerted effort to me."

"That's a pretty good description, poetry lady."

I move my arms around the front of him and squeeze, and then rub his chest.

"What's that?"

"What?"

I pat his pocket.

"I don't know."

He pulls out a feather.

"My feather, Daddy. My feather," Faith exclaims and takes it from Jack's hand.

"Imagine that. No worse for the wear."

"And neither are we," I say.

"Whatever worse for the *weigher* means," Faith says.

"Smarter perhaps." I say.

"Fatter perhaps." Jack pats his belly.

"And happier, for sure." I say, rubbing his shoulders.

Hope and Faith stand up and dance a jig.

"Can we yell, Daddy? One great big yell?" Faith asks.

"Why not?" Jack says. "Who can hear us?"

"AHHHHHHH," Faith yells.

"AHHHH," Hope yells, but softer. And then Faith joins again with an enormous noise.

"Wow, that was a sound blaster," Jack says.

"I've been wanting to do that for like a hundred, million, zillion years," Faith says.

And the house is filled with laughter once again.

Epilogue

Dearest Jack:

This letter is for you to read on hay where it is soft and sweet. I have left you a blanket and enclosed a flavored lollypop that will stain your tongue blue.

Having you back is having a dream revisited, so tell me again who you are.

How you used to think the stars would taste like candy; how frogs jump happily from lily pad to lily pad; how you would watch the clouds dance in the sky on a lazy day. Speak from the deepest places of your soul about the things you love.

Let's plant lilacs, pale lavender in color, and watch them grow to their seven-year blossom. You'll take the fragrant flowers and put them in beautiful vases and fill the rooms with the scent of beauty.

The girls will be going to college one day, but we won't be lonely. I'll bake you cookies, and we'll do crossword puzzles. We'll watch the Northern Lights from the Igloo. I'll read to you Whitman, Frost, and poems by poets never well known but who should have been. You'll read to me from the Bible, and love God more than you do now.

At twilight, in all the months of twilight, we will dream

golden dreams and talk about years past and years to come. We'll have no regrets, like drops of water on glass they will slip down to our pool of blessings.

Promise me you'll think I am beautiful even when I no longer look like Audrey Hepburn. I promise you that I will love you even if your hairline recedes, your memory fades, and you are cantankerous because your oatmeal is cooked too hard.

Promise me we'll grow old together. That you will paint my toenails in the moonlight and kiss them barely dry; that we'll share fondue toothpicks; that you'll sing to me even when your voice is cracked. You'll sing to me with your guitar, your fisherman songs in your own tune. And you'll never stop whistling again. Not for a single day.

Tell me, Jack, we'll never leave Alaska. We'll travel and see new places and adore them. Romantic places. Historic places. Places far away and mysterious. But tell me we'll never leave again for good. Tell me with your most authentic voice that we shall die in Alaska happy and wrinkled souls with children and grandchildren sharing in our pleasures, loving each other supremely.

Promise me true, and I'll promise, too.

Readers' Guide

For Personal Reflection
or Group Discussion

Readers' Guide

Concessions is the story of losing yourself and finding yourself again, only stronger and better. Without God this would be an empty story. He is the catalyst behind Karan and Jack's newfound truths. God works through a process. Rarely do we receive the rich reward of revelation without hardship.

Hopefully, you have learned from the experiences of the characters in *Concessions* and can relate to their struggles. Look at life a little differently, at yourself differently. And understand that change—expected or unexpected—can reap benefits if we are willing to learn the hard lessons and love unceasingly.

Reflect on the following questions:

1. Jack's discontent was full blown before he shared it with Karan. How do you think it got to that point? Should Karan have seen it coming?

2. Karan makes the comment, "Maybe my world is small. But is that wrong?" What does that tell you about her? How do you feel about her small world? Is it wrong?

3. Karan was drastically affected by Jack's spontaneous choices. What happens to us when we feel we aren't making our own choices anymore?

4. When life started spinning out of control for Karan, she went through a period of rebellion, refusing to give herself fully to Jack. Was this a proper response, or not? If not, what might have been?

5. At her lowest point Karan found it difficult to pray. Why do you think it is sometimes our tendency to avoid God when we need him most?

6. Creativity was an important aspect of Karan's personality. In what ways can creativity aid us in knowing God and ourselves better?

7. In the midst of her pain what Karan needed most was a sense of security. Could Jack have provided that to her? How do we go about finding security in insecure circumstances?

8. Karan had a happy life in Alaska as a homemaker. When she was forced to go to work she was forced to change against her will. How can we make the best out

of an unwanted situation? And how can we include God in this process?

9. Determination and perseverance were key factors in Karan's survival through her months of loss and change. However, she sought God in her responses and was obedient to him. In this age of embracing female empowerment as the answer to creating positive change, how does a Christian woman, strong in her opinions, strike an appropriate balance?

10. Karan asked God a lot of questions. Was this a good thing or bad thing? Do you think God wants us to ask questions? Can we cross the line from questioning to disrespecting our Creator?

11. Karan gained new friends, family, and experiences she would not have known if it hadn't been for the move. What did she gain by having had these people added to her life?

12. No doubt, Karan's experiences changed her. Looking back, think of an experience that changed you. Did the circumstance lead to a change in heart and a change in view? Did it cause you to grow in your faith and your love of God, or the opposite?

13. Karan had a "cast of characters" to deal with in her
    jobs, most of them non-Christian. What did Karan
    learn from them? How can we learn from those who do
    not share our beliefs?

14. A main lesson in this book is that material things cannot
    fill the void in our lives. How is this evident in some of
    the lives of the characters in the book? How do you deal
    with the accumulation of things in your life?

15. At one point, Karan washes Jack's feet in an act of love
    and servanthood. What do you believe is the signifi-
    cance of this scene? What impact did it have in tearing
    down Jack's walls?

16. Many of the secondary characters in this book present
    different views of life. (Such as Karan's mom, the voice
    of reason; Cindy, the carnal Christian; Candy, the con-
    fused seeker; Delilah, a woman of worldly values.)
    Explore these characters further. Do you see mirrors of
    them in your circle of friends? Or, perhaps, do you see
    elements of each in your life?

17. Jack struggles for his worth outside of God and family.
    Why do you believe some of us go looking in the wrong
    places for a sense of self worth?

18. It took tragedy for Candy to see that God was the answer to her big question mark. What might have held her back for so long?

19. Faith and Hope, two very different sisters, reacted in different ways to change. Had their differences not been recognized by Karan there might have been deeper wounds. How can we as parents celebrate the differences in our children?

20. Karan had forsaken female friendships because her own family relationships were so satisfying. What do you think she was missing out on?

21. Helpless to hurry along Jack's learning process, Karan discovered new emotions, weaknesses, and vulnerabilities in her time of waiting. What have you learned about yourself in times of necessary waiting?

22. One of the central themes in this story is discontent and the havoc it causes. Paul says in Philippians 4:11 that he has achieved contentment in *whatsoever state I am.* How can we achieve contentment in our lives, even when we would like to have a different life than the one we have?

23. Jack was from Louisiana, and Karan was from Alaska. How do our backgrounds influence what we want out of life?

24. Obviously, Karan had some misconceptions about California and life in general. What were some of these misconceptions?

25. The author brings out the many differences between men and women in this story. Did you see some truths? If so, consider them.

26. Children are resilient, as demonstrated by Hope and Faith. Do you believe God instills this gift in children? What have we lost as adults that children maintain which allows them to be more adaptable?

27. Karan refers to Jack's search as "Solomon's crooked road to fulfillment." What other biblical characters can you think of who learned lessons similar to Jack's by taking the wrong path? What was their outcome?

28. Humor was one of Karan's saving qualities. How can we choose to view bad situations with humor? Do you think we sometimes take ourselves too seriously?

29. In the end the LaRue family unit is stronger than ever before and Karan, too, is stronger and wiser. What role did truth, loyalty, and love play in this outcome?

30. If Karan were a real person, how might she live her life differently today than she would have before the changes took place in her life? Would you consider these positive changes?

The Word at Work Around the World

A vital part of Cook Communications Ministries is our international outreach, Cook Communications Ministries International (CCMI). Your purchase of this book, and of other books and Christian-growth products from Cook, enables CCMI to provide Bibles and Christian literature to people in more than 150 languages in 65 countries.

Cook Communications Ministries is a not-for-profit, self-supporting organization. Revenues from sales of our books, Bible curricula, and other church and home products not only fund our U.S. ministry, but also fund our CCMI ministry around the world. One hundred percent of donations to CCMI go to our international literature programs.

CCMI reaches out internationally in three ways:

· Our premier International Christian Publishing Institute (ICPI) trains leaders from nationally led publishing houses around the world.

· We provide literature for pastors, evangelists, and Christian workers in their national language.

· We reach people at risk—refugees, AIDS victims, street children, and famine victims—with God's Word.

Word Power, God's Power

Faith Kidz, RiverOak, Honor, Life Journey, Victor, NexGen — every time you purchase a book produced by Cook Communications Ministries, you not only meet a vital personal need in your life or in the life of someone you love, but you're also a part of ministering to José in Colombia, Humberto in Chile, Gousa in India, or Lidiane in Brazil. You help make it possible for a pastor in China, a child in Peru, or a mother in West Africa to enjoy a life-changing book. And because you helped, children and adults around the world are learning God's Word and walking in his ways.

Thank you for your partnership in helping to disciple the world. May God bless you with the power of his Word in your life.

For more information about our international ministries, visit www.ccmi.org.

Additional copies of *CONCESSIONS*
and other RiverOak titles are available
from your local bookseller.

If you have enjoyed this book,
or if it has had an impact on your life,
we would like to hear from you.

Please contact us at:

RIVEROAK BOOKS
Cook Communications Ministries, Dept. 201
4050 Lee Vance View
Colorado Springs, CO 80918
Or visit our Web site: www.cookministries.com